Finding Freedom

Finding

Freedom

Jeff Barrows

Finding Freedom

Copyright © 2019 by Jeff Barrows

ISBN-13:9781694506030

To my lovely bride Kathy,

who provides loving support for all my adventures.

Acknowledgements

First of all, I want to thank Terry Reeder for her kind diligence in reading and correcting my initial drafts. You helped curb my ellipsis utilization dramatically! A heartfelt thanks to Yolanda Schlabach for her unceasing excitement regarding the unfolding drama in the book. Your ongoing encouragement kept me writing when I might otherwise have put the work aside.

I sincerely appreciate the prayer support of my men's group and my home church. Prayer produces the power for any spiritual endeavor, so many thanks to Mark, Larry, Phil, Andy, Patty, Joni, Sheri, Cheri, Bethany, Terry, Ariel, Tom, Rita, and John Paul. The regular fellowship with all of you keeps me grounded and spiritually directed.

Finally, I want to thank my family for their encouragement, especially Kathy, who has remained at my side through all my escapades.

Chapter 1

The Mistake

Heather Wallace stared up at the clock above the door, willing the hands to move faster so that she could get out of this place. Heather sensed the cauldron of emotions churning within her, threatening to erupt at any time. She only had to make it through this final class of the day, and then she could get away and develop a plan that would get her through this. Heather knew the day would be stressful, but she couldn't believe how close she came to a near-meltdown early this morning when Mrs. Wilson asked if everything was fine. Then Sue had to go and stir things up during lunch.

"What's going on with you?" Sue had asked. "You look like you didn't sleep a wink last night. Did your mom and Ted get into another fight?"

"Something like that," Heather had answered reluctantly. "I don't want to talk about it right now."

"Heather, we've been through this before. You hate talking about their fights, but once you talk it through, you always feel better. Today, let's skip the first part and jump to the second so that you can be halfway normal this afternoon."

"You don't understand. Something has changed, and I have to work through what I'm going to do about it."

"OK…if that's the case, why don't we get together and talk about it after school."

"I just can't today. And I can't take an interrogation right now, so please; I need you to drop it. And I know I promised to work on that paper after school, but there's no way I can today."

Heather remembered Sue's concerned look and how it almost caused Heather to dissolve into tears right there at the lunch table. Fortunately, she had managed to keep herself under control and somehow even convinced Sue not to press further.

Now at the end of the day, Heather was exhausted.

Why wouldn't she be exhausted? It was true that she had hardly slept last night. After all, who could sleep after what she experienced?

Heather looked at the clock again…just three minutes had passed. She pulled her dark hair back from her face and stared at the floor, unable to comprehend anything Mr. Blake was saying. She usually enjoyed world history, especially when Mr. Blake became animated as he told a story about a world-changing event.

But today, the minutes had turned to eons.

What was she going to do?

Should she tell her mother?

What if her mother didn't believe her?

Had Heather done something to encourage it?

Tears came to the surface again, and she struggled to keep from letting out a sob. She just had to hold herself together a few minutes more.

When the bell finally rang, Heather grabbed her backpack and walked directly outside, not bothering to go to her locker. She knew Sue would be there waiting, and she still wasn't ready to face her. She'd make it up to her later.

Beginning her walk home, Heather knew she had an important decision to make. Her mom would be waking up soon after working the night shift at the hospital, and Ted would be at the factory for another two hours. If she was going to tell her mom, it needed to be soon.

Heather knew it would devastate her mother since she and Ted had only been married for six months. Just last week Heather had come home to find them giggling and tickling each other on the couch like lovesick teenagers.

Sure, they had had their fights, like the big blowup two weeks ago when Heather's mom found pornography on Ted's phone. Heather had never seen her mother so angry, screaming, and throwing the phone at Ted when he walked into the room.

But that was nothing compared to what Ted...

Suddenly, Heather was overwhelmed with shame and guilt, no longer able to hold back the tears. The sobs came out uncontrollably, causing Heather to stop and fall to her knees, feeling sick all over. She desperately wanted to hide somewhere...anywhere.

How could she face her mother after what had happened? She couldn't think of anything she had done to encourage Ted. After all, she was only 15 years old, twenty years younger than Ted. Why would he have any interest in her?

The events of the previous night swept over Heather as she continued kneeling on the sidewalk. She had gone to bed at her usual time just before her mom left to start her night shift at the hospital. She had done some bedtime reading before turning out the light to go to sleep.

And then Ted came in.

The continuing cinema of memories brought increasing shame to Heather, making her feel like a dirty piece of clothing, while also creating anger and loathing for Ted.

How could he do that to her?

How could he do this to her mother?

Thoughts of Ted having an accident at the factory entered her mind, bringing a twisted sense of hope to Heather. That would certainly take care of her problems.

Heather slowly eased her crying as she stood and resumed her walk home. She had a lot to think through. There had to be a way to make sure last night never happened again. As she turned the next corner, Heather remembered her mother was working that night, and the thought immediately flooded her with fear and anxiety. She fought an almost overwhelming desire to turn and run away.

No, she had to hold herself together and get through this somehow.

The best thing to do would be to tell her mother.

But what would she tell her?

Heather couldn't even remember everything that had happened. It was all a strange blur beginning when Ted came into her room and ending when he left. She remembered strange sensations and the fear filling her. There was also the sensation of being trapped and overpowered by his strength. Finally, she remembered the threat Ted made as he left.

"If you tell your mom about this, I'll deny everything. I'll even tell her that you act like a slut when she's not around."

As she thought about it now, Heather was confused. Why would telling her mother that her daughter acted like a slut with Ted somehow protect him? Heather had never acted like a slut, and there was no way her mother would believe him.

Then she remembered the fights with her mother.

Their relationship had become strained in the past couple of months. The divorce from Heather's abusive father had been trying for both Heather and her mom. They had never been close, but immediately after the divorce, they had forged a special bond since it was only the two of them. Heather enjoyed that time immensely and even thinking back on it now caused her mood to lift slightly.

But then Ted entered the picture, and her mother began spending all her free time with him. At first, Heather tried to understand, recognizing her mom needed some adult companionship. But when Ted and her mom got married, Heather began to feel like she was a piece of unwanted furniture. She couldn't help it that she had let out her anger and frustration with her mom.

Ted had witnessed many of those fights.

Her mom's words still echoed in Heather's mind, "If you don't like staying with me, maybe you should go live with your father!"

The words had stung deeply since her mother knew how dangerous Heather's father was when he was drunk. How could she forget the violence that had finally ended the marriage? After drinking all day, her father had suddenly become enraged at her mom over some minor thing. He began hitting her before turning toward Heather as she screamed at him to stop. She would never forget the look of hate and viciousness in his eyes.

Fortunately for them both, when her dad turned towards Heather, her mom was able to grab the skillet and knock him out. Heather shivered at the memory, afraid to imagine what would have happened if her mother hadn't stopped him.

There was no way she could ever live with her father.

But now her mother had changed. She focused all her time and affection on Ted, causing Heather to wonder whether her mom might prefer Heather lived somewhere else. She recalled the annoying look her mother gave her when Heather recently interrupted an intimate moment in the living room. Heather had initially been puzzled by the look since she didn't mean to barge in on them. But now thinking back on it, Heather remembered several similar glances from her mom over the past few months.

Heather began to realize not only that her mother might prefer that Heather live somewhere else, but also that she might actually believe Ted's accusation. The more she thought about it, the more confused and frightened Heather became. Up until this moment, it would have seemed impossible for her mother not to believe her about something so important. But the more Heather thought about the recent changes in her mother, the more she recognized that Ted had become her mother's whole world.

So maybe she shouldn't tell her mother.

Besides, maybe last night was a fluke and won't ever happen again. Maybe Ted realizes he made a huge mistake and even feels terrible about what happened. Certainly, he won't say anything about it. And if it doesn't happen again, it might be better if her mom never knew.

No, she shouldn't tell her mother.

Finding Freedom

Floating ten feet above Heather, Taron struggled to maintain his angelic peace as he watched Kul passed his long spindly fingers through Heather's head from his perch on her right shoulder. Taron's long white robe flowed gracefully around him as he kept reminding himself that he had no authority to intervene. Taron placed his hand on the hilt of the long sword at his right side, suppressing his instinct to knock Kul to the other side of the city. Heather's mother Nancy had inadvertently given Kul, and his fellow demons access to Heather when she invited Ted to live in their home nine months ago. Since neither Heather nor Nancy belonged to the Lord, Taron was forced to keep his distance for the time being, even though he knew Heather was making one of the most important decisions of her life. Nothing would have pleased Taron more than freeing Heather from the influence of Kul, who no doubt was swaying Heather's decision to align with the plans of the enemy. If only Heather would reach out and pray for guidance, Taron would have the authority to end this evil session and send Kul whimpering back to his master.

Taron passed through tree limbs above Heather as she continued walking, his luminance radiating the nearby spiritual realm. His ten-foot frame was massive compared to Kul, who appeared more like a shrunken dark malformed specter, clinging tightly to Heather. Eighteen months earlier, during the divorce, Taron was assigned to Heather after she began regularly praying for her mother. At that time, Nancy was suffering from depression and had withdrawn from everyone, even Heather. Heather's ongoing prayers enabled Taron to fight off a demon of depression and suicide, establishing a new level of peace and stability in their lives. They had even started attending Brookview Community Church, a Bible-believing church named after their town.

But as is often the case with those not born of the Spirit, when stability returned to their lives, they stopped attending church, causing their prayers to lessen until they finally ceased. Shortly after that, Nancy met Ted, and their rapid romance ensued. Within a couple of months, they had moved in together, granting Kul and his fellow demons access to the home and Heather.

Taron wasn't surprised that Ted's evil behavior had quickly re-surfaced with Nancy working nights at the hospital, leaving Ted alone with an attractive 15-year-old girl. It created a temptation too strong for Ted to resist, especially with the increasing demonic influence Ted was accruing through his addiction to pornography. Taron knew that it was only a matter of time before lustful thoughts turned into wicked actions.

With the signs of an impending assault, Taron asked the Lord for the authorization to intervene. There was no question he could handle both Kul and Bazen, Ted's demonic companion. However, the Lord had refused. Taron wasn't surprised since the home was now void of any spiritual pursuit or prayer. Nancy had willingly brought Ted into the house, and for now, the Lord was respecting that decision. Therefore, Taron was forced to assume his least favorite role as an angel, spectator rather than a warrior. He maintained that role even now as he watched Kul manipulate Heather's thoughts during this critical moment of decision.

Thankfully, he knew the Lord had a plan.

*****

As she walked through the front door, the aroma of freshly cooked bacon and eggs alerted Heather that her mother was awake and in the kitchen. Heather immediately turned to go up the stairs, hoping to gain some time before talking.

"Heather, how was school today?" her mother called from the kitchen. "Come and sit with me while I finish my breakfast."

"I'll be right down, mom," Heather yelled from the stairs. "I just need to do a couple of things."

Swollen eyes looked back at Heather from the bathroom mirror as she washed her tear-stained face. Heather realized there was no way she could easily cover up the aftermath of her emotional release and hoped that her mother's usual busyness would prevent her from paying too much attention.

Heather took several minutes to gather her thoughts and prepare to face her mother for the first time since the assault. As she walked down the stairs, Heather reminded herself of her decision not to tell her mother, strengthening her limited resolve.

"My day was OK," Heather replied as she sat down at the kitchen table. "How was your shift last night at the hospital?"

"It was a busy night. We ended up having two emergency C-sections," answered her mother as she rinsed her dishes in the sink. "A mother came in bleeding shortly after my shift started, and it wasn't long after we took care of her that another woman came in with a breech baby. Before I knew it, the shift was over, and I had to get ready to give report."

Heather's mom turned back toward the table where Heather was sitting.

"Heather, have you been crying?" she asked.

"Oh, I had an argument with Sue," Heather replied, trying not to lie. "It was no big deal, and I don't even know why I ended up crying. I'm sure we'll get everything worked out tomorrow."

"Well, I hope so," her mother said as she finished the dishes. "Listen, Ted has his softball league tonight and won't be home till later. I've got some shopping to do before I go to work, so I'll be leaving soon. There's some leftover casserole in the refrigerator for you for dinner. You can have a quiet evening here catching up on homework and that report you and Sue are doing together."

Heather watched her mom walk up the stairs, still wondering if she was doing the right thing by not telling her. She was glad her mom accepted her explanation, but part of her was disappointed that her mom hadn't asked more questions. It might be a good idea to follow her upstairs and continue the conversation. Then an image of her father's threatening look suddenly popped into her thoughts, reminding Heather she had made the right decision.

*****

Taron watched from the upper corner of the kitchen as Kul continued to wiggle his finger inside Heather's head. Corel floated through the kitchen ceiling from the upstairs bedroom to join Taron, his luminance adding to Taron's. Corel and Taron often worked closely together, since they were both under the authority of Solen, their local commander.

"Kul seems to be having his way for the moment," Corel observed.

"Unfortunately, a very key moment," replied Taron with some frustration.

Kul looked up, giving them both a hideous, broad smile. He was clearly enjoying this rare opportunity to manipulate a subject while two angels watched helplessly.

Both Taron and Corel passed through the kitchen wall into the back yard to gain some separation from Kul.

"How does Nancy seem today?" Taron asked.

"As you just witnessed, Skulty is successfully keeping Nancy distracted and self-focused. Short of an outright confession by Heather, it was highly unlikely she was going to notice the depth of Heather's emotional pain today."

"Solen warned us that the increased demonic activity in this home would focus on Heather," replied Taron. "With the addition of Skulty, Nancy's ability to empathize with Heather has been further mitigated."

"I will update Solen about the assault last night so that we can refine our strategy to respond when prayers provide the opening."

"The darkness that came with Ted at the invitation of Nancy has settled over this home and will continue to bring unforeseen suffering," Taron sighed. "Thankfully, the Spirit has shared that Heather's salvation will come from outside this home."

"No doubt that is part of the Father's plan," agreed Corel. "For now, it seems we must continue observing until prayer or the Spirit disrupts the authority of the dark forces."

As they floated together in the backyard, they turned their attention to the throne of God, lifting their hands in praise and worship, vastly increasing their brilliant radiance.

"For the Lord and His glory!"

Chapter 2

Hope Arising

Eric finished the last email just as his mobile phone began ringing. He looked at his watch, pleased to see that the call was right on time.

"This is Eric Stone," he answered. "Is this Ellen?"

"Yes, it is. How are you this morning, Mr. Stone?"

"I'm doing well, thank you. And thank you so much for working with my schedule in arranging this call. We're in a critical phase of getting the house open, and I've been overwhelmed with meetings."

"No problem. I know you're super busy and I appreciate you taking time for this interview."

"It's my pleasure. I was a high school teacher before this job, so I put a priority on helping students whenever I can."

"Really, what did you teach?"

"U.S. history, which is quite different from what I do now."

"Well, I'm looking forward to hearing more of your story, Mr. Stone."

"Certainly, and please call me Eric. Before we get started, it would be helpful for me to get a little more background on both this assignment and you, Ellen," Eric replied.

"Sure…this interview is for a paper I'm doing for my class on the nonprofit sector."

"And you're working toward a degree in social work, correct?" Eric asked.

"Yes. I have one more year to complete at the university, and then I'll graduate with my bachelor's degree in social work."

"What made you choose our work here at Hope House for this paper?"

"Well, ironically, it was you. I already knew about the issue of human trafficking through my studies, but I became especially passionate about child sex trafficking when you gave a moving presentation at my church a few weeks ago. That's when I found out about Hope House and came up with the idea of interviewing you for this paper. Again, I'm so glad that you agreed."

"So, are you a believer?" Eric asked.

"Absolutely! I've known the Lord since I was twelve years old, growing up in a Christian home."

"That's terrific. We need more committed Christians engaged in this issue, especially as social workers. I hope you'll consider joining the anti-trafficking movement, once you've graduated."

"That certainly is a possibility, which is one reason I'm so excited to talk with you."

"Well, now that I know a little more about you, I'm ready for your questions any time," Eric replied, waving at Melinda as she came into the office.

"First, could you give me your title and role with Hope House?"

"Sure, I'm the Founder and Executive Director of Hope House, which essentially means I make sure everyone on staff gets paid," Eric said with a laugh.

"When did you start Hope House?"

"It was a little over five years ago, about a year after I first learned about child sex trafficking."

"Could you tell me a little more about how that happened?" Ellen asked.

"Well, as I mentioned, I used to teach high school history, and toward the end of the school year six years ago, someone from the county juvenile court came to the school to talk about child sex trafficking as part of a prevention program. I'd never heard of it before that day and was shocked to learn something as horrific as this was happening right here in our city. But what shocked me the most was learning how little was being done to help these young victims."

"So, is that when you decided to start Hope House?"

"Oh no," Eric chuckled. "That decision didn't come until much later. Even though everything I heard that day moved me deeply, I wasn't ready to change the whole course of my life quite yet."

"So, what did happen after that presentation?"

"Since it was the end of the school year, my focus was on finals and then posting grades for all my students. However, after having some time off during the summer, I began to think more about what I learned during that presentation. I realized that the students I was teaching were the same age as the victims of this horrendous crime. That realization prompted me to start researching the issue of child sex trafficking. Through that research, I learned that the average age for a minor to first enter trafficking is thirteen. I also began learning about the warning signs of child sex trafficking."

"Could you share some of those warning signs with me?" Ellen asked.

"One crucial sign within the school setting is a student from a lower-income home who begins wearing the latest designer clothes or carrying the latest smartphone. A few of my students had exhibited that sign, and I completely missed it. I remember wondering how they were able to afford those expensive items, and now I know. But at the time, I was clueless."

"Are you saying that most of the boys and girls who end up trafficked come from low-income homes?"

"Not at all. Students possessing items they normally can't afford is just one of the many red flags that might reveal a child is a victim of trafficking. The main risk factor for child trafficking is abuse within the home."

"So, did you decide to start Hope House when you learned about the association with abuse?"

"Not entirely, but it did lead me to further research, including a pivotal phone conversation with a representative named Adam from the national office of the Salvation Army. I vividly remember talking to him one afternoon late that summer, asking him what these victimized kids needed most. When he told me they needed specialized residential treatment, I sensed the Lord call me into this work, giving me the name Hope House. And yes, that's when I decided to start Hope House. I took most of the next school year to lay the foundation necessary to start the nonprofit that would become Hope House."

"Since this paper is for my nonprofit class, could you tell me about your experience laying that foundation?"

"Sure...I have a friend who is an attorney, and she helped me with the incorporation papers and writing the bylaws for the nonprofit. Then I began the process of choosing board members. As you are no doubt aware through your studies, a nonprofit, tax-exempt organization, must be under the authority of a Board of Directors," Eric replied as he saw Connie, Rachel, and Marge enter the office together.

"What happened after you got the nonprofit up and running?" Ellen asked.

"We spent the first year raising funds through our awareness campaign. Thankfully, the Lord brought us a survivor of child sex trafficking, Gloria, who bravely agreed to speak publicly about her experience. Through Gloria's efforts and my speaking at churches, we were able to raise enough money by the end of our second year to purchase an existing house and add one additional staff person."

"Wow, it sounds like things took off quickly."

"Initially, there were a lot of people who, like me, had never heard of child sex trafficking. When we estimated there were approximately one hundred girls in our city currently entrapped in child prostitution, audiences I spoke to began feeling compelled to do something about it. Since we had a mission to help these young girls, many donated generously to our work."

"And what exactly is your mission at Hope House?"

"Our formal mission is to prevent child sex trafficking and assist survivors in our area. We accomplish that through our outreach program to all the junior and senior high schools, and through our case management program. When we finally open the house, we'll be able to offer comprehensive residential rehabilitative care."

"You mentioned that you started Hope House five years ago. Does it usually take that long to open a specialized facility?"

"It does when you're working with minors. We spent a significant portion of our third year renovating the house to meet state codes. Also…"

"Sorry to interrupt you, but to which state codes are you referring?" Ellen asked.

"The state has established building codes for facilities such as group homes that house minors. For example, we had to install a fire suppression system in the house."

"I had no idea it could be that complicated to start a home for minors."

"And that doesn't include the license that is required. We started working on the license application two years ago, while we continued to raise funds to support our resident staff once the house opens."

"Aren't funds available from the state and county to help rehabilitate these girls once you open the home?"

"Yes, but they don't cover all our expenses, so we'll need to supplement those funds even after the house is open."

"When do you expect that to happen?"

"It could happen soon. We submitted our license application six months ago, and once our license is approved, the only remaining barrier to opening will be hiring and training the residential staff."

"Well, this has been very helpful, Mr. Stone. Thank you again for taking the time to talk with me," Ellen replied. "May I email you if I come up with any further questions?"

"Absolutely. Best wishes on your efforts to complete your degree. And by the way, when you do get finished, please stop by our office. You never know, we might be hiring at that time."

"That would be great…thanks again."

Eric put his phone down and glanced at his watch. He had twenty minutes before the weekly staff meeting.

Opening his laptop, he brought up the agenda and began reviewing it, when a sudden whoop from Melinda startled him.

"What's going on?" Eric asked as he joined the others around Melinda's desk.

"We finally got it!" Melinda cheered. "I just received an email from the state telling us our license was approved, and we should receive a paper copy in the mail within a week. Finally!"

"Great news!" exclaimed Eric as he high-fived the rest of the staff. "Congratulations, everyone. Melinda, as our program director, you've taken the lead in writing the application, but everyone has worked hard for this day!"

"I was beginning to think I had done something wrong since it was taking so long," Melinda replied.

"I had faith in you girl," Rachel responded.

"We knew it was going to take some time since we're a new organization," Eric chimed in. "By the way, where is Gloria?"

"She was asked to speak at a school function this morning," Connie answered.

"Too bad she's not here to join in the celebration. Her speaking engagements have been instrumental in making this happen."

"I'll text her to let her know."

"Well, now that we have our license, we can finally begin planning our final steps for hiring and training the residential staff," Eric said. "I'll make a coffee run and be back in time for the staff meeting."

"This should get our creative juices flowing," Eric said as he returned with six variations of coffee and latte and placed them around the table. "Before we dive into planning our next few weeks, I think we need to give thanks and praise where it is due…to our Lord who has made all this happen. How about I open in prayer and then close after giving time to anyone else who wants to pray?"

"Absolutely," they all agreed.

"Lord, we come before you this morning recognizing that you have called us into this issue, and we thank you for everything you have accomplished through us, including this approval of our license. We recognize that we could not have done any of this without Your help and provision. We praise You that You are a God who cares for these girls, and we are humbled that You have chosen us to be Your hands and feet for them."

*****

Riel joined Adren, Joft, Nefa, and Jehos above the conference table raising their hands in praise and worship, enjoying the prayers of the saints below. The brilliance of their shimmering raiment increased through the prayer time as each staff member took their turn to pray and give thanks to the Lord. Beams of spiritual light radiated upwards toward heaven as the prayers lifted to the throne of heaven. Like a signal fire, the brightness of the angelic group sent a clear message of spiritual vitality and strength throughout the nearby spiritual realm.

The angels relished these periods of weekly corporate prayer, drawing the necessary power for their ongoing struggle against the forces of darkness. Even now, they were aware that demons were witnessing their brilliance, powerless to overcome it. When the time of prayer concluded, the angels turned their attention to their leader.

"Praise the Lord for this victory," Riel began. "We've all had a part in the battle against our spiritual adversaries working their will in various governmental agencies. And while this truly is a victory, opening Hope House will bring new and more powerful enemies, increasing the intensity of our spiritual battle."

"Riel, where do you expect the next point of attack?" Joft asked.

"I'm not entirely certain yet. But I am concerned about the spiritual state of a couple of the board members. Their pride has opened them to possible manipulation by the enemy. Also, I've noticed that Eric is beginning to idolize his executive director role, gaining worth from his position in Hope House instead of his role as a son of the Father.

That could be extremely dangerous, especially if his time in prayer continues to decrease. I don't need to remind you of the various vulnerabilities within the staff, so there are multiple openings our enemy could choose to exploit for his purposes."

"Melinda will need additional prayer support as she begins the process of hiring the staff," Jehos suggested. "I could update the overseeing angel at her church to request additional prayer from her Bible study group."

"That's a great idea that we should apply to the entire staff," Riel responded. "We can coordinate increased prayer support within each of the staff member's churches until we know the enemy's next point of attack. Be sure to quickly communicate any perceived shift in the enemy's strategy or new vulnerabilities, so that we can respond appropriately."

"For the Lord and His Glory," they all exclaimed, racing away to complete their tasks.

*****

When their time in prayer concluded, Eric pushed his now outdated agenda aside and looked around the table at his staff. Melinda was his go-to person when it came to the treatment program for the girls. Not only did she have her master's degree in social work, but she had also helped lead a therapeutic program for adult survivors of sex trafficking in another state. Eric remembered reading her resume for the first time, recognizing that Melinda would be the perfect program director for Hope House. When he found out she was willing to relocate to Brookview, he understood she was a gift from the Lord. It didn't hurt that she was still single since Eric knew that when the house first opened, Melinda would have very little free time.

Marge was the other licensed social worker Eric had hired. Having just graduated from college with her social work degree, Marge was very passionate about helping victims of child sex trafficking. When the Lord blessed Hope House with a local government grant to provide case management to underage survivors of sex trafficking, Marge was thrilled to join the staff.

But none of this would have been possible without Connie, Eric's trusted administrative assistant. When Eric had an administrative task that needed completing, all he had to do was give it to Connie, and Eric knew it would be done and done correctly. Hope House would be a jumbled mass of unorganized papers and emails without Connie.

Rachel was the latest hire as director of development. It was a considerable step to hire someone full time to raise funds for the work of Hope House, but Rachel came with plenty of experience and passion. She seemed to know everyone in the philanthropic world within Brookview and the surrounding cities, helping her stay connected with donors that might be interested in supporting Hope House.

Yes, Eric thought, turning toward Melinda, the Lord had provided the perfect staff for Hope House.

"Melinda, how many applicants for the resident assistant positions have you screened so far?"

"At this point, we've received twenty-five applications, and I've been able to interview ten of those women," Melinda responded.

"How many of those ten do you feel would be good hires?"

"I especially liked eight of them."

"That's the number of RA's you wanted to have hired and trained before we take our first girl, right?"

"Yes, taking into account sick time, time off, and calculating that each RA would work thirty-two hours a week."

"Why only thirty-two hours instead of forty?" Eric inquired.

"To lessen the risk of secondary trauma to the new staff. Remember we talked about that a couple of months ago."

"That's right…that's the trauma someone may get from working with traumatized individuals. I forgot about that. Just to make sure I'm not missing anything, if we end up hiring and training these eight individuals, we'll be ready to open, right?" Eric asked.

"Essentially. We'll need to do a few minor things like buying some fresh groceries, but we'll otherwise be ready," Melinda answered.

"That's great news! Go ahead and set up a second interview with them, and I'll join you to make the final decision on hiring. It might be a good idea for you to go ahead and interview a few of the remaining fifteen, just in case one or two of the others don't work out."

"I can do that," Melinda replied. "I'll let you know when I have those interviews set up. I assume you'll be here at the office for the rest of the week?"

"I don't have any planned outside meetings at this point," Eric answered. "I'll make sure to keep it that way since completing these hires is a priority. How is the training preparation coming?"

"I've stepped in to help with that," Marge answered. "Since I only have three girls and one boy currently on my case management load, I have some time to help out. I've adapted some previous experiences interacting with the survivors in the past year to provide good examples for our training curriculum. Since our policies and procedures are already in place, we should have these additional training modules completed by the end of the week."

"How many hours of training are you planning?" Eric asked.

"At this point, we have fifty hours of training for new hires. We'll be supplementing that training with regular quarterly updates," Marge answered.

"It sounds like we're on track to begin training just as soon as we complete the hiring process," Eric responded. "Now, we need to get the announcement about our licensing out to our donors. Rachel, could you put together a formal looking announcement to send out via email?"

"Absolutely," Rachel answered. "But I still haven't mastered the email listserv."

"No problem. Connie can help you with that," Eric replied, giving a knowing look at Connie. "No one has the email listserv mastered like Connie, the one who keeps everything here running smoothly."

"I'm glad to help," Connie replied quietly as she made a few notes on the ever-present pad of paper in front of her.

Eric looked at the staff gathered around the table, silently thanking the Lord again for bringing this team together.

"Well, I think we're all going to have a busy week. There's only one more important piece of business we need to take care of," Eric said with a big smile. "How does Wednesday noon sound for a celebration lunch on me at The French Connection?"

As Eric started his drive home that evening, he shook his head, remembering how hesitant he had been when he began to sense the Lord leading him to start Hope House. He was a schoolteacher after all, not a social worker. Add to that his complete lack of experience with nonprofits, and it was a recipe for disaster. It logically made more sense for God to lead a wealthy lawyer or at least someone with a background in social work to start Hope House. But since his calling, Eric had learned that God's logic was very different from his logic. God's reasoning was to find someone with an attitude of submission and humility and then empower them to carry out His plan.

Eric thought back over the many hours he had prayed about the decision to start Hope House that summer after first learning about sex trafficking. He had cornered his pastor Jason on several occasions after church asking about knowing God's will.

With Jason's help, Eric finally accepted the idea that starting Hope House was God's plan for him. Now here he was, five years later, working full time as Executive Director of Hope House with a staff of five women.

Only God could have done that.

But there had been difficulties along the way. Eric was having trouble keeping up with everything as word about

Hope House spread around the city. He felt a pressure to try and answer every email and return every phone call, which interfered with his ability to stay connected with the staff. He felt an increasing distance, especially from Marge and Rachel. Now that their license was approved, it would only get worse.

I guess I'll have to get up even earlier in the morning to get to the office Eric thought as he parked his car in the garage and carried his computer bag into the kitchen where Maggie was finishing dinner.

"How was the staff meeting today Handsome?" Maggie asked.

Eric shook off his thoughts and smiled as he leaned down to kiss his wife.

"The license came through this morning!" he announced.

"That's wonderful!" Maggie exclaimed as she gave Eric a big hug. "You've worked hard for this. I'm so proud of you and your team."

"It is a great step forward, but it also means that I'm going to be a lot busier now that we have a green light from the state to open our doors. I'm not sure where I'm going to find the time to keep up."

"I'm sure you'll find the time somewhere…you always do."

"All I can say is it's a good thing I didn't know it would be this difficult when I started Hope House."

"You know that wouldn't have mattered. The Lord called you into this work, and whether hard or easy, you had no choice but to follow His lead," Maggie responded.

"That's probably why the Lord doesn't tell us everything ahead of time; otherwise, we'd get caught up worrying and thinking we can't do it. But honestly, if I had known five years ago what I know now, I may have tried some negotiation with the Lord before accepting the call," Eric replied with a smile.

"We need to have a celebration dinner and invite Jason and Heidi over to join us," Maggie said as she put the dinner plates on the table, shifting the tone of the conversation." Jason deserves to be part of the celebration since he was so helpful in the beginning."

"That's a great idea," Eric answered, following Maggie's positive turn. "What about this coming Friday evening?"

"That works for us. I'll call Heidi after dinner and see if they're free Friday."

"I told the staff I'd take them out for a celebratory lunch at the French Connection on Wednesday. You should join us. Jason's not the only one who helped me with this assignment," Eric said as he kissed Maggie on the cheek. "You've supported me through thick and thin these past five years, so you should be there with us."

"I think I can convince Mr. Thomas he can do without his legal aide for a little while on Wednesday," Maggie answered, smiling.

"Let's pray before the food gets cold."

Chapter 3

Ted's Treachery

Heather clicked off the TV and went into the kitchen to clean up her dishes from dinner. She found herself relishing the quietness of the house, which was something new for her. Up until a week ago, she didn't like to be alone, but that was just one of the many things that changed since that terrible night.

Fortunately, her life was slowly returning to some form of normality. Throughout the week, Ted had focused on work and softball, so there had not been any further nighttime visits. Heather had resumed having her regular lunch with Sue the past couple of days, and today, she'd even played basketball with friends after school to get ready for team tryouts. As long as she kept busy, Heather could keep looking forward and ignore the past.

She rinsed her dishes, put them into the dishwasher, and looked in the special drawer for some chocolate.

Thankfully, her mom also had a thing for chocolate, so the drawer always had something to offer.

Heather thought briefly about studying for the history exam Monday morning but quickly dismissed the thought. It was Friday night after all, and besides, the last time she tried to read about the French Revolution, the violence brought back her memories of that terrible night. It was as if she was reliving the assault all over again.

No, tonight she would check out the latest movies on Netflix. Heather was just about to turn on the TV when she heard a knock at the front door.

"My mom and stepdad have friends over, so I thought I'd come by and hang out," Sue said as Heather let her in the door out of the rain. "I thought the rain had stopped, but luckily I wore my raincoat just in case. Where are your mom and Ted? I only see one car in the driveway."

"Oh, Ted surprised mom with a so-called romantic getaway in a cabin somewhere south of here. I'm just glad to have the house all to myself for the weekend," Heather answered.

"Great! We can have a party!" Sue exclaimed. "I could post something on Facebook, and we'd have this place hopping in no time!"

"Absolutely not. I'm not going to spend all day tomorrow cleaning up after your friends trash this house. Besides, I'm in no mood for a party."

"Hey ...what's gotten into you? You love parties! And they're not just my friends; they're your friends too. You know, you've been acting very different lately. Almost like you're here one moment and then spaced out the next."

Sue came in and plopped down in her favorite chair, wearing her usual dark gray yoga pants along with a bright top and Asics running shoes.

"I'm sorry; you know it doesn't have anything do to with you," Heather answered as she sat down on the couch across from Sue. "It's just that some things have kept me preoccupied recently."

"No kidding! You haven't been yourself all week. What's going on?"

Heather grabbed a hairband and pulled her hair back into a ponytail as she considered what to tell Sue. She smiled to herself as she noticed they were both wearing similar yoga pants and shoes. Heather had known Sue since third grade, and Sue was not only her best friend, but she had also been a faithful friend through the years. Heather didn't doubt Sue would keep her secret. What she didn't know was how Sue would react.

"If I do tell you, you absolutely can't tell anyone," Heather said slowly and deliberately.

"Wow...you sound serious. Of course, I won't tell anyone. But now you're scaring me."

"Something really...really horrible happened to me last Sunday night." Heather began, starting to feel her emotions churn as the memories of that night floated to the surface again for the umpteenth time.

"I don't know any other way to say this..." Heather continued, struggling to keep from crying. "That night...Ted came into my room...and raped me." As Heather said that word for the first time, she felt a profound shift within her, as if she were finally acknowledging what had actually happened. Her anger, shame, and disgust came rushing back, causing her to break down in a gush of tears.

Sue sat stunned for several seconds, working through the shock of what she had just heard. Then she quickly climbed onto the couch next to Heather, holding and comforting her. It took a few minutes before Sue could say anything.

"I...I'm so sorry, Heather. Why didn't you tell me? I had no idea something that horrible had happened to you. I can't imagine how terrifying it's been for you. And you've been dealing with this all by yourself."

When several minutes had passed, and Heather had slowed her crying, Sue asked, "Did you tell your mother?"

"I thought about it and almost told her the next day. But Ted threatened to tell a bunch of lies about me if I told her," Heather answered, wiping the tears from her cheeks.

"What kind of lies?"

"Ted said that if I told Mom, he would tell her that I've been acting like a slut when she wasn't around, trying to seduce him," Heather answered, starting to cry again.

"That's ridiculous!" Sue exclaimed. "How could she ever believe anything like that about you? You've never acted like a slut. You're the one who gets weird and nervous when you're around a guy you like. Besides, it's totally creepy that you'd like someone as old as Ted."

"But she might think I was trying to come between them," Heather answered, pulling away from Sue.

"I don't understand."

"You know how my mom has been ignoring me since she married Ted, especially lately and all the fights we've had because of it."

"Yeah," Sue said as she returned to her chair.

"Well, not long ago, Mom threatened a couple of times to send me back to live with my dad."

"I still don't get it."

Heather looked at Sue, then turned away, gathering her thoughts. "Mom knows that I don't like Ted and that I want to go back to the time when it was just the two of us.

I'm afraid she might start thinking that I've come up with a plan to get rid of Ted by seducing him."

"Why would she think that?"

"Ted overheard some of those fights, and I think that's where he got the idea that he could threaten me by telling my mom that I'm trying to seduce him."

"It's still absurd," Sue replied. "I can't believe your mom would choose to believe Ted over you."

"That's because you and your mom are close, Sue. Besides, you didn't see how needy Mom was right after the divorce."

"What do you mean?"

"She was different; it's hard to describe. After the divorce, when dad wasn't around, Mom loved hanging out with me whenever she wasn't working. We'd have fun doing girl things. But it was also kinda weird because it seemed like she wanted to be my best friend, not my mother. Don't get me wrong, I really loved spending all that time with Mom, but it was as if she needed something from me. Then Ted came along, and everything went back like before, with Mom essentially ignoring me."

"So you think your mom might actually believe Ted?" Sue asked.

"I can't take that chance. There's no way I can go back living with Dad. He scares me to death when he's drunk."

Sue looked out the front window processing this latest tragedy in Heather's life. She thought back to the many hours she had spent with Heather after one of her father's raging episodes, and how terrified Heather had been. Sue knew what it was like to grow up in a home with an angry man. It was the main reason she and Heather had bonded so many years ago. Sue's stepfather also had a temper, but at least he didn't hit anyone. He would yell, slam doors, and sometimes bang his fist against something, but that was all he did.

"Now you have Ted to be afraid of as well," Sue sighed, not knowing what else to say.

"I know," Heather answered quietly. "But he's left me alone since that night, and I'm hoping it will never happen again. Besides, I don't know what else to do."

"You can't go to the police if you don't want your mother to know, so I can't come up with anything either at the moment. But there's no way you can't tell your mother if Ted ever shows any sign of doing something like that again," Sue replied.

"Don't worry…I plan to."

"I don't like talking about this creepy stuff so what do you think about binging on The Vampire Diaries?" Sue suggested.

"Great idea," Heather answered, relieved that Sue finally knew the truth about what had happened to her.

The rest of the weekend passed uneventfully, allowing Heather to catch up on homework before Ted and her mom returned home on Sunday evening. Their mushy talk and giggling when they walked in the door, told Heather the weekend had been good for both of them. By the time she went to bed Sunday night, Heather had realized that much of the dread she was carrying had lifted to the point that she began to believe things might work out. The talk with Sue had helped Heather release some of the shame from the attack, while also helping her feel more confident that she had made the right decision not to tell her mother.

By the following Wednesday, Heather was feeling hopeful about her life, anxious to try out again for the basketball team. She just missed making the team the previous year, and since two of the starters had graduated, her chances of making the team this year were looking good. She might even end up starting as a point guard.

After her mom left for work late Wednesday evening, Heather decided to take a quick shower before going to bed. Ted had been quiet most of the evening, off by himself in the living room. A few minutes after getting into the shower, Heather heard the bathroom door open.

She suddenly froze …she had locked the door!!

How did he…suddenly the shower curtain was thrown aside as Ted stood leering at her.

"Get out of here!!" Heather yelled as she tried to cover herself.

Ted smiled malevolently, slowly reaching for a towel as he continued to stare.

"If you tell your mother anything, I'll just lie about it," Ted threatened as he left the bedroom. "Your mother is going to believe me long before she believes you. I made sure of that this past weekend."

As Ted left, Heather lay in the bed, crying and shaking all over. She worked to quiet her sobs so Ted wouldn't hear. After several minutes, she put on her pajamas and sat in the bed with her knees drawn up so she could wrap her arms around her legs and quietly cry. Heather felt flooded once again with shame and anger, unable to think clearly. She needed to make a plan and get her thoughts together. If only she could calm herself down.

"God, I know it's been a long time, but I need your help…"

*****

Taron quickly flew into Heather's bedroom from the backyard, his sword shining brightly in front of him as he came straight at Kul, who was hovering on Heather's shoulder with both hands plunged deep into her skull. The sudden appearance of Taron caught Kul off guard, and before he could defend himself, Taron knocked Kul off Heather with the hilt of the sword before expertly placing its point under Kul's oversized chin.

"Now it's my turn," Taron exclaimed. "Back away and keep your filthy hands out of her head."

"You have no authority here," Kul whined in his high-pitched voice, as he slowly backed further away, grasping his small sword.

"That just changed. While you were trying to plant your poisonous thoughts, Heather prayed and asked for help, so now I have all the authority I need," Taron answered. "Get out of my way before I let you draw that puny thing and show you how quickly I can separate your hand from your wrist."

Kul continued backing away, cringing at Taron's greater size and strength, while also shielding his eyes from the brilliant light around Taron. He slowly rose to an upper corner of the room, perching himself in a position facing Taron, determined to stay as close to Heather as possible. Taron settled himself behind Heather, laying his sword next to him as he glanced up at Kul. Taron then placed his enormous hands around Heather's head and began massaging, allowing his peace to soak into Heather.

Taron had lacked the authority to prevent the assault, but he was now thrilled to be able to provide comfort to Heather during this difficult time. When he saw Bazen arrive earlier to join Ted, he had decided to wait outside the house, surmising what was going to happen. Taron was familiar with Bazen and his habit of using addiction to pornography to gain access to his human instruments. Over the past couple of years, Bazen had been a frequent companion of Ted's, facilitating numerous sexual assaults.

Taron looked down tenderly at Heather, gently stroking her face, sensing her emotions of shame and terror slowly empty out of her as a tear rolled down his cheek.

*****

As Heather sat in the bed, she began to feel much better, as if all the bad emotions were draining away. The memory of the terrible attack remained, but now the shame and terror weren't nearly as prominent. Her crying eased considerably, and Heather found that her shaking had also stopped. A peace slowly settled over her, and she found herself strangely comforted. Maybe she would get through this after all, she thought.

As her thinking cleared, Heather realized that she had to make a plan to tell her mother. She was never going to be safe alone in the house with Ted, and only her mother could help her. She would have to tell her soon, and tell her is such a way that she would have no choice but to believe her. Heather drifted off to sleep as the strange peace continued to envelop her.

The next day, Heather hurried home after school, anxious to get things out in the open with her mother. But when she walked into the house, Heather found a note on the kitchen table:

> 'I'm out shopping and will be meeting Ted for dinner later this evening. There's leftover casserole in the fridge. Enjoy your evening. Mom.'

Of all the nights to have yet another date with Ted! Heather slumped down in the chair to think through her next steps. It was less than an hour before Ted got off work, and there was no way she wanted to call her mom's cell phone and tell her about this over the phone. She had no choice but to wait until they both got home after dinner and try to get her mother alone. The private conversation with her mother was not turning out the way Heather had envisioned.

After finishing dinner, Heather paced around the house, unable to concentrate on any homework or even watch TV. She carefully thought through the approach she would take with her mother, knowing it was essential to include some details from each assault. However, the attack last night was still blurred in her mind after Ted dragged Heather out of the bathroom. She would tell her mother everything she could remember, making the point that it was Ted that had initiated both attacks. Her mother had to believe her.

When Ted and her mom came in around 8 o'clock, they were both laughing and being affectionate with each other. When her mom saw Heather standing in the living room, her facial expression quickly changed, and she suddenly became serious. Ted looked at Heather and gave her a sly smile before walking up the stairs to their bedroom.

Heather was confused by her mother's sudden change in expression but decided to press ahead anyway.

"Mom, we need to talk," Heather started.

"I agree, we absolutely should talk," her mother answered. "Ted's been telling me about some alarming habits you've taken up lately while I'm at work."

"Mom, it's not like that," Heather replied, growing more anxious. "Ted is not the same person when you're not here.

He's been staring at me for several weeks now and the other night..."

"Don't be ridiculous," her mother interrupted. "Ted has no interest in you! He's very much in love with me. I finally have someone who loves and cares for me, and here you are trying to mess it up."

Heather was startled at the sudden change of attitude in her mother and the approach she was taking. She began to shake all over, realizing this conversation wasn't going at all as she had hoped.

"Mom! He raped me the Sunday before you went on your getaway," Heather said as she began to cry.

"I've heard enough!" her mother screamed. "If that actually happened, why didn't you tell me right away? Why wait until now? No...you didn't tell me because it never happened! It never happened because this is all something you've made up in your mind so that I'll get mad at Ted and make him go away. You've never liked him, and apparently, you don't want me to be happy. He told me you might try something like this after all your slinking around trying to seduce him. I won't have it, you hear! I won't have it. Any more of this, and I'll send you to your father!" With that, Heather's mom turned and walked up the stairs, leaving Heather in a state of shock.

Ted had outsmarted Heather and turned her mother against her. He must have been planning this all along. Heather couldn't believe how suddenly everything in her life had turned upside down. She sat on the floor crying, completely overwhelmed. She had no idea what to do now.

After some time, Heather gathered herself up and slowly walked up to her room. She felt a sense of darkness and fear slowly descend on her as she realized the terrible truth. If her mother didn't protect her from Ted, Heather only had two terrifying options. Either she could stay in this house with the ongoing possibility of another assault by Ted, or she could leave and try to somehow live on her own.

If Heather knew one thing for sure, she never wanted Ted touching her again.

*****

"It's always difficult to watch a parent ignore the needs of one of their children, especially when those needs are so desperate," Taron said as he floated next to Corel, looking down on the scene below. Taron glanced over at Kul in the corner of the living room, placing his hand on his sword to remind Kul not to bother trying to attach himself to Heather during this vulnerable moment.

"When humans are sinfully obsessed with meeting their emotional needs, they become blind to the needs of those around them," Corel noted. "This wrong decision to believe Ted at the expense of Heather is the culmination of increasing self-centered behavior on Nancy's part. She has repeatedly made decisions that are opposed to God's will for her life, providing Skulty the ongoing authority to influence her. Until Nancy's attitude changes, there is no need for my presence in her life, so I'm returning to Solen to seek a new assignment."

"When you update Solen, tell him I would appreciate additional prayer support as I pour into Heather the comfort and peace she will need to make it through this difficult time," Taron replied as he floated over to join Heather in her room, and relieve some of her suffering.

"For the Lord and His glory"

Chapter 4

Battle Preparation

Eric opened the front door to let Jason and Heidi come in out of the rain. "Come in you two before you get soaked."

"I can't believe it's been raining continuously for three days," Heidi replied as she walked into the entryway. "If I didn't know better, I'd start looking for an ark."

"I don't mind the rain as much as the chill telling us winter is coming," Jason added. "But I checked the forecast, and we're finally going to see the sun tomorrow, just in time for me to catch up with some of my outdoor chores." They both shook their umbrellas out the front door before handing them to Eric, who placed them in the closet.

Jason was a gifted pastor with a golden retriever personality that made him a friend of everyone he met.

Though he had not started Brookview Community Church, it had thrived under his dynamic leadership the past eight years, nearly doubling in size. Heidi was his anchor; his best friend who kept him grounded and wouldn't let success go to Jason's head. Together they were raising a family of three girls of their own, and two adopted boys from Ethiopia.

"Thank you for giving up a Friday night to come to join us," Maggie said as she walked in from the kitchen.

"Are you kidding? We've been looking forward to this celebration for months. Besides, I've earned this meal with all the encouragement I've poured into this guy," Jason said as he slapped Eric on the back.

"Just to be clear, there was at least one time when I encouraged you," Eric laughed.

"Yeah, wasn't that three years ago when I was depressed about turning 40?" Jason retorted as they walked into the kitchen.

"Your timing is perfect," Maggie said. "I just took the pizza out of the oven. Come on into the dining room and find a place to sit down."

"We're having your famous homemade sausage pizza?" Jason asked excitedly.

"Nothing but the best for our dear friends in the Lord," Maggie smiled. "Besides, it's one of Eric's favorites as well, so what better way to celebrate!"

They all sat down around the table, and after a prayer of thanks, Eric passed the pizza to Heidi. As she took the pizza, Heidi asked, "So Eric, what does this mean for you and Hope House, now that you have your license?"

"Getting the license to care for minors was the last barrier preventing us from opening. So now we can begin hiring and training the women we need to staff the house."

"So, have you set an opening date yet?" Jason asked.

"Not officially, but we should be able to open in two or three weeks."

"That's terrific," Jason replied. "All kidding aside, I know that you both have had to overcome many challenges to finally reach this point."

"Tell me about it," Maggie interjected. "These past several Fridays, Eric's come home frustrated that another week went by without any word from the state. I was beginning to dread Fridays."

"Sorry…I've been trying hard not to be impatient, but apparently I wasn't successful," Eric replied, giving Maggie a repentant glance.

"So Eric, what do you think your greatest personal struggle is going to be, now that Hope House is about to open?" Jason replied, asking one of his usual penetrating questions.

"Wow, that's going deep fast, even for you, Jason," Eric responded.

"One of the prerogatives and perhaps the dangers of being a pastor," Jason smiled back as he looked around the table, catching a warning look from Heidi.

"Well, since I haven't even finished my first piece of pizza, I'd have to stop and think about it," Eric chuckled. "My first thought is just finding the time to do everything I need to do."

"Have you thought about the possibility of increased spiritual attack?"

"Jason, you don't always have to get so intense so fast," Heidi said as she gave her husband her 'back off' look.

"I recognize that the work of Hope House is going to stir up many of the enemy's forces. Frankly, I'm a little worried about you, Eric," Jason answered as he gently smiled back at Heidi.

"What exactly are you worried about?" Maggie asked. "Do you think he's in some form of spiritual danger?"

"Well, I wouldn't put it precisely that way. However, no one can argue that sex trafficking is evil and therefore facilitated by the enemy. What Eric and Hope House are doing is redeeming young lives from the enemy's control. That makes them a target, so Eric and his team should be careful not to underestimate the enemy's response. As Eric's pastor, I see one of my roles as preparing him for that battle."

"I'm glad you asked that Jason," Eric responded. "In spite of not getting the license until this week, I've been way too busy writing grants and digging out from the onslaught of emails that seem to increase every day. Three weeks ago, I began to go into the office an hour earlier to keep up. But unfortunately, it's cut into my devotional time."

"That's what I'm worried about," Jason responded. "It's easy to focus time and effort on what's immediately in front of us. But we often do that at the expense of our relationship with Jesus. That's just what the enemy wants. I'd be happy to begin meeting with you weekly to help you keep that spiritual focus if that would help."

"Well, I don't really have a time slot available, but I also can't afford to get ambushed by an unexpected spiritual attack," Eric answered. "Can you do an early breakfast on Monday mornings?"

"For you brother, that time slot just happens to be open. How about the Red Lantern at 6:30 AM?"

"Perfect!"

*****

The brilliance of the two angels floating up through the roof of Eric and Maggie's home radiated across the spiritual realm surrounding their house. As the commanding angel of the city, Solen was larger than Riel, with a brightness that matched his authority. Typically, an angel with Solen's status would confine his efforts to overseeing the angelic nexus of the city. Instead, Solen chose to spend much of his time in the company of Jason. Solen believed that it helped him maintain a more accurate sense of the spiritual condition of Jesus' local flock.

Jason didn't have the largest church in the city, but he was fully consecrated to the Lord, daily offering himself to the service of Jesus.

Additionally, his many hours of prayer each week allowed Jason to maintain a closeness to the Spirit that was unrivaled in the city.

Riel had been assigned to Eric more than 20 years previously, diligently assisting his spiritual growth and maturity through the years, as well as fending off the occasional unwarranted spiritual attack. Riel was quite proud of the fact that his charge had been chosen by the Lord to start Hope House.

"Meeting regularly with Jason will further enhance his preparations for spiritual battle," Riel noted. "Jason's aggressive questioning tonight exposed Eric's complacency enough for him to see his need for help. Planting the idea for a weekly meeting during Jason's prayer time this morning was brilliant, Solen."

"The Spirit has been bringing Eric to Jason's attention these past several weeks, so it was an easy addition," Solen responded. "I'm thankful they had this time together tonight in a setting outside the church."

"What are the plans for increasing prayer support for Eric and his staff, now that they've crossed this latest threshold?" Riel asked, turning toward his commander.

"I've instructed the angelic nexus to increase the prayer burden for Hope House within our prayer warriors throughout the city. The nexus will also begin promoting prayer requests for Hope House in all the praying churches through their social media platforms."

"I've noticed a decrease in demonic activity against both Eric and his staff recently. I'm wondering if it might be a prelude to a much larger attack," Riel pondered. "Has the Spirit told you anything about such an attack, and how it might present?"

"The Spirit has chosen not to inform me yet. However, the Lord has placed enough importance on the mission of Hope House to send a Watcher to help monitor the movements of the enemy around the city," Solen noted.

"It's been decades since I was involved with a mission that included a Watcher."

"Yes, it's tangible evidence that the Lord has prioritized helping Eric and his team begin gathering in His future daughters."

"If the Lord has sent a Watcher, it's likely the enemy is planning a major attack against Hope House."

"That shouldn't surprise us," Solen answered. "As Jason pointed out, the mission of Hope House is in direct opposition to the enemy's strategy, forcing them to respond. And centuries of warfare have taught us that their response to opposition is never weak."

"But regardless of how violently they react to opposition, the Lord's will is always accomplished."

"For the Lord and His glory!" exclaimed both Solen and Riel.

*****

Eric took a sip of coffee as he gazed out the window of the Red Lantern restaurant, reviewing the many tasks awaiting him that week. However, his first task was to decide on what to have for breakfast. Glancing down at the plastic-covered menu in front of him, Eric settled on the Farmers Special, a three-egg omelet, ham, fried potatoes, and a glass of OJ. That should give him a good start for the day.

"Good morning brother," Jason said as he sat down in the booth across from Eric. "I see you've already got your coffee."

"Just trying to get myself geared up for whatever comes this week," Eric answered. "Say, was it my imagination, or did you preach about spiritual warfare yesterday because of our work at Hope House?"

"I've actually been planning to talk about spiritual warfare for several months, but I do think the timing was providential," Jason responded. "Anything strike home for you?"

"Not really. I remember what you said the other night at dinner, but I still have trouble imagining that the enemy is all that concerned about me and the work of Hope House."

"Are you kidding? I don't know anyone in our church more likely to encounter spiritual warfare than you in your work fighting sex trafficking. Don't you understand you are a prime target?"

"Well…I guess I'm still getting used to that idea."

"Eric, it would be helpful for you to expand the way you look at the world to include the spiritual realm. There is far more going on around us than what we see physically."

After the waitress had taken their orders and walked away, Eric asked, "OK, what should I know about spiritual warfare, especially since according to you, I'm a prime target?"

Jason took out his ever-present Bible and opened it. "One of the best places to begin is the passage I referenced yesterday in Ephesians chapter six. There, Paul wrote:

> 'We do not wrestle against flesh and blood, but against the rulers, against the authorities, against the cosmic powers over this present darkness, against the spiritual forces of evil in the heavenly places.'

So, my point is that the Bible makes it clear that there are spiritual forces at work all around us."

"But aren't those spiritual forces focused on Christian work that you do in the church, rather than what the rest of us do."

"Eric, what is your ultimate goal for Hope House?"

"To restore girls who are survivors of sex trafficking."

"And as part of that restoration, won't you be introducing them to Jesus Christ?"

"Sure...but..."

"Then, what's different between that goal and what we do in the church?"

"Well...not so much, I guess."

"Eric, you plan to restore girls coming out of the control of the darkest powers active in our world today. Then you plan to lead them to Jesus Christ. Don't you think that will get the attention of those dark powers?"

"Now that you put it that way, I suppose it probably will get their attention."

"Not probably...definitely."

"I get that, but I'm still not sure why you are worried about me. I'm a faithful member of our church; I read the Bible and pray regularly. I should be protected, right?"

"Not necessarily, especially with the level of evil you will be encountering."

"Now you are beginning to make me nervous, Jason."

"I don't want you to be nervous, but I do want you to be alert and prepared as Peter tells us in his first letter."

"So, how do I go about getting prepared?"

"First and foremost is prayer. And speaking of prayer, let me pray before we eat," Jason responded as the waitress brought their food.

They both spent a few minutes quietly eating before Eric continued the conversation. "So when you say prayer, do you mean spending more time in general prayer, or that I should be praying in some specific way?"

"A little of both. I would describe it as developing an attitude of prayer."

"How do I do that?"

Jason paused to collect his thoughts before continuing. "An attitude of prayer begins with the realization that we don't ever accomplish anything of eternal value without God's help. Someone who fully understands this will possess a natural inclination toward prayer to the point that prayer becomes an ongoing habit throughout the day."

"There's no question I need to work on that," Eric replied. "Last month, I was halfway through our board meeting when I realized that I hadn't started the meeting with prayer. As if that wasn't bad enough, I also realized I hadn't prayed ahead of time for the meeting."

"That's a perfect example of my greatest concern for you. The likely reason you didn't pray in preparation for the meeting was self-reliance rather than relying on God. That attitude creates vulnerability to the enemy's attack."

"OK, but praying frequently throughout the day sounds difficult, especially when life gets hectic like mine has become these past few months."

"It's not as difficult as you might think," Jason answered. "The prayers don't have to be long and involved. It starts with an attitude that over time, becomes a habit."

"So, have you developed this habit in your own life?" Eric asked.

"I'd say that I'm still in process. But I can tell you that the longer I work at it, the easier it gets. For instance, even during our conversation now, I've asked the Lord to give me the wisdom to say the right things. I've learned the hard way that left to my own devices, I usually mess things up."

"Really...I've never imagined praying during a conversation."

Eric sat quietly eating his omelet, collecting his thoughts, before asking his next question. "OK, so I need to work on developing an attitude of prayer, which again, will not be easy. What else?"

"Do you remember the passage in Matthew seven where Jesus tells us to remove the log from our own eye before we attempt to remove the speck from someone else's eye?"

"Yeah, but I'm not sure what that has to do with spiritual warfare," Eric replied.

"Believe me; it has a lot to do with spiritual warfare. Jesus is telling us that before we can help someone else, we must first fully understand ourselves, most importantly, our personal faults."

"Great. I was hoping for a few pointers to help me be a better spiritual warrior, but instead, you're asking me to self-psychoanalyze!"

Jason chuckled as he pushed his plate away and looked directly at Eric.

"No, Dr. Freud, I'm not asking you to self-psychoanalyze, but you do need to understand what motivates you."

"Shucks…I was hoping that after I mastered the art, I could turn my attention to you," Eric chuckled.

"Oh, don't you worry…I'm still learning my faults the hard way as a pastor, believe me," Jason laughed. "But seriously, when we understand our weaknesses, or to put it into warfare terminology, our vulnerabilities, we can better prepare ourselves for a spiritual attack."

"So you're saying that if I know myself well enough, especially my weaknesses, I'll be better prepared for spiritual warfare," Eric replied.

"That's it in a nutshell."

"So as my pastor, what weakness or vulnerability do I have that I should be concerned about?" Eric asked, looking directly back at Jason.

"Since you've brought up the example of neglecting to pray before a board meeting, I'm concerned that you are becoming too self-reliant as you lead Hope House. That may be because you struggle with something common to many people, including myself."

"What struggle would that be?"

"Deriving your sense of identity or worth from what you do, or in your case, your role as executive director of Hope House. Far too many men and women derive their worth from their jobs or status in society, rather than their adoption as God's son or daughter."

"Wow, that sounds deep, but I think I know where you're going with this. How can I know whether or not I'm deriving my identity from Hope House?" Eric asked.

"You'll be able to gather clues by watching your emotional state."

"Now you've lost me. Can you give me an example?"

Jason took a few minutes to think through his answer. "When you derive your sense of worth from your role at Hope House, you'll feel like you're on an emotional roller coaster. When things are going well, you'll feel good. When problems arise, or something doesn't go the way you want, you'll feel frustrated. Does that make sense?"

"Yes, it does."

"But when you are fully living out of your identity as a son of God, you will only want what the Father wants. Since the Father always accomplishes His will, there's no need to worry or become anxious. Therefore, instead of having your emotions go up or down, you should experience profound peace."

Eric sat thinking through Jason's explanation for several minutes. "I theoretically understand what you are saying. But actually living that way is not easy."

"I agree; it is difficult...but you can accomplish it with persistent practice, and the result is rewarding. Your life will radiate with the fruit of the Spirit, especially peace. Do you understand now?"

"Yeah...to some degree, but I'll have to think about it more on my own. Maggie can confirm my emotional lability the past couple of months. Which if I understand you correctly, means that to some degree, I've been deriving my worth from my identity as ED of Hope House."

"It's easy to fall into that habit, but if you recognize it, there are things you can do to realign your heart to live your life as a son of God. We'll talk about those things next week. In the meantime, I would suggest spending some time meditating on Colossians chapter three, verses one to four."

"Sounds like a plan. Thanks brother!" Eric replied.

*****

"Jason's instinct that Eric is deriving his sense of worth from his role with Hope House is right on target," Riel observed, floating next to Solen near the ceiling of the restaurant. "If Eric successfully realigns his identity as a son, he will be far more resistant to an attack from the enemy."

"Eric's greatest challenge will be the lack of time in the coming weeks," Solen responded. "It will be helpful if you can find a way to create more flexibility in his schedule."

"Good idea…I'll discuss it with the Hope House nexus. We'll look for opportunities for the staff to free up Eric's schedule."

"Also, please pass on the message that last evening, the Watcher reported a new demonic presence around one of the board members," Solen added. "The enemy must be detecting some spiritual vulnerability with this board member, and is planning to exploit this weakness."

"Which board member is it?"

"Abigail Wilson."

"Did the Watcher give details about this presence?" Riel inquired.

"He did mention a prominence of pride and secrecy, but couldn't elaborate further, which is unusual."

"That fits the news I was going to bring you this morning. Joft just told me that Marge has met with Abigail on several occasions, discussing concerns regarding Eric's methods."

"This is a worrisome development," Solen responded. "It confirms that the enemy is centering on Abigail, and may somehow be using Marge."

"We haven't noticed any unusual demonic presence around Marge beyond her small demons of selfishness and self-pity. Has the Watcher observed anything that we've missed?"

"He hasn't seen any new demonic presence around Marge either. Perhaps the enemy is attempting to probe Marge regarding her allegiance to Eric."

"That probing could produce some nasty fruit if the influence of self-pity increases significantly," Riel noted. "It could result in pride that allows further manipulation by the enemy. Does the Watcher have any idea of the enemy's plan for Abigail?"

"No. The Watcher mentioned that the demonic presence has some form of barrier preventing him from accurately discerning the spiritual activity around her," Solen answered.

"What can block the vision of a Watcher?" Riel asked incredulously.

"Another Watcher, or in this case, a fallen Watcher."

"If the enemy is using a fallen Watcher, it's likely that this upcoming attack will come at a time and manner that will be hard to predict."

"Which is why we must be vigilant in all our efforts."

"Joft also informed me that Marge recently met with Rachel secretly. But according to Joft, Marge didn't say anything untoward about Eric or the rest of the staff."

"Secrecy is always from the enemy. Tell Joft to immediately report any further secret meetings Marge undertakes with any of the staff. Now that we've established a direct connection between Marge and a board member the enemy is manipulating, we'll need to observe her closely. I'll send out an additional prayer alert to Marge's church for them to pray for her protection against the attack she's come under."

"I'll let Joft know right away to report any further secret meetings."

"For the Lord and His glory!"

Chapter 5

The Gateway

Heather waited impatiently at Sue's locker, trying not to make eye contact with her friends as they walked by. She needed to talk to Sue, but she didn't need the prying questions from her other friends, especially not today.

"Where have you been all day?" Sue exclaimed as she came up behind Heather.

"We need to talk."

"I'd say...but seriously, where have you been? I barely saw you yesterday, and I haven't seen you at all today. I texted several times, but you never responded."

"I've been home. I didn't want to come to school today, so I faked an email from my mom saying I was sick. She was gone shopping all day since she didn't work last night. I'll tell you more once we're outside," Heather answered.

Sue quickly put some books into the locker, slammed the door closed, and walked outside with Heather, slinging her backpack onto her shoulder.

"Did something happen with Ted again?" Sue asked as they made it to the sidewalk.

"Yeah," Heather replied, trying not to get too emotional. She quickly described the shower episode from Wednesday night, leaving out the worst details. Heather finished by mentioning the strange sense of peace that came over her afterward, adding that it had helped her get through the past couple of days.

"What do you think caused this feeling?" Sue asked. "I hope you're not going crazy with all that's happened to you."

"Thanks for the confidence," Heather replied, smirking at Sue. "As I've thought about it, I remembered that the peace came over me after I prayed."

"Really! You think the feeling was an answer to prayer?"

"I don't know...I'm just glad it happened. I honestly don't know what I would have done without it."

"Ted's worse than a pervert. He's a predator. I hope he goes to jail for a long time for this. You told your mom, right?" Sue asked.

"Yeah, but it didn't go well. Ted had just taken her out to dinner and managed to convince her that I was trying to seduce him. He gave her the whole spiel about how I wanted to get between the two of them so she would get mad and make him leave."

"She actually believed that?"

"Unfortunately..."

"So what did she do when you told her about Ted coming into the bathroom?"

"I never got that far. When I started to tell mom what Ted had done, she was already mad at me and didn't want to listen. She just yelled at me and went upstairs."

"Man, I'm so sorry, Heather. It's hard to believe your mom would be so blind."

"I know…it took me some time to pull myself together after that. Thankfully, that peaceful feeling came over me again."

"So now what are you going to do?"

"The only thing I can think of is talking to mom again at a better time. I need to convince her of the truth," Heather replied. "Luckily, mom was off last night, so I didn't have to worry about Ted, but she works this weekend. I was wondering if I could come and hang at your house until Sunday evening when she's home again?"

"I don't think that will be a problem. Why don't you go home and grab your things and then come over. I'll work things out with my mom in the meantime."

"Perfect…thanks Sue."

*****

Corel joined Taron far above the two girls as they continued walking down the street.

"Solen sent me to investigate your plans to help Heather through the weekend since her mother is working," Corel inquired.

"Earlier today, I successfully planted the idea for Heather to stay at Sue's for the weekend, and Sue just informed Heather she could make it happen."

"Good…that means she'll be safe for at least a few nights. When I told Solen that Bazen didn't follow his usual pattern of leaving Ted after inciting him into an attack, he agreed that Bazen was probably planning an additional assault this weekend," Corel commented.

"Well, I'm sure Ted will be quite upset when he finds out we've interfered with those plans."

"It looks like Kul is also dismayed at being preempted by you because of Heather's prayer," Corel noted, as he looked back at the demon following at a distance.

"Kul's a low-level demon with no appetite for combat. He's been sulking ever since I surprised him the other night. But Bazen will not take the disappointment so lightly. What if he plants the idea for Ted to look for Heather?"

"Solen asked me to help you protect Heather from Ted this weekend. I could stay at Heather's house and keep Bazen distracted so that he's unable to cause any further problems with Heather. I've met Bazen in battle before, and I'm sure he remembers who got the best of whom," Corel replied.

"Heather is going to need this quiet weekend. Her pain and suffering are just beginning, and she could use a couple of peaceful days to allow me to build some inner strength into her so she doesn't succumb to depression and despair," Taron noted.

"Solen assigned you to Heather for a reason, Taron. He has complete confidence that you will be able to get Heather through this difficult time. Besides, the Spirit will enable you as always. In the meantime, I'll get this positive news back to Solen."

"For the Lord and His glory!" they both exclaimed.

*****

"You're just in time for dinner," Sue replied as she led Heather up the stairs toward her room. "Go ahead and throw your things into your usual spot in my room. I just finished making the extra bed."

"Thanks. So your mom was OK with me staying over?"

"Sure...I told her things aren't good at your house right now, and she understood. It didn't hurt that she and Bill had a blowup a few weeks ago."

"You never told me that," Heather replied.

"You were going through your own troubles, remember? I didn't want to bother you with it. Besides, it didn't last long, and I think they've worked everything out."

"I'm sorry I wasn't available to help during that time," Heather replied.

"No worries...it wasn't your fault. Besides, my small stress here doesn't even compare to what you've been through these past few weeks."

Heather and Sue walked into the kitchen. "Hello, Mrs. Johnson. Thanks for letting me hang out for the weekend."

"Please, I've told you before Heather, call me Julie. Besides, you're almost family. We love having you stay with us, so it's no problem."

"What's for dinner, Mom?" Sue asked.

"Roast chicken, mashed potatoes, and vegetables. You've got impeccable timing Heather," Julie smiled. "I wanted to cook a big meal for Bill tonight since this has been a busy week for him. He should be walking through the door anytime."

Just then, Julie's phone beeped with a text. Julie's smile quickly faded as she read the message.

"It appears that Bill won't be home for dinner," Julie said with slight anger in her voice. "I don't know why he can't let me know sooner. You girls can grab what you want and eat in the living room where you can watch TV. I'll put the rest of this food away."

Sue and Heather grabbed some plates and loaded them with food, quickly disappearing into the living room.

"Sounds like more trouble is brewing," Heather observed.

"He's been doing this lately. I'm not sure what's going on, but I hope it blows over fairly quickly," Sue answered with a concerned look. "Let's not think about it and just watch TV."

Later that evening after Heather and Sue were in bed, Heather heard Julie and Bill arguing downstairs after Bill had come home. She looked over at Sue and saw her eyes were open in the dim light.

"Sorry, Sue," Heather whispered.

"Yeah, it sounds like they're back at it again. Mom lost a lot of trust in men when she caught Dad in an affair. Since that time, she's been super suspicious whenever Bill comes home late. I really hope it doesn't end up ruining our weekend together."

"So what do you do when they're fighting like this?"

"I just try and stay out of the way until the storm clouds leave."

"How long does that take?"

"Sometimes just a few hours, but sometimes it can be a few days. The longest I've seen them fight like this was a couple of weeks. I was afraid Bill was going to leave, then suddenly they worked things out."

"It sounds like you're glad your mom married Bill."

"Yeah, for the most part. He's stable and mostly good for Mom. He does have a temper, though, but he's never hit either Mom or me. It would be nice if he were open to going to church. Before Mom married him, we used to go to church most Sundays. The messages helped with the stress of Mom and Dad's divorce, and I even began reading the Bible. But after Mom and Bill got married, she quit going. It's too far for me to walk and Mom didn't want to take me each week. I kinda miss it," Sue replied.

"I know what you mean. When my mom and dad got divorced, Mom and I used to go to Brookview Community Church. They gave away Bibles, and I still have one somewhere. After church, Mom would take me to lunch at whatever restaurant I wanted. I really miss those times with my mom."

"Too bad Brookview is also on the other side of town. I wouldn't mind finding a good church nearby," Sue said.

"Yeah, me too. In the meantime, since I didn't get much sleep last night, I'm fading fast. Goodnight Sue, and thanks again for letting me stay with you this weekend."

"I'm glad it worked out. I hope the emotional weather around here is better tomorrow," Sue answered.

When Heather and Sue walked into the kitchen the next morning, they found Julie making coffee in her bathrobe.

"Morning, Mom," Sue said.

"Morning," Julie responded, without turning around.

"Should we just get some cereal for breakfast?" Sue asked.

"That's probably best. I don't feel like fixing anything this morning after I spent all that time in the kitchen yesterday. Besides, Bill took off early this morning before you two got up."

"Cereal's one of my favorites," Heather replied, trying not to make the situation more awkward.

"I'm going to run some errands this morning, so you two can just hang out here doing whatever," Julie said. "Just like usual, I don't know when Bill will be back, but you should have the house to yourself most of the day."

Jeff Barrows

"Sounds great; thanks, Mom," Sue replied.

Sue and Heather grabbed some bowls, cereal boxes, and milk, and sat down at the kitchen table, while Julie went upstairs to get dressed.

"She's a little upset isn't she," Heather asked quietly.

"She gets like this when she's mad at Bill. She'll go shopping, spend too much money, and end up taking back most of what she buys."

"Beats a lot of other ways to deal with stress. So what should we do after breakfast?" Heather asked.

"I know...I found this great free app that lets us broadcast video onto the Internet. It has chatrooms with all kinds of guys," Sue exclaimed. "I've downloaded it, but haven't had a chance to try it out. What do you think?"

"That sounds great! Who knows, we might even find some boys from around here. What's the name of the app?"

"You'reOn," Sue replied.

*****

Taron descended through the roof of Heather's house to come alongside Corel.

"I see you've been successful keeping Bazen occupied, so Ted isn't searching for Heather," Taron said as he looked down at Ted lusting in front of his computer screen with Bazen at his side.

"It only took a couple of reminders for Bazen to remember his defeat the last time we met," Corel chuckled. "Once he realized my blade hadn't slowed in the interim, he gave up the idea of having Ted find Heather, and is content just helping him indulge in his favorite pastime."

Bazen looked up at the two angels and spat angrily, before placing one hand on his sword, and the other on Ted's shoulder, intimating that they shouldn't try to take his prey from him.

"He's so absurd when he pretends to be brave," Corel commented as they backed to the far side of the house. "Any developments with Heather?"

"We've been unsure of the timing regarding Heather's introduction to You'reOn, but unfortunately, it will occur during her time with Sue today. This development accelerates our need for additional prayer support since it will be her gateway into a level of darkness few have experienced."

"And you will need all the prayer we can raise to get her through that difficult time. I need to notify Solen about this. Can you stay here for a few minutes while I go pass this information onto him?" Corel asked.

"Sure...I don't think Bazen will be a problem for me. Besides, I wouldn't mind a little sword practice if he decides to try something."

"When I update Solen, I'll remind him to have the prayer warriors pray not only for the future staff of Hope House but also for the future residents."

"For the Lord and His glory!" they both exclaimed.

*****

Sue and Heather giggled as they read the chat alongside their image streaming across the Internet. They were both lying on the floor of Sue's bedroom, still wearing their pajamas. They hadn't even taken the time to fix their hair, choosing instead to jump online right after breakfast. It was their attire that was drawing so much attention from their

Jeff Barrows

Internet admirers. They were amazed at how just doing a few little things like winking or blowing a kiss would create a surge of responses from the guys who were watching. They never got this kind of attention in school, which is why they had spent most of the morning and afternoon flirting online. One boy was especially attentive to their antics. He had been online most of the day as well and called himself SBC. Sue typed into the chatbox:

'So what does SBC stand for?'
'Shy but cute…'
'How do you know you're cute?'
'That's what some girls tell me.'
'Maybe you should be SBB…'
'What's that stand for?'
'Shy but boastful…'

Sue chuckled as she typed in the last line.
"Ask him how old he is," Heather replied.

'So, how old are you?'
'I'm 18, a senior in high school.'

"We're chatting with a senior!" Sue exclaimed. "I can't remember the last time any senior said anything to me at school, much less one that could be cute."
A new line appeared in the chatbox from SBC:

'Where do you both go to school?'
'We're students at Brookview.'

"Smart not telling him we're in ninth grade," Heather replied.

'Really…I'm only an hour away in Williamsburg.'
'Wow, what a coincidence!

"Ask him to send a picture," Heather said.

'Can you send a pic?'
'Do you want it with or without clothes?'

Both girls gave each other a confused look before Sue continued typing:

'With clothes of course…'

Within a couple of minutes, a picture appeared in the chat window. It was too small to make out very well, but Sue opened it with another program that allowed her to enlarge it. They found themselves looking at a handsome young man who could easily have been 18 years old. Sue quickly typed:

'Wow…you are cute!'
'Why thank you. Now, do you still think I'm boastful?'
'Well, you might be a little boastful, but maybe there's a reason.'
'So, do you think I could get one or both of your cell phone numbers?'

"Mom's told me never to give out my number to a stranger," Sue said as she turned to Heather. "What about you?"

"I feel a little uncomfortable doing that. But we could ask for SBC's number. It might be fun to talk to him on the phone sometime," Heather answered.

Sue turned back to the laptop:

'What if you give us your number, and maybe we'll call you sometime?'
'Sure…here it is.'

Heather and Sue both giggled as they wrote down the number. Heather then took her turn typing:

'Thanks, SBC. Since we have your phone number, could you tell us your real name?'
'I don't know…'
'Come on….pleeease.'
'Well, since you asked nicely, it's Derrick.'
'Thanks Derrick, you're the best. We have to grab some lunch, but we hope to be chatting/talking soon.'
'Until then, my sweet ladies.'

"Why'd you have to sign off so quickly?" Sue asked. "I was just getting warmed up, and see what he called us…his sweet ladies!"

"I'm sorry, I ran out of things to ask. Besides, we've been at this for hours, and I'm getting hungry. We can go back online after we eat. Maybe we'll even connect with other older boys who live nearby."

"Alright. Just in case Derrick's still online, we can decide what other things we want to know about him while we get some food," Sue replied as she looked at her watch. "Wow, it's almost 4 o'clock! I can't believe we've been online that long. We'd better get changed before we get something to eat."

As the girls came down the stairs, they heard Julie come in from the garage. She was carrying several packages from the mall, with an unhappy look on her face.

"What's wrong, Mom?" Sue asked.

"Nothing I want to talk about right now," Julie answered. "I thought I'd feel better after shopping, but I just had another fight with Bill, so I'm not in the best of moods. I don't feel like cooking tonight, so go ahead and order some pizza for delivery."

"OK...thanks Mom, and...sorry about Bill," Sue replied as she watched her mom go up the stairs. "It always bums me out when they fight like this," Sue said as tears formed in her eyes. "I just can't stand the thought of going through another divorce, especially when I think about what it did to Mom last time."

"Why can't adults get past themselves," Heather answered with a sudden burst of frustration. "My mom is so caught up in her private world, she doesn't see what's happening to me, and Ted ...he's just plain evil."

"I'm sorry, Heather, it's selfish of me to focus on my problems. At least Bill hasn't done anything close to what Ted's done to you. So when are you planning to talk to your mom again?"

"I have to find a time before Tuesday evening since she works that night."

"And what will you do if she still doesn't believe you?"

"I was thinking of asking if I could come and stay with you for a while, but with what's happening with your mom and Bill, it may not be a good idea."

"Unfortunately, you're probably right. The more normal things are around the house, the more likely they'll be able to work everything out. I wish things were different right now, Heather."

"It's OK. I'll find a way to convince my mom of the truth."

Chapter 6

The Betrayal

E ric unlocked the door of the office and put his computer bag on the large meeting table. He looked around the office, observing several messy desks, trying not to become frustrated. The staff had forgotten his request to clean up before the monthly board meeting. Eric berated himself for not arriving earlier, so he could straighten up if necessary, but now he didn't have time.

Eric found the coffee, measured his preferred amount into the filter, and started the coffee maker after filling it with water. He then began clearing scattered papers from the conference table, placing them on his desk. After putting the fresh Krispy Kreme donuts in the middle of the table, Eric set up his laptop at his usual spot at the table. He then took out the copies of the agenda and laid them at each of the other six seats.

Just as he was pouring a cup of coffee, Tom Anderson walked through the door wearing his police uniform.

"Hi Tom, are you just getting off a shift, or about to start one?"

"Morning, Eric. Fortunately, I don't have to do night shifts that often anymore, so I'm just starting my day shift."

"Help yourself to some coffee; I just finished making it."

"Thanks…I could use a fresh cup."

"I'm so glad you agreed to join our board. Your experience in law enforcement will bring a critical perspective to the organization, and I'm sure your passion for helping young girls will be infectious. Since this is your first meeting, I was going to ask you to share a little about yourself, if that's OK."

"Sure, I thought you might do that."

As Tom found a seat at the table, the rest of the Board members began filing in, some going to grab some coffee, while the others went and greeted Tom.

"Welcome everyone. I know that some of you don't like this early hour, especially on a Friday, but the Lord recognizes your sacrifice," Eric said, smiling, as he sat down. "We have a new Board member to introduce this morning plus a full agenda, so we'll get started as soon as everyone has a chance to get their java juice."

After everyone found their usual seats around the table, Eric opened the meeting with a quick prayer and then turned to Tom.

"This is Tom's first Board meeting, so I thought we would start by allowing him to tell us a little about himself, and then have each one of you take a few minutes to introduce yourselves, so he has an idea of just what kind of group he's joined," Eric started.

"Thanks, Eric," Tom began. "There's not a lot to tell you. As you can see, I work in law enforcement for the city, which is how I first learned about child sex trafficking. About three years ago, I was involved in a vice raid at a hotel in the city where neighbors had been complaining about drugs and prostitution. We initially thought we were going in to break up an adult prostitution ring, but we were also shocked to find fourteen, fifteen, and sixteen-year-olds working as prostitutes. None of us thought that type of thing happened here. That raid caused me to begin researching how young teenagers get caught into prostitution, and I've since learned that it's occurring in every major city in our state. About a year ago, I began training some of my fellow officers, and one day, I'd love to be able to focus on this problem full time."

"Could you give us a little information about your faith background, Tom," Eric asked.

"Sure, I grew up in the Grace Brethren Church and have known the Lord since I was in high school. I still attend there and have been teaching a Sunday school class for young adults for about ten years. I truly believe the Lord called me into the fight against child sex trafficking, so I'm honored to help Hope House out in whatever way I can. Thanks for asking me to join this board."

"Tom, we're honored to have you," Abigail replied. "As Board Chair, let me start our introductions. I've been on this board since Hope House started five years ago. My background is in business. I work at a local bank, and I learned about this issue through Eric's presentation at our church. When I first heard him, I knew I had to be involved in some way, so I was thrilled when Eric asked me to join the board as Hope House was starting up. My role besides chairing the board has been helping Eric and his staff network with various businesses around town."

"Well, since I'm sitting next to Abigail, I'll go next," Steve said. "My name is Steve Taylor. I am an accountant and have an accounting firm here in town. I go to the same church as Abigail, and I also learned about trafficking through Eric's presentation at our church. I've been on the board for about three years trying unsuccessfully to get Eric to move these meetings to a more decent hour," Steve chuckled as he looked at Eric. "I'm not a morning person like most of the rest here, but I'm honestly honored to be part of Hope House. As you can imagine, my role is to help with the financial side of the organization."

"Thanks, Steve, we're glad you're here, and I'm very thankful for your monthly sacrifice of getting up early, in spite of your regular complaints," Eric teased, giving Steve a quick smile. "Janet, would you go next?"

"Sure. Tom, it's great to meet you finally and have you become part of this team. I'm Janet Morris, and my husband is the pastor of Brookview Fellowship Church. Eric came to our church about four years ago and gave a very moving presentation on the need for a rehabilitative facility here in Brookview. His vision not only captured the hearts of many within our church, it completely captured my heart as well. I was utterly unaware that child sex trafficking was occurring in our city, so when Eric asked me to join the board, I gladly agreed. My main role is to help Eric and the staff network with other churches in the community."

"Tom, my name is Ruth Thompson. I'm a realtor here in the city, and just like everyone else, I learned about this problem through Eric's presentation at our church several years ago. It especially hit home for me since I have a history of abuse in my childhood, something I've been open about since joining the board. I was fortunate to help Eric find the house that is now Hope House. And since I'm also fairly well connected into the business community here, Eric asked me to join the board two years ago."

"Well, I guess I'm the only one left, so I'll finish up. Tom, I'm Cheryl Givens, and I know Eric because we attend the same church. I'm an attorney, so when Eric decided to begin Hope House, he connected with me early on for legal advice about starting a nonprofit. I'll never forget the conversation we had over coffee six years ago. I was completely clueless about child sex trafficking, but Eric opened my eyes to the problem, and when he asked for my legal help getting Hope House started, I gladly agreed. I've had the privilege, like Abigail, of serving on this board since the organization started five years ago. Welcome to our modest team; we're honored to have you."

"Thanks, everyone," Eric replied. "It's always an encouragement to me to introduce new board members since God uses it to remind me of how He has been the one to build this organization from the start by bringing the right people at the right time."

"Thanks, Eric, but now I think we need to get moving on the agenda since there's a lot we need to cover today," Abigail interjected. "Is there a motion and second to approve the minutes from the last meeting?"

Once the previous minutes were approved, Abigail efficiently moved through the agenda until all that was left was the financial report.

"Steve, can you give us your financial report from last month?"

"At the end of last month, Hope House had a total of $474,797.21 in its accounts, which is satisfactory to meet all current debts and payroll, including Eric's proposed staffing level for up to 5 months," Steve concluded.

"Any questions on the financial report, or for Steve?" Abigail asked.

"Not hearing any questions, before we conclude the meeting, I have a couple of questions for Eric," Abigail began. "Eric, I understand from the staff that they need updated laptop computers to perform their tasks better, but so far you've refused to purchase them. With these significant funds in the bank, can you tell us why you've decided not to purchase new computers?"

Eric was taken aback, not only by the question but also by Abigail's manner in asking the question in front of the whole board. She could easily have asked him this question during one of their many private meetings. He took a few minutes to collect his thoughts before answering.

"Eventually, we could use some new laptops for some of the staff, but I don't think it's urgent at this time. Their current computers are completely adequate, even though they are older and a little slower. With so many unknowns regarding how quickly we'll receive funds from the state once we open, I've decided it's best to hold off upgrading the computers at this time."

"Well, I know that several of the staff don't agree with you," Abigail replied. "Besides, there have been some grave allegations made to me recently that have me and some of the board members very concerned."

"What type of allegations, and what do you mean by some board members?" Eric asked, becoming more alarmed.

"I've had the opportunity to meet personally with some staff members to hear their concerns, and I felt it was necessary to share those concerns with a few of the board members. There have been allegations of poor staff oversight, and some staff have come to believe that you may not have the expertise necessary to lead the organization through this next step of opening," Abigail replied. "I'm wondering if it may be time for you to consider resigning as ED to let someone else take over the leadership of Hope House."

Eric sat stunned, looking around the table at the board members. Several were glancing down the floor with uncomfortable looks on their faces. However, Cheryl was staring directly at Abigail with an expression of concern. Tom almost appeared as shocked as Eric felt. Eric could sense his neck getting warm and his face becoming flushed as the anger grew within him.

"You've been having meetings with my staff without informing me?" Eric asked slowly, trying to control his emotions.

"Yes, I felt it was necessary, due to the impending opening of the house," Abigail answered.

Eric looked down at his hands, now tightly clenched together. He couldn't believe this was happening. He knew from his reading on nonprofit management that it was entirely inappropriate for board members to meet privately with nonprofit employees other than the Executive Director. Eric gathered his thoughts, holding his anger in check, and began to speak slowly and deliberately.

"So you have made the determination that I should consider stepping down as ED without giving me a chance to face my accusers or answer any of their accusations?"

"Well, I'm bringing it up to you now," Abigail answered.

"Yes, after you've suggested that I should resign," Eric responded, unable to keep the anger out of his voice.

"Eric has a point," Cheryl replied. "And for the record Eric, I wasn't part of any of those meetings. I just heard about this new development last evening. If there have been accusations of incompetence on Eric's part, I believe we should give him a chance to answer them as well as know the source of those accusations."

"I'm not ready to give up my sources just yet," Abigail replied. "But I will give Eric a list of the accusations. Since it appears there is a desire on the part of some for Eric to respond to the accusations made to me, I move that Eric write up that response by the next board meeting."

"I second that motion," Ruth replied.

A vote was held regarding the motion, with all in favor except Cheryl. Tom abstained since he was new to the board. The meeting then ended quickly, and all the board members left except Cheryl, who drew up a chair next to Eric, who was still sitting in a state of shock.

"I'm so sorry Eric, I had no idea this was coming until last night. I thought about calling you, but it was late, and I knew there was nothing we could do to prevent this from coming up this morning. I think they've kept me out of the loop on purpose because they knew I'd be on your side. I'm not sure exactly what's going on, but I can promise that I'll help support you in whatever way I can."

"Thanks, Cheryl...I don't know what to think. I had no idea any of my staff felt this way. I knew that some of them have been holding the old 'meeting after the meeting,' but I never dreamed it would lead to something like this. And I never imagined the board would abandon me after all I've done for this organization. I'm sorry. I'm just a little overwhelmed right now."

"Remember Eric; there may be a component of spiritual warfare coming into play here, and Jason talked about last Sunday."

Eric sat, staring at the wall. A couple of minutes passed before he answered.

"You may be right. Coincidentally, I just met with Jason this past Monday, and we talked about spiritual warfare. He gave me a reading assignment, but I haven't had a chance to do it."

"Sounds like today is a good day to get that done before you start working on your response. If you'd like me to help with it, or review it, I'd be glad to help."

"Thanks, Cheryl. I'm very thankful I'm not alone in this battle."

"You're absolutely not alone, Eric."

*****

Riel and the other angels floated back through the office roof, having removed themselves earlier when the massive darkness appeared with Abigail. They had been warned by Solen not to confront the evil being until they knew more about him and could develop a strategy for his defeat.

"It's been a long time since I've encountered a demon of that nature," Adren replied. "He reminds me of someone I once fought centuries ago in the Holy Land."

"I was involved in a fight against a fallen Watcher in my previous assignment," Riel noted. "To defeat them, you must first learn their unique vulnerability. This one's ability to hide his purposes has caught us all by surprise. We should have known they were planning a full-frontal assault once a fallen Watcher appeared."

"I'll get word to Solen right away about this latest development," Joft announced.

"Ask him if we should assist Eric in discovering that Marge is one of the key staff working against him," Adren replied.

"Good idea. I'll stay here to help Eric get through this shock," Riel said. "We need to find the identity of that fallen Watcher as soon as possible. His control of Abigail as Board Chair could bring about a coup far quicker than we imagined."

"I'll bring back an update as soon as I can," Joft replied.

Joft flew at high velocity toward Brookview Community Church where Jason was currently at work. After Joft came through the church walls, he immediately went up to Solen near the ceiling above Jason, who was finishing an extended time in prayer.

"What news do you have from the board meeting?" Solen asked.

"The dark Watcher has made his move. He convinced Abigail to question Eric's ability to continue leading the organization in front of the entire board. She has accused Eric of incompetence, demanding a response from him by the next board meeting. It appears that she has the support of enough board members to remove Eric if he doesn't adequately respond."

Solen was quiet for a few minutes.

"The Spirit has allowed these events to move forward without giving us advanced warning, probably to build more character into Eric. I expected the enemy to use Abigail to create a distraction for Eric, but I didn't expect an attempt to remove the God-called Founder so quickly. How is Eric holding up?"

"Riel is attempting to encourage him, but he's in a state of shock and may need some form of divine intervention if he's going to recover quickly from this."

Solen closed his eyes, spending time in communion with the Spirit. After several minutes, he finally turned to Joft.

"Good insight Joft. The Lord is planning to give Eric a direct word of prophecy. It will come quickly and in a manner that will strengthen Eric's faith."

"That's excellent news," Joft replied.

"In the meantime, I'll notify the angelic nexus to prompt the prayer warriors into earnest prayer, seeking wisdom and empowering for Eric. Joft, I need you to remind the angelic nexus at Abigail's church that we will not confront this dark Watcher until I give the order."

"Absolutely. Is there anything else?"

"Yes…have them encourage the prayer warriors in that church to pray that the Lord will help us learn the identity of this dark being so that we can begin planning how to defeat him."

"Should we assist Eric in knowing the identity of the staff members opposed to him?"

"Not at this time. It could cause Eric to have difficulty working with them in the future."

"For the Lord and His glory," Joft cried as he sped away.

*****

Eric slumped in his favorite chair in the living room looking out the window as Maggie started preparing dinner. He had been in the chair most of the day, since coming home right after the board meeting to avoid interacting with the staff. Maggie had been her usual supportive self when Eric told her about Abigail's accusation and the board's request for a formal follow up report. But he had witnessed her frequent glances into the living room revealing her worry for him.

Where had he gone wrong?

Was he really incapable of leading Hope House through the opening process?

If that was true, why would the Lord call him to start Hope House, and then push him out of the way just as they were ready to open?

Who on the staff had made these accusations?

Then Eric considered the complete change that had come over Abigail recently. Before, Abigail had been very supportive of Eric and his work. But since her transformation, Abigail had been increasingly critical of small things Eric was trying to accomplish. She had canceled several of their weekly meetings for no reason. Eric could tell that something had changed with her.

These thoughts and questions had been recycling through Eric's mind most of the day without any resolution. He tried to break the pattern a couple of times by attempting to pray but had minimal success. Instead, he found himself alternating between anger, confusion, sadness, and frustration.

A couple of times, he thought he might get started on his response to the board, but then the questions would resurface, and his thoughts would spin-off once again.

Eric's phone rang, and he looked at the caller ID. It was Bob, an old teacher friend he hadn't spoken to in many years. He almost sent the call to voicemail, but something made him answer.

"Hello Bob, it's been a long time."

"Hi Eric, I hope I'm not interrupting dinner."

"No, Maggie just started getting it ready. What can I do for you, Bob?"

"Well, it's actually something I'm supposed to do for you."

"I'm not sure I'm following you."

"I know we are brothers in the Lord, so I hope this doesn't sound too strange to you, but I believe the Lord is telling me to say something very specific to you."

"Really...actually, that's not as strange as you might think. Do you want to tell me over the phone, or in-person?"

"I think it would be better to tell you directly. Is it alright if I come over now?"

"Absolutely, Bob. I'll be here waiting."

"Thanks, it shouldn't take me very long."

"Who was that honey?" Maggie called from the kitchen as Eric hung up the phone.

"You won't believe it. That was Bob Farley, who used to teach with me at Eastside years ago. He says he has some word from God to give me."

"That's quite a coincidence. Is there any way he could know about what happened this morning?" Maggie asked as she stood in the doorway.

"No way that I can imagine. I'm not even sure that Bob's aware of what I've been doing these past five years. I bet it's been ten years since I last talked with him."

Eric got up from the chair and walked around the living room, feeling a glimmer of hope, yet wondering what this could mean. After about ten minutes, there was a knock on the front door.

"Come on in Bob; it's good to see you again after all these years."

"I don't mean to barge in or sound like some crazy religious nut," Bob answered as he took off his coat.

"Bob, I don't know if you've ever met my wife Maggie," Eric said as Maggie came to the door of the living room.

"No, I haven't. Nice to meet you, Maggie."

"Very nice to meet you as well. We appreciate your prompt obedience to the Lord. I'll leave the two of you alone while I finish making dinner. You're welcome to join us for dinner if you're available, Bob."

"Thank you so much, but my wife told me I have an hour before she's expecting me back for our dinner."

Eric motioned for Bob to sit down on the sofa while he sat down across from him.

"So, do you get these words from God very often?"

"No, not really. But when I do receive what I consider to be words of prophecy, they come to me clearly with a distinct impression of who needs to hear them. I hope you don't think I'm crazy, Eric."

"Not at all. I do believe that prophecy still exists today, though I'll admit I've never heard or been given a prophecy before. What's crazy about this is that I had a significant event happen earlier today."

"Well I don't know what's happening currently in your life, but earlier this afternoon, the Lord told me to tell you two specific things. First, He wants you to stay true to the calling He's given you. Second, while there will be struggles within that calling, the Lord will be with you and will support you through all of it."

As Eric sat quietly, tears began to form in his eyes. "Wow, Bob...you have no idea what an encouragement this is for me."

"Well, my hope and prayer are that the words have some meaning for you."

"Oh, there is no doubt what these words mean. This morning I had something happen that has caused me to question everything I've done for the past five years, and what you just shared will help me tremendously as I move forward."

"I'm so glad to hear that. Since I'm only the messenger, I never know the context of what's happening in the rare instances the Lord gives me these words."

"Believe me; it couldn't be more clear. But it's not just the words themselves; what also encourages my heart is that the Lord took the trouble to speak these words to me through you. That means more than anything to me," Eric replied as he wiped some tears from his cheeks.

Eric went on to tell Bob a summary of his work at Hope House and the events of the board meeting that morning.

"Before I leave, I'd like to pray for you, Eric."

"I'd be honored."

"Lord, I thank you for allowing me to play a small part in getting your message to Eric. I praise You for the work he's doing on your behalf, and I pray that through Your Spirit, You will uphold him during this difficult time. Give him the wisdom to respond in a godly manner to this accusation, and enable him to write a report that completely removes any shadow of doubt regarding his ability to continue as Executive Director of Hope House. We ask all of this in the name of your precious Son Jesus, amen."

Chapter 7

The Trap

Heather came through the front door late Sunday afternoon to find her mom and Ted sitting on the couch watching the football game. When she turned to go upstairs, her mother called out, "Where have you been all weekend?"

"At Sue's. I left you a note on the kitchen counter."

"I never saw any note."

"I'm sorry Mom. I did leave a note," Heather replied, going into the kitchen to see if she could find it.

"Well if you left one, it sure wasn't obvious."

"I left it right out in the open where you would be sure to see it," Heather said as she turned over everything on the counter, unable to find it.

Ted must have taken it!

"I'm not sure what happened to it, but I stayed over at Sue's all weekend," Heather replied, thinking now was not the best time to accuse Ted.

"Notes don't just get up and walk away now, do they? It seems to me that you don't care all that much about letting me know what you're doing, as if you think you're old enough to take care of yourself."

"I'm really sorry, Mom, but honestly, I did leave a note," Heather replied as she came into the living room.

"Doesn't help me much now, does it? Good thing I wasn't too worried. Dinner will be ready in 30 minutes unless you happen to have other plans," her mother said as she continued to watch the game, refusing to look at Heather.

"Thanks, Mom."

Heather stood there for a couple of minutes trying to think of something else to say before she turned to go upstairs. Why did everything seem to be working against her?

The frosty tone in her mother's voice told her that the distance between them had grown even greater. She had a lot of work to do before she could bring up Ted again.

As Heather climbed the stairs, she realized her mother hadn't made any effort to find her. If she was worried, she could at least have texted Heather's cell or called Sue's mom. It was as if she didn't care. What if something had happened to her?

Heather tried to push the thoughts out of her mind as she dropped down on her bed, feeling dejected. Maybe her mother didn't want her around after all. Feeling herself rapidly spiraling down, Heather spotted her desktop computer and decided to get online. Perhaps she could still access You'reOn even though this computer didn't have a camera.

After Heather downloaded and installed the app, it opened without any problem, showing a blank space on the left side of the screen where her video image should have been. Heather navigated to the same chat room she and Sue had used previously, looking to see if SBC happened to be online. Her pulse quickened when she saw SBC listed in the chatbox.

'Hey SBC, this is Heather from yesterday,' she quickly typed.
'Heather...Oh yeah, one of the twins from Brookview. How are you?'
'Well, not so good today.'
'Oh, why is that?'
'Things with my mom and stepdad.'
'That's a bummer. So your parents are divorced?'
'Yeah, they divorced about a year ago. It's a long story.'
'I'm happy to 'listen' if you want to chat more about it.'
'I don't think everyone in this chat room wants to know my history.'
"Here, this link will take you to a private chat room with just the two of us.'

Heather felt honored that a good-looking senior in high school was willing to spend so much time with her. She spent the next hour telling SBC about her parent's divorce and the fights with her mom since Ted moved in. She didn't tell him about the assaults but mentioned feeling like her mother didn't want her around.

'Heather, if you ever need a place to stay, I have an older sister who lives in an apartment with a spare bedroom. I'm sure she'd be willing to put you up.'

'Wow, that's nice SBC.'

'No problem. I think you'd like my sis. If there's ever a need, just give me a call or find me here, and I'll introduce you.'

'Thanks again for taking the time to "listen" :). I feel a lot better. But I probably should go and get something to eat. Hope to catch you soon :).'

'Sure…you know how to reach me.'

Feeling a renewed sense of hope, Heather walked into the kitchen to find her mother finishing the dishes, having put away all the food.

"I thought you decided not to come down for dinner, so I packed everything away," her mother stated flatly. "If you're hungry, you can reheat something. I fixed it once, so I'm not fixing it again."

"That's fine Mom, I just got caught in something, but thanks for fixing it," Heather replied, trying to overcome her mother's cold demeanor.

"Work wore me out this weekend, so I'm going to bed. Ted, are you coming up?"

"I'll be up shortly," Ted replied from the dining room as he stared at Heather.

Heather grabbed some leftovers from the fridge and put them into the microwave, before looking over at Ted.

"So did you miss me this weekend?" Ted asked after Heather's mom had gone upstairs.

"I think even you are smart enough to figure that out," Heather replied in a sarcastic tone.

"So you did miss me, how nice. We can always make up for it the next time your mom works. When is that by the way? Oh yeah, Tuesday night. I'll be counting down the hours until then," Ted sneered as he walked past Heather to go upstairs. Just as Ted passed her, Heather felt a sudden rush of cold fear come over her, followed by a quick thought to pray.

"Help me, Lord," Heather prayed silently, leaning against the counter as Ted started up the stairs. Just as the cold fear threatened to overwhelm Heather, she felt the fear drain away as quickly as it had come, replaced by a strong sense of peace. It took several minutes before Heather had the strength to take her food out of the microwave and sit down to eat. She didn't know what had just happened, but she didn't have time to figure it out. Her priority was to develop a plan to convince her mother of the truth about Ted, and Heather only had forty-eight hours to do it. She needed to find the time when she could talk alone with her mother. As Heather thought about the next couple of days, she quickly realized that the only time to speak with her mother alone was tomorrow after school. She'd have to skip basketball practice to make sure Ted didn't interrupt them, but it was worth it. Now she just needed to figure out what she could say that would convince her mother of the truth.

*****

Taron kept his hand on Heather's shoulder, pouring his peace into her. He was thankful that Heather had responded to his prayer prompt, reasserting his authority to protect Heather in this home now dominated by darkness. Bazen's bold attack had taken him by surprise, but with the flash of his sword, Taron was able to prevent Bazen from passing his grisly hand through Heather's head a second time.

"Try that again, and you'll lose that hand," Taron declared.

Bazen gave Taron a sneering smile. "We'll get her yet, and there's nothing you can do about it."

Taron returned his sword to its sheath after Heather sat down at the table and looked to heaven's throne, thanking the Lord for the strength and agility to respond quickly to Bazen's attack. Taron knew Bazen was right, but he certainly wouldn't admit it to him. Nancy's abdication of authority over this home to Ted and his evil companions had created this opening and mitigated the ability of Taron and his angelic partners to prevent the coming cascade of events. Regardless, Taron's assignment was to use every possible means to lessen Heather's suffering throughout the upcoming ordeal, and Taron would fulfill that role to the utmost of his ability.

*****

As soon as the last school bell rang, Heather quickly stopped by her locker before heading out the door. Over lunch, she had reminded Sue to tell the coach that Heather wouldn't be at practice today because of illness.

As she walked home, Heather thought through her approach with her mom. First, she would thank her for her hard work, and for everything she does to provide for her. Then Heather would remind her mom of the great times they had together after the divorce when they were like best friends. Hopefully, those thoughts would bring back warm memories to her mother, allowing Heather to bring up the changes in Ted. She could remind her mom about the time she caught Ted looking at porn. That should help her understand that Ted might have a different side to him.

It had to work...it just had to.

Heather came into the kitchen and was relieved to find her mother awake and alone.

"Hi Mom, did you get some sleep today before work?"

"I got a nap in. Why aren't you at basketball practice?"

"I decided I'd come home and spend a little time with you."

"Oh..." Heather's mom replied, giving her a suspicious look. "Why the sudden change?"

"I just feel like maybe I've taken you for granted a little too much, and wanted to tell you thanks for all you do."

"That's nice of you, but I get the feeling that there's something you want from me... like a new pair of jeans."

"No Mom... I'm serious. I know you work hard to make money and I just wanted you to know I appreciate that. Plus with Ted around, I don't get to spend much time alone with you."

"So that's it ...you're still jealous of Ted."

"I just like spending time alone with you," Heather replied, beginning to feel somewhat frustrated. "Is there anything wrong with that? Don't you remember how we used to hang out right after your divorce from Dad?"

"Yes, but that was a different time. Ted and I are married now, and I owe him my time and attention. Besides, you know he makes me happy. So I hope you'll quit any stupid antics to try and make me jealous of Ted."

Heather began to feel a growing sense of desperation.

"Mom, you remember that time you found porn on Ted's phone?"

"What's that got to do with anything?"

"It's just that Ted's different when you're not around."

Jeff Barrows

"He told me that was just a fluke. I've checked his phone several times since then, and I've never found anything resembling porn."

"When you're working, he looks at porn on the computer," Heather replied, trying to keep herself calm.

"I don't believe you. Ted's perfectly happy with me, so he doesn't need pornography. He also told me that you would make that accusation," Heather's mom replied with increasing anger.

"Mom, I really need you to believe me. Ted changes when you leave."

"From what he tells me, it's you that changes young lady. How can you prance about in your underwear and expect me not to hear about it?"

"Mom, why don't you believe me? I know I should have told you about the first time Ted assaulted me, but..."

"I've heard enough. I don't appreciate you making up stories about the man I love."

Heather sat down at the kitchen table with tears forming in her eyes before her mother continued.

"I know you want to go back to that time before Ted moved in, but it's not going to happen. Now I don't want to listen to any more of this, you hear?" Heather's mom declared as she turned and walked out of the kitchen.

Heather sat at the kitchen table with her head in her hands, crying softly. After some time, Heather walked upstairs to her room and sat on the bed. It was clear she wouldn't be able to convince her mom of the truth before she had to work the following night. Heather needed to find someplace to stay to avoid Ted, and Sue's home wasn't an option anymore. Where could she go? Heather looked at the computer and remembered SBC.

Heather turned the computer on and closed the door to her room as it was booting up. She navigated to the chat room where she had encountered SBC before, and thankfully saw that he was online.

'Hey SBC, it's Heather.'
'Hey Heather, how's it going?'
'Listen, can we chat privately?'
'Sure, follow this link.'

Heather entered the private chat room and waited for SBC to show up.

'What's going on, Heather? More trouble at home?'
'Unfortunately. Were you serious when you said your older sister would be willing to put me up?'
'Absolutely. She often has people stay with her. Do you want me to contact her and have her get in touch with you?'
'Could you? Or I could give her a call if you gave me her number.'
'Tell you what. Give me your number, and I'll have my sis call you.'

Heather hesitated a few minutes, thinking through her limited options. Realizing she didn't have much choice, she typed her number into the computer.

'Great! I'll let her know about you, and she should call in about an hour or so.'
'Thanks, SBC, or I mean, Derrick.'
'Sure, no problem. Sorry about things at home, but you'll love my sis.'
'OK. Thanks again. I'll be waiting for her call.'

Heather felt a sense of relief now that she might have somewhere she could go. She began packing what she could into her backpack, in case she didn't come home after school tomorrow.

*****

Taron turned from watching Heather pack as Corel came through the ceiling into the bedroom.

"Has she made contact with Derrick yet?"

"Just a few minutes ago. Heather's belief that Derrick wants to help her is fueling a false sense of hope."

"She has little choice at this point but to latch on to whatever hope she can, since her mother has failed to protect her," Corel replied. "Nancy's self-centeredness has blinded her to the truth about Ted and will cause Heather to fall under the control of an evil she has yet to imagine."

"I will never get used to the careless decisions humans make regarding their children," Taron replied with some frustration.

"Without the opening of their spiritual eyes, or as the great Apostle Paul put it, the eyes of their heart, they have limited ability to look beyond themselves."

"Self-centeredness is also evident in Sue's home, destroying that marriage and preventing it from being the place of refuge that Heather needs right now," Taron noted.

"Yes, leaving Heather with very few options. God's will is always a mystery, but we can draw encouragement from His plan to redeem the evil Heather is about to experience."

"I will be reminding myself of that promise as I help Heather endure what's coming through the next several weeks."

"I came to tell you that since Nancy has chosen to resist the Lord's will for her life, Solen has reassigned me to relay messages about the progress at Hope House, and assist in the upcoming battle," Corel announced.

"Is everything progressing with Hope House as planned?"

"Not quite. There has been a troublesome development recently. An unknown dark entity has influenced the Board Chair to make grave accusations of incompetence against the God-called-Founder."

"I thought a Watcher had been assigned to assist us in locating and identifying the dark forces. Why hasn't the Watcher been able to identify this dark entity?"

"Solen believes it is a fallen Watcher with the ability to shield his identity."

"Will this delay the opening of Hope House?"

"No doubt that is the intent of the enemy. But the Watcher has informed Solen that in time, he should be able to learn the identity of this dark being. Then Solen will be able to strategize how to defeat him."

"Praise the Lord that he has appointed Solen as our leader. Heather will desperately need Hope House to be open after she undergoes her upcoming ordeal."

"Solen is more than capable of thwarting any plan the enemy concocts. If only Nancy hadn't abandoned her search for the Lord, we could protect Heather from experiencing the evil that lies ahead," Corel noted.

"Their free will is part of the dignity our Lord has bestowed on them, and thus He will respect Nancy's decision to essentially abandon her daughter."

"Allowing you to fight and keep Heather from falling into despair."

"One of the privileges we possess as angels."

"For the Lord and His Glory!"

*****

"How are things at home, Sue," Heather asked as she sat down at the lunch table across from her.

"Not good. My mom and stepdad are both still fighting. It's been four days now, and I'm doing everything I can to stay out of the way in the hope that they will work everything out."

"I'm so sorry, Sue. You know that I've been there and understand exactly what you're going through."

"Speaking of which, how did your talk with your mom go last night?"

Heather looked across the lunchroom and quietly sighed, "Not well."

"She still didn't believe you?"

"Ted has her completely fooled. Remember when I told you I had left a note telling mom that I would be at your house for the weekend?"

"Yeah,"

"Well, Ted found it and threw it away. Mom didn't know where I was the whole weekend. The worst part is she didn't seem to care. She never bothered calling around to find out where I was."

"That doesn't sound like her."

"Actually, more and more, it does seem like her. Over the past couple of months, she's acted as if she could care less if I'm around."

"I'm so sorry, Heather, I had no idea. So what are you going to do now?"

"Unfortunately, Mom works tonight, and Ted's already acting like a jerk, so I can't stay home tonight. But I did connect online with Derrick, and he has an older sister who is willing to take me in."

"Who's Derrick?"

"Remember...SBC...in the chat room...online."

"Oh yeah, I forgot his name was Derrick. That's way cool. How do you know she's willing to have you stay with her?"

"I talked with her on the phone last night."

"Really! You've already talked with Derrick's sister! What's she like, and what's her name?"

"She's OK. Her name is Melanie. She didn't seem overly friendly, but she said I could stay. I wanted to check how things were at your house before I made a final decision."

"Well, if I were you, I'd pick Derrick's sister. You know I'd love to have you, but things aren't the best right now. Besides, you might get to meet Derrick."

"Yeah, like that's my top priority. But I did want to thank you for letting me stay this past weekend."

"Sure. So when are you going to call Melanie?"

"Right after school today, I suppose."

"Well, if you meet Derrick, don't make any moves on him right away," Sue smiled.

"You really do have a one-track mind," Heather smirked.

Heather started up her phone as she left the school building and called Melanie.

"Hello," a male voice answered.

Heather was startled and almost hung up, thinking she had called the wrong number.

"Is Melanie there?" Heather replied after a long pause.

"Sure, just a sec."

"Hello," came Melanie's voice after a couple of minutes.

"Melanie, this is Heather. Remember we talked last night?"

"Sure, I remember. Do you need to come and stay tonight, Heather?"

"Yes, I guess so. Is it still all right?"

"Absolutely. Since I live in Springfield, you'll probably need a ride to get here."

"I didn't know you lived in Springfield. I assumed you were in Williamsburg where Derrick lives."

"No. We...I mean I...live in Springfield where I work. Since it's only 45 minutes away, I can come to pick you up. I have an errand to run near there anyway."

"You sure that's OK? I don't have any money to reimburse you for gas."

"No problem at all. I should be there in about an hour. Where should I come to get you?"

"I'll be at the high school, near the parking lot. By that time, it should be empty since everyone will have gone home."

"Perfect. See you then."

Heather walked around the neighborhood surrounding the high school, hoping she wasn't making a mistake. She'd have to figure out how to get back to school in the morning, but that wasn't a priority right now. Something didn't feel quite right. Why had a guy answered Melanie's phone?

As she walked, she went over her options again. She definitely couldn't take a chance at home with Ted. Sue's house wasn't an option, at least right now. Maybe her parents would work things out in the next few days, and she could stay there over the weekend. Heather couldn't think of any other friends she could ask for help. So it seemed that Derrick's sister was her only option for now. At least she would try to stay as few nights as possible.

After Heather waited about sixty minutes, a woman drove up in an old gray Honda Accord to where Heather was standing.

"Are you Heather?" the woman asked as she rolled down the window.

"Yeah, you must be Melanie."

"Yep. Glad to meet you. Jump on in."

Heather walked around the front of the car, a little surprised at how old Melanie looked. She could have easily been twenty-five or even older.

"Thanks again for coming to get me," Heather said as she got into the front seat, putting her backpack on her lap.

"Sure. As I said, I had some business to take care of up here anyway," Melanie replied as she pulled out of the school parking lot.

"Oh, what kind of business do you work in?"

"I suppose you could say the entertainment business," Melanie replied as she turned to give Heather a strange smile.

Heather decided not to ask any more questions, becoming more uncomfortable as time passed. She took a deep breath and mostly kept her eyes on the road ahead, occasionally glancing over at Melanie.

Melanie looked to be at least twenty-five, with bony cheeks and a small nose. Her hair was stringy blonde with dark roots revealing it was colored. She had a natural attractiveness that was marred only by a single missing front tooth, suggesting she had been through a lot in her life.

"Mind if I smoke?" Melanie asked as she took out a cigarette.

"I guess not."

"You sure are a quiet thing. What grade are you in?"

"Ninth."

"Really. Derrick thought you were a little older. But that's fine. You must be what, fifteen or sixteen?"

"Fifteen."

"Well, I must say you are a pretty little thing."

"Thank you…" Heather replied, feeling more and more awkward.

The rest of the 45-minute drive was spent in silence before they pulled into the driveway of a small home in a middle-class neighborhood. Heather followed Melanie into the house and was startled to find a man who appeared to be in his mid-thirties sitting in the living room working on a laptop. He looked up and eyed Heather carefully, eventually smiling at her.

Heather gave Melanie a confused look, "I didn't know you were married."

"Actually, I'm not married. Derrick and I live together."

Heather felt her legs weaken as she stood with increasing confusion. She looked back and forth between Melanie and Derrick, who were both smiling slyly. Fear began to creep into Heather.

"So, are you the Derrick I've been chatting with?"

"Yep…that's me. As a matter of fact, I'm online right now."

"But why did you tell me you were in high school? And why…?" Heather struggled to grasp the truth as she looked over at Melanie, her fear and anxiety growing.

"It's really quite simple, Heather," Derrick answered. "If I had told you the truth, you never would have come, now would you?"

"No…but…what…what do you want with me?"

"Oh, you'll find out soon enough," Derrick replied. "In the meantime, you can leave your cell phone with me. You don't need it now. Melanie will take you up to your room."

Heather looked back at the front door to see if there was any way she could run out of the house, but Melanie had moved to block her. Melanie pointed to the stairs, and as Heather walked up the stairs, she held tightly to the railing to keep from passing out as fear, anxiety, and doom settled over her.

She had walked into a trap, and no one, not even Sue, had any idea where she was.

Chapter 8

The Enemy's Plan

"That's quite a story," Jason replied as he sat across from Eric at the Red Lantern restaurant.

"I have to admit, I don't know what I would have done without the Lord using Bob to bring me that message," Eric responded. "The timing was impeccable, coming just a few hours after the board made their accusation against me. There was no way that Bob could have known what had happened, so I'm convinced it was truly from the Lord."

"Sure sounds that way," Jason answered, sipping his coffee. "Brother, I'm so glad God gave you that gift. It's a great example of what I mentioned last week, how there is always far more going on around us than what we see."

"So, do you think spiritual warfare triggered this accusation?" Eric asked.

"No doubt about it in my mind. Remember, the enemy desires to seek and control all of us, but especially our youth. The mission of Hope House is in direct opposition to that plan, so it's foolish not to expect some form of spiritual attack. From what you've told me, it appears the enemy has been planning this attack for some time."

"So, how would you suggest I proceed?"

"Have you written your response to the board yet?"

"No, but I've been praying about it."

"Good. Have you spent any time looking over my assignment from last week, the first four verses of Colossians chapter three?"

"Not as much as I would have liked, but I did read through it slowly a couple of times."

"That's a start. My purpose for having you read and study those verses was to have you begin thinking about developing a spiritual mindset. I had expected to have more time to develop a foundation for understanding spiritual warfare, but the enemy has shortened that timeline. Thankfully, the Lord is never surprised by the enemy's plans."

"Which brings up a question I wanted to ask you, Jason," Eric replied after the waitress brought their breakfast orders and they finished their prayer. "If God knew this was going to happen, why didn't He prevent it, or at least give me some warning ahead of time?"

"What you are asking gets into the long-debated issue of why God allows bad things to happen to good people. In other words, it's the question of why evil exists in the world."

"Well, I'm more interested in my particular situation than exploring some abstract theological concept."

"Eric, I don't have an absolute answer for you, but I do have a possibility. Do you remember Hezekiah in the Old Testament?" Jason asked.

"He was a king, wasn't he?"

"Yes, one of the few good kings to come after David. I won't go into a history lesson-"

"Not that I don't love history, since I used to teach it," Eric interrupted.

"We could save that for another time," Jason suggested. "Back to my point, Hezekiah was a king who diligently sought God and was faithful throughout most of his reign. However, the Bible tells an interesting story about Hezekiah near the end of his life. A group of emissaries from Babylon visited Hezekiah, and he foolishly showed them all his treasures."

"That does sound rather foolish."

"So foolish, that it helped bring about the later Babylonian invasion," Jason continued as he took out his Bible, turning to the book of Second Chronicles. "In spite of being a godly king, God allowed Hezekiah to forget all common sense, and verse thirty-one of chapter thirty-two tells us why:

'…God left him to himself, in order to test him and
to know all that was in his heart.'

My point is that God allowed Hezekiah to make that foolish mistake to test him and find out what was in his heart," Jason finished.

"So you're saying that God has allowed this episode with the board to test me?"

"I'm saying that it's a possibility."

Jason waited a few moments before continuing, allowing Eric some time to consider this prospect. "It's not that

God needs to learn what's in your heart since He already knows everything about you. Rather, He may use an incident like this to show you what's in your heart. Does that make sense?"

"Yeah, unfortunately, what came out of my heart was a lot of anger and frustration."

"Anything else?"

"Well, I also had some doubt about whether I had misunderstood God, at least until Bob talked with me."

"Do you think it's possible Eric, that you've made Hope House into an idol?"

"What do you mean?"

"An idol is anything or any person we use to gain something we should only receive from God."

"I thought an idol was something we worshipped."

"Yes, but worship takes many forms. Remember when we talked last week about living out of your identity as God's son rather than as the ED of Hope House?"

"Yeah…"

"When you derive your sense of identity as the ED of Hope House instead of being God's son, you have essentially made Hope House an idol."

"Are you saying that deriving my sense of identity from anything other than God is a form of worship?"

"That's exactly what I'm saying. Many Christians today engage in this kind of idolatry and don't even realize it."

"I remember you also talked about having peace when we live out of our identity as God's son or daughter."

"That's right. We have peace because, when we live out of our identity as God's child, we desire only His will, no matter how it affects us."

"Hmmm…but isn't it difficult to get to the point of desiring only God's will?"

"Absolutely. It can take decades for some Christians, but it's something we should all strive for."

"I can understand the concept, but desiring only God's will continuously is a different matter. There are occasions when I truly want what God wants regarding Hope House. But then there are also periods when my plans and desires for Hope House seem to take over."

"That's natural, especially since you've invested so much time and effort into starting Hope House. What would be unnatural is letting go and giving God complete control regarding the outcome of this allegation."

"What would that look like?"

"It would mean that after you write your response to the board, you place the outcome completely in His hands. If He wants you to continue as Executive Director, He will make that happen. If for some reason He wants to replace you, that's His prerogative, since the organization belongs to Him."

"I agree it belongs to Him, but for me to just sit idly by as they replace me is, as the old saying goes, a lot easier said than done," Eric replied.

"Actually, it would be impossible without the Holy Spirit. That's why Paul reminds us in Philippians chapter two, verse thirteen:

'For it is God who works in you, both to will and to work for His good pleasure.'

So remember, the Holy Spirit is working to help you follow God's will."

"Is there anything I can do to help that happen?"

"Have a prayerful attitude," Jason smiled. "Remember, we talked about that as well last week."

"Yeah, I just thought I'd have more than a week to develop that habit."

"So did I, brother, so did I. But remember also, the Lord is never surprised by events, which means that His plan, whatever it may be, will come about. In the meantime, the prayer warriors at our church, and I will be praying for you."

"Thanks, I don't doubt that I'll need it."

*****

Floating high above the breakfast table at the Red Lantern, Riel turned to Solen, "How are preparations proceeding for the attack against the dark being controlling Abigail?"

"The angelic nexus requested that the prayer warriors within the city add fasting to their prayer efforts, expecting a difficult upcoming battle."

"When do you plan to engage this dark being?"

"We've little doubt that this is a fallen Watcher, which means he is a powerful being. We won't be able to successfully attack him until we learn his identity and therefore, his weakness. I'm hoping our Watcher will give us that information soon," Solen responded.

"Has the Watcher relayed anything further regarding the demonic forces influencing Marge?"

"Yes. There has been ongoing communication between this fallen Watcher and the demons attached to Marge. Also, he related that the demon of self-centeredness has grown in power and influence."

"I've witnessed some of that growth," Riel replied.

"For now, I've decided that we not interfere with that connection until we defeat the fallen Watcher."

"Since you've assigned Joft to assist Marge, I'll give him that message and report back any other changes with her. Are there any other suggestions you have for me to keep Eric encouraged, other than reminding him of the Lord's prophecy?"

"As this morning's discussion clarified, Eric is going to need help developing a prayerful attitude. Perhaps you could temporarily enhance that process, Riel."

"Absolutely! For the Lord and His glory!"

*****

Eric entered the office and gave his usual morning greeting to everyone as he walked to his desk. Instead of their typical response, however, Eric heard only a few muted greetings as the rest of the staff stopped all conversations. The awkward silence that followed indicated that something unusual had happened.

Eric realized that everyone might know more than they should about the board meeting the previous Friday. One primary reason he had gone home right after the meeting was to keep the staff from sensing the discord Eric currently had with the board. The only way they could have found out about the meeting was through some illicit backchannel communication. As the awkward silence continued, Eric quickly decided to have an impromptu staff meeting, before becoming more frustrated.

"OK everybody, let's all gather around the table for a quick meeting," Eric replied after he put his computer bag on his desk.

He walked over to the conference table and sat down at the head, waiting for the rest of the staff to gather. While they all quietly found their seats, Eric prayed silently for wisdom and calm.

"It seems that all of you are acting a little differently this morning, so I want to clear the air. Would this have anything to do with the board meeting last Friday?"

The uncomfortable glances and silence around the table confirmed to Eric that they were definitely aware of what happened at the meeting.

"This is something we've talked about before. All communication between the board of directors and staff should go through me as the executive director. Also, all business conducted at board meetings is confidential, and should only be shared with staff as it directly pertains to them. Apparently, someone has not followed these common procedures."

Eric took a few moments to collect his thoughts and pray again for calm while looking around the table.

"At this point, I'm not going to try and discover how you all know about the meeting, though again it is completely inappropriate. All I will say is that a disagreement has arisen between some of the board members and me. It has nothing to do with any of you at this point."

Eric saw a quick smile flash across Marge's face, causing Eric to wonder whether his staff caseworker might be the one responsible for the breach of confidence.

"For now, our goal should remain opening Hope House as soon as we can," Eric continued. "Melinda, what interviews do you have lined up with potential staff?"

"I have two interviews this afternoon, and, if both of those candidates work out and accept a position, we should have our full complement of staff ready to train," Melinda answered.

"Great! How are preparations coming on the training curriculum?" Eric asked.

"It's all set except for a few modules I've turned over to Marge," Melinda answered.

"When do you expect to have those done, Marge?" Eric inquired.

"It shouldn't take me too long...maybe by the end of the week," Marge replied.

"If at all possible, I need you to complete the training curriculum by the end of the week," Eric responded, annoyed by Marge's complacency. "The training curriculum is a priority since we're so close to having all the staff hired."

"I'll do what I can, but I don't want to have to sacrifice quality just to get it finished," Marge replied with firmness.

"I'm not saying you have to sacrifice quality, Marge. I'm simply saying that getting the curriculum done is critical, and I know your caseload is down right now. I'd like you to focus all of your efforts toward getting the curriculum completed by the end of the week," Eric replied, trying not to let his frustration show.

Marge didn't respond but gave a quick smirk toward Rachel. Eric happened to see that smirk, further confirming his suspicions about Marge.

"Are there any questions from anyone?" Eric asked. "OK, if there aren't any questions, let me say thank you, again, for all your work to get us to this point. Just a little more concentrated effort, and Lord willing, we'll soon be opening Hope House."

*****

Buzel gave the angelic gathering above him a gruesome grin as he freely worked his talons in and out of Marge's head. He then looked over and gave an encouraging nod to Raz who had settled comfortably on Rachel's shoulder.

The group of angels floated out through the ceiling of the office.

"Abigail's repeated compliments and the individual attention she has shown Marge have created the opening Buzel needed to attach himself to her," Joft replied. "A demon of pride was the last thing she needed."

"Solen just informed me this morning of the close communication between Marge's other demons and the dark entity influencing Abigail," Riel announced. "There is no doubt that Marge found out about the board meeting from Abigail, and was probably encouraged to share that gossip with the rest of the staff. I'll need to update Solen of this latest development."

"Marge has been resistant to my efforts to remind her of the Lord's assistance in enabling her to receive her social work degree," Joft noted. "Buzel has now convinced Marge that she is a social worker because of her superior intellect."

"Marge's pride has also enabled her to criticize Eric's actions with the rest of the staff whenever Eric is not in the office," Nefa said.

"Marge's criticism of Eric is also increasing Rachel's preexisting doubt about some of Eric's methods," Adren added. "Raz is taking advantage of that doubt to spread further discord."

"Now that Abigail gladly shared the results of the board meeting with Marge over the weekend, those seeds of doubt and discord have nearly grown into a full rebellion among the staff," Joft observed.

"We've seen this pattern throughout the ages," Riel commented. "When humans begin depending on themselves rather than the Lord, they are easily swayed from the Lord's plan for their life. Because our Lord values free will so highly, He allows his children to pursue their plans in spite of the damage it causes. For now, our efforts must be limited to simply reminding them of God's grace and goodness in their lives, as you rightly attempted Joft."

"I doubt this brief staff meeting will do much to slow the spread of rebellion," Joft noted. "If Hope House is going to open on time, we'll need to separate the powerful demonic influence from Abigail, and stop its poisonous effect on Marge and Rachel."

"What is Solen's plan regarding the darkness surrounding Abigail?" Nefa asked.

"This morning, he told me that before he plans an attack, he wants to identify the being behind this darkness, to make a victory more likely," Riel responded. "In the meantime, he has notified the angelic nexus to request that all regional prayer warriors also begin fasting in preparation for the eventual battle."

"Did he give any time frame regarding the battle," Joft asked.

"He expects the Watcher to identify this being soon. In the meantime, I suggest that we keep the rest of the staff focused on their responsibilities as much as possible so that they have little time to be influenced by Marge or Rachel."

"For the Lord and His glory!"

*****

Abigail sat in the restaurant drinking her tea, thinking about how her opinion of Eric had changed in the past several weeks. She still respected him for taking the initiative to start Hope House. But now he was hopelessly out of his depth trying to run what was essentially a social work organization. He was a teacher after all, not a social worker. It was a good thing she had agreed to join this board in the beginning, since she had been the first to recognize Eric's deficiencies. Now it was up to her to save the organization from almost inevitable failure. It was fortunate she knew just the person who could take over for Eric. She was a true professional who had begun her career in social work and had since become a very successful businesswoman in the community.

Abigail had been introduced to Charlotte a year ago at the annual Chamber of Commerce dinner. She was bright, well spoken, and well connected, making her perfect for the job. She did attend a more liberal church, but that was less important than her other credentials. Most importantly, Abigail had come to believe that a woman, not a man, should lead Hope House as the nonprofit's influence continued to grow. In addition, Charlotte had an excellent reputation as CEO of the city's United Way Campaign. Abigail's main obstacle was successfully persuading Charlotte to leave the United Way, with its multi-million dollar budget. Hope House was a new organization and therefore much smaller. Abigail hoped that what Charlotte previously shared might be enough to motivate her to join Hope House.

The two of them were together at a community luncheon the previous month when the idea of approaching Charlotte first occurred to Abigail. Charlotte shared how excited she was about Hope House's mission to save young girls out of sex slavery. Charlotte even expressed some envy that she couldn't somehow be more involved.

Well, maybe there was a way she could become very involved.

Abigail looked up to see Charlotte approaching the table.

"I'm so glad you could make it," Abigail said. "Thank you for taking time out of your busy schedule to meet with me."

"Oh, my pleasure," Charlotte answered as she sat down. "You know that my interest in the work of Hope House has increased as I've learned more about sex trafficking, especially as it relates to young girls. I'm looking forward to hearing the latest news about your upcoming opening."

"Well, fortunately, there is a lot of news. But before we dive into it, may I suggest that we decide on what we want and order so that we can talk without being interrupted?"

"That sounds great; I'm famished."

After they spent a few minutes looking over the menu and ordering, Abigail started the conversation back up.

"Well, the good news is that Hope House received its licensure from the state a couple of weeks ago. We've now entered the final phase of preparations before opening the house very soon."

"That's wonderful. I'm so excited for you and your team. I know you've been part of this project for what, four years?"

"Well, actually I'm finishing my fifth year on the board, serving as Chair for that entire time."

"And from what I hear, you've done an excellent job leading the organization to where you are today."

"That's kind of you to say," Abigail responded. "I will say that it's been more complicated than any of us first suspected when we started Hope House five years ago."

"Well, regardless, receiving your licensure is quite an accomplishment. But I can't help but notice you said 'good news' as if implying that there was also some 'bad news'.

"As I expected, you are very perceptive, Charlotte. Yes, I'm afraid there is some bad news, and that's why I wanted to talk to you. Our executive director, Eric, is a very nice man, but his background is teaching, not social work. I'm afraid that he's taken the organization as far as he can professionally. It's my opinion that we now need someone with a strong social work background to take Hope House to the next level. I also think Hope House should have a female executive director."

"I see…"

"I remember talking with you last month about our work, and I was struck by how much passion you showed for the issue of sex trafficking. I even remember how you mentioned you were sorry you couldn't be more involved. So with that in mind, I wonder if you would consider coming over from the United Way to become Executive Director of Hope House?"

Charlotte sat quietly for a few moments, sipping her tea. "Well, I certainly hadn't expected an offer like this. As you might imagine, I'll need some time to think it over."

"That's only natural."

"You are right; I have become passionate about this issue. But let me ask you, what does Eric think about having someone else take over for him?"

"He doesn't know anything about this yet, so please keep this completely confidential between us."

"Really!" Charlotte responded with a surprised look. "If that's the case, how exactly do you envision this transition proceeding?"

"I've been able to persuade most of the board that Eric doesn't have the credentials necessary to take Hope House to the next level. We discussed this with Eric at our last board meeting, and I believe it's only a matter of time before he will be leaving us."

"You said most of the board…"

"There is one member of the board who disagrees with our concerns because of her close friendship with Eric. However, I believe we will be able to overcome her misgivings by our next board meeting. That's why I wanted to sit down with you now as my first choice as Eric's replacement."

"Well, naturally, I'm honored that you've considered me for this role. It's definitely something I'll have to think over carefully. I've enjoyed my time at the United Way, but lately, I've begun to sense that it's time for a change, both for the organization and for me. And please keep that completely confidential between us as well."

"That won't be a problem, Charlotte."

"May I give you my decision in, say, two weeks?"

"That will be in plenty of time for us. And please let me know if you have any other questions I can answer. We'd absolutely love to have you as our new Executive Director."

*****

Solen and Aland continued watching the large cloaked demonic being below from high above the restaurant, to lessen their chance of being detected. In addition to the unknown fallen Watcher, they could see several other lesser demons congregating around both Abigail and Charlotte.

"This fallen Watcher has worked hard to keep me from identifying him," Aland started. "As you know, there are relatively few Watcher angels and even fewer fallen Watchers. Initially, I had hoped to recognize him by his specific patterns of movement, but that has proved unsuccessful."

"I hope you've discovered another means to identify him," Solen responded as he turned to the larger Watcher.

"Indeed, I have. Another identifying characteristic of powerful demons is the surrounding company of lesser demons that usually follow them. By carefully observing this demonic horde, I've identified this fallen Watcher as Travoz. He normally operates in Europe, so I'm surprised to find him here. He is very subtle, yet powerful and almost always successful in leading his subjects to do his bidding through pride, arrogance, and vanity."

"I've never encountered Travoz before. How difficult will he be to separate from Abigail?"

"Unfortunately, it will be challenging, requiring a great deal of prayer and fasting. Also, we must coordinate the timing of the attack with a confrontation with Abigail in which she is somehow profoundly humbled. Profound humility substantially weakens Travoz's hold on his subjects."

"That's very helpful to know. It will allow us to make plans accordingly," Solen replied. "As always, I thank the Lord for your assistance; this should give us the advantage we need."

"I serve at His pleasure, as do you. Please let me know if I can be of any further assistance in your efforts to protect this worthy cause."

"I will keep you informed of our plan to free Abigail since we might need your assistance in escorting Travoz from the region."

"That would certainly be my pleasure," Aland replied.

"For the Lord and His glory!"

*****

Travoz looked over at Dazon, who was hovering next to Charlotte and gave him a congratulatory nod. His plan was progressing just as he had hoped.

"You have done well preparing this woman to consider what normally would appear to be a lesser opportunity," Travoz said.

"Thank you, Mighty One. Once I helped her imagine what it would be like to be the savior of these girls, it became quite easy to manipulate her. She has been particularly susceptible since the Enemy does not indwell her," Dazon added.

"How right you are to acknowledge that difference, Dazon. While your subject does not belong to the Enemy, mine does, requiring someone of my stature to manipulate her."

"Quite correct, but might I inquire as to your wondrous methods, so that I may learn from you, O Great One?"

"Your effort at flattery is pathetic, Dazon. But you have proven yourself useful, and clearly, there are many things I could teach you."

"Thank you, my liege. I am humbled by this opportunity."

"When dealing with a subject who is indwelled by the Enemy, it is critical to move slowly and subtly. They must not even suspect in the slightest the source of your thought suggestions. They must be convinced rather, that these suggestions arise out of their spiritual growth and superiority."

"And how do you accomplish that, O Great One?"

Ignoring the obvious attempt at flattery, Travoz continued, "It requires knowing your subject well. Do not quickly rush to implant some foreign thought that might alert them to your presence. Instead, work to know them well enough to implant thoughts that seem natural to them. And certainly, don't be a fool and implant a thought that is clearly contrary to the Enemy's dreadful book. That will only alarm them. The thought must only be slightly at odds with the Enemy's plan, yet natural enough to the subject that they accept it. Then once that thought is accepted, suggest another further at odds with the Enemy's plan until the course of the subject is more in alignment with us than with the Enemy."

"What specific thoughts did you implant in this woman's mind, O Great One?"

"This woman's success in business made it easy to suggest she might be smarter than most people. Once I repeated that suggestion a couple of times, she quickly accepted it. From there, it was only a series of small steps to inflate her pride by encouraging her to compare herself favorably to others, including the other board members."

"How did you get her to turn on the executive director?"

Travoz stared intently at Dazon, becoming more suspicious of his motives for this interrogation.

"And why are you so suddenly interested in all my methods, Dazon? Are you planning something I don't know about?"

"Certainly not, Master," Dazon replied with surprise. "I simply want to learn from you so that I may serve you better."

Travoz grunted, still very suspicious. "If I find out you plan to share this with another dark lord who might be after my position, you'll wish you never met me."

"Never, my lord, never!" replied Dazon, now beginning to shake with fear.

"Very well, Dazon, I'll continue…for now. So, once I fooled this woman into thinking that she was smarter than the others, I subtly suggested that she was the only one who knew what was best for the organization. She quickly accepted that suggestion when I reminded her of everything she had done in her role as Board Chair. After that, I helped her take the final step of placing herself in the role of savior of this nasty organization by emphasizing her differences with the Enemy's Founder and Executive Director."

"Sheer genius, Master. I will certainly remember this valuable lesson and put it to good use as soon as possible. I have one final question."

"And what would that be?" Travoz asked warily.

"How did you initially get access to this follower of the Enemy?"

"That, Dazon, I will not answer, since I must keep some of my secrets," Travoz replied.

"I understand, Master, though I am disappointed. Do you have any other orders for me?"

"Make sure this Charlotte is ready to accept Abigail's offer within the next two weeks. You can guarantee her acceptance by suggesting to her that she might be the only woman who can save these poor girls. Never underestimate the corrupting power of pride."

"Brilliant, Master."

"Then, as my perfect plan to replace the Enemy's Founder, His plans will be thwarted, and all the spiritual impact of this dreadful organization will slowly dissolve."

"I will make sure of it, my liege."

Chapter 9

The Enemy's Enterprise

Prince Valden floated high above the city gazing out over his reign. His twenty-one-foot humanoid frame made quite a silhouette in the nighttime sky, a useful tactic to motivate his captains. Tonight, they needn't worry since he was in a pleasant mood, relishing his recent victories.

Indeed, since he took over this region some two hundred years ago by human time, he and his syndicate have made steady progress in their efforts to capture and control the population below.

Prince Valden knew his success was in part due to his superior organizational ability. But even he knew the best organization would eventually fail if he didn't make the requisite decisions to fill leadership roles correctly. No, he quietly mused, his overwhelming success showed that he possessed not only an administrative genius, but an executive genius as well.

Even his provincial overlord had been impressed with Valden's decision to give his most promising captain oversight of wealth expansion. Unlike some other princes, Valden understood that wealth was the wellspring from which every other form of evil would flourish. After all, he chuckled to himself, how could there be materialism and greed without first having wealth. And how he enjoyed watching materialism ripen into vanity and selfishness, further increasing the shallowness of their pitiful lives.

They deserved their addiction to alcohol, drugs, and of course, his favorite-pornography. He couldn't understand why the Enemy had created such weak and vulnerable beings. Oh, but he wasn't complaining, he thought with another chuckle. Their weakness made it almost effortless to draw them into addiction, making it that much easier to control them.

Valden continued smiling as his thoughts drifted to the new digital devices. Undoubtedly the master himself had assisted in their development. Who knew how quickly the young would become so easily manipulated through their superficial, meaningless interactions. They were even using them to send pictures of their nakedness to one another. These new technologies had the capacity to corrupt, even without the help of his demonic hordes.

Sexual promiscuity was gloriously epidemic, bringing the magnificent mayhem of its emotional aftermath, not to mention the associated infections, unwanted pregnancy, and abortion. Infidelity was also on the rise, causing havoc in families, producing more and more fatherless homes. Yes, things were going gloriously well.

His musings were interrupted by the arrival of Benzal.

Finding Freedom

"My prince," Benzal declared as he bowed before his larger master.

Prince Valden looked down on his captain for youth recruitment. "What success do you have to report this week, Benzal?"

Benzal stood slowly, with his head still bowed before his prince. "The rates of abuse and neglect among our youth remain high enough to exceed all enlistment quotas."

"That is good news...perhaps it's time to increase those quotas."

"My prince is always wise," Benzal responded, immediately regretting his overly positive phraseology. "If that is your desire Master, what increase are you considering?"

"Let's see how you do with a five percent increase."

Benzal was relieved the answer wasn't higher.

"Excellent, my Master. I believe these youths' increasing dependence on screens will assist us in meeting your new quotas."

"Yes, and you can thank Lozel for his part in bringing about that increasing dependence. You remember he recently achieved a 92% ownership rate among your youth," Valden responded. "That certainly has helped make your job easier."

"Yes sire, I'm very thankful for Lozel's efforts in wealth creation."

"As you should be. And what of your efforts to boost recruitment into sexual bondage through these digital devices?"

"Excellent news, my prince. The development of new digital applications and their wide dissemination have successfully increased youth enlistment by seven percent. We continue to be pleasantly surprised at how the gullibility and naiveté of this young generation make them particularly susceptible to manipulation with these devices. By focusing our efforts more specifically on abused and neglected youth, we have decreased our resource utilization by five percent."

"Ah yes, and don't forget how the work of my captain over adult recruitment reinforces your labors. Every parent his team distracts or leads into some addiction makes your job that much easier."

"I am always very aware of your superior organizational skill, Master, and the benefit it provides to all of us."

"With that in mind Benzal, it appears you have continued to thrive in your role in overseeing youth recruitment. Is there anything else?"

"Yes Master, there is a minor matter that I wish to bring to your attention."

"Yes?"

"A new organization in this city is attempting to combat our youth recruitment efforts into sexual bondage."

"And why do you bring this to my attention?"

"Because my prince, the organization was started by the Enemy-"

"The Enemy! How long have you known about this?"

"We have been watching this organization closely for the past six months."

"Benzal, you didn't answer my question," Valden replied as he looked down with increasing anger at his captain.

"My prince, we first became aware of this organization four years ago, but because they didn't pose an immediate threat to our efforts, I didn't believe it was worth bringing to your attention."

"You fool! Any organization started by the Enemy is automatically a threat in my region!" Valden thundered. "If the delay in reporting this treacherous organization causes any harm in my region, I will hold you personally responsible! Do you understand Benzal?" Valden threatened as he bent low over the cowering captain.

"Yes, my prince."

"Now tell me, what are you doing to eliminate this organization?"

"I recruited a Watcher from Europe with special deceptive abilities to disrupt the leadership of this organization."

"You recruited a powerful demon from outside my region without first notifying me?" Valden responded with increasing fury.

"I acted only to keep from concerning you unnecessarily," replied Benzal, expecting a hard blow at any time.

"You would be better off worrying about my concern, Benzal," Valden roared angrily. "I don't like potential spies coming in without my permission. Who is this specialized Watcher?"

"His name is Travoz."

"And what exactly did you promise this Travoz?" Valden asked with his massive arm raised threateningly above Benzal.

"He seeks to increase his power in Europe by learning from your great success."

"Hmmm; are those his words or yours?"

"He speaks of your growing reputation in Europe, Master. He was quite eager to come, once I informed him you were my prince."

"Is that so?" Valden replied, straightening up and bringing his arm back to his side.

"That better be his plan...for your sake."

"I'm certain it is, Master."

"It would be wise for you to be completely certain he has no other plans. I want regular reports on his activities, and I don't want him connecting with any neighboring prince. Is that understood?"

"Absolutely, my prince."

"And what exactly is his strategy?"

"He has successfully deceived a woman with oversight of this organization, and plans to replace the Enemy's chosen leader."

"And…"

"His replacement will not belong to the Enemy, rendering her more easily deceived and manipulated by us."

"I see. Do not fail to bring me regular updates on this matter, Benzal."

"Yes, my Master. I will notify you once we have successfully replaced the Enemy's leader."

"And be certain to report anything that does not go according to your plan," added Valden with a menacing voice.

"Of course, my prince."

Benzal took his leave of Prince Valden, flying to his headquarters in the heart of the city. His smaller lieutenants clamored for his attention, each trying to win the favor of their master. But before Benzal could address the gathering, his lieutenants began parting to allow a massive demon to pass through their midst. Benzal recognized the fifteen-foot humanoid figure that stood before him.

"Well, Travoz. I just finished speaking about you to Prince Valden," Benzal commented, as he carefully scrutinized his peer. "He is anxious to get your report."

"Anxious no doubt, so that I will soon be out of his region," Travoz responded with a sly grin. "I hope you reassured him that I have no interest in staying once we conclude our agreement."

"He is aware. And how are your efforts with this woman progressing?"

"Exactly as I have planned. I have complete control of this 'so-called' female leader. She has started the process of recruiting the replacement for the Enemy's Founder that I suggested to her."

"I'm very pleased to hear that. How soon do you anticipate the completion of your operation?"

"Quite soon. No more than two weeks from now. Which means that if you want me to depart from this region quickly, you'll need to begin holding up your side of our agreement."

"Are you implying that I might try and deceive you?" Benzal asked with irritation.

"Not at all. I simply know that my continued presence here might become, shall we say…delicate, if I stay too long," Travoz answered with a cunning tone.

"That is not your concern. I will deal with any complications of your stay, Travoz. Now regarding our contract, since your plan appears to be progressing well, I will grant you access to the lieutenant in charge of sexual exploitation," Benzal replied, as he motioned for a large demon to come forward. "This is Dravon. He will show you our latest techniques in youth corruption through sexual coercion. Dravon, describe our strategy to Travoz."

"Certainly, Master. We have found great success enhancing the corruption of both boys and girls by facilitating their sale for sex," Dravon started.

"This is nothing new; we've been selling children for sex for centuries," Travoz interrupted with a loud growl.

"Let him finish!" Benzal demanded. "There are new techniques we've developed that greatly facilitate the process."

"Yes," Dravon continued. "We've assisted in the development of a whole line of applications for use on the

Internet, which have increased our recruitment numbers tenfold."

"Such as?" Travoz interjected.

"One of our most successful is Instachat. It automatically destroys any image or writing sent via digital device within one minute of sending. This automatic destruction has emboldened youth so that their exchange of sexual imagery has increased fifty-fold since its introduction."

"What does this have to do with selling children for sex?" Travoz asked impatiently.

"Recruitment; it's all about recruitment," Benzal answered firmly. "To sell children for sex, you must first get them away from their protectors."

"And Instachat does this how?"

"It allows risk-free communication, protecting our recruiters, as well as being very versatile," Dravon continued. "If a recruiter convinces a youth to send sexual imagery, we've taught them how to capture that image to use in further persuasion. We've also trained them on the methodology of mimicking compassion, guaranteeing a steady stream of recruited youth."

"I see. And what other tools do you have?" Travoz inquired with increasing interest.

"Our latest success is called You'reOn," Dravon answered. "We wisely made it free, designing it with special appeal to female youth, our most valuable commodity."

"Go on…"

"It allows the user to broadcast themselves on the Internet within specialized chat rooms," continued Dravon. "We've populated these chat rooms with our human recruiters, who have proven to be extremely successful deceiving these youth, allowing us to exceed all demand quotas in our region."

"This is promising," Travoz responded, softening his tone. "I would like the schematics for these applications so that I can take them back to my own region. They will help compensate for my work here."

"Very well. We will arrange it, but only after you complete your assignment successfully," Benzal answered firmly.

"Of course. I will be returning soon to collect these applications as well as a few others," Travoz replied as he turned to leave. "Just make sure everything is ready."

As soon as Travoz had departed, Benzal turned to Dravon.

"How dare you tell him about You'reOn without my permission," Benzal barked as he grabbed Dravon by the throat, lifting him to his eye level. "I told you to speak only of Instachat."

"I'm sorry, my Master," Dravon choked. "But he seemed unconvinced of the utility of these new tools. I thought…"

"You thought!" Benzal thundered. "It's not your role to think, you moron!"

"Yes Master, forgive me," Dravon begged as he hung from Benzal's powerful arm, feeling the pressure tighten around his throat.

Benzal looked around the room, satisfied he had reasserted the necessary fear among his lieutenants, after the appearance of Travoz.

"Your recent successes will save you for the time being, Dravon," Benzal replied, as he tossed Dravon aside. "But stray from my clear instructions again, and it will end differently next time."

"Of course, Master," Dravon answered as he picked himself up, massaging his throat.

"Oh, and by the way, all quotas are now increased by five percent," Benzal commanded.

"What!!" the deputies screamed. "Why? We didn't do anything wrong!"

"It's very simple, you idiots. Prince Valden has commanded the increase, and I'm passing that command onto you. Now, stop whining, and start making the necessary adjustments, before I decide I've been too lenient on all of you," Benzal ordered.

As Dravon left the gathering, he continued to massage his throat and sent an aide to order all his deputies to come for an emergency meeting. He was confident he would be able to meet the new quota with the help of the latest technologies. But it never hurt to prepare for unseen complications, especially with that Travoz around.

Dravon waited impatiently at his underground headquarters, pacing back and forth until all thirty of his deputies had gathered.

"I've just come from a meeting with our captain, Benzal. He informed me that Prince Valden is demanding a five percent increase in all quotas."

A murmur of growls spread among the group. Dravon stamped his foot, waiting for the noise to subside.

"Of course, this increase applies to our division of youth recruitment into sexual exploitation."

The growls returned...

"Since we've had outstanding success with our new digital applications, I don't expect a problem meeting the new quota."

Dravon waited for silence, glowering over the group.

"However, I want to be prepared for any unforeseen circumstances such as the laziness and incompetence I've recently witnessed among you. Therefore, I want to streamline our operation further and improve our efficiency."

The growls grew loud again.

"Silence!" Dravon yelled as he began walking among the group, anxious for a chance to redeem himself after his incident with Benzal. He spotted a smaller deputy whose growl had been especially loud, and grabbed him by the throat, lifting him off the ground. "You seem particularly unhappy about this news Taz. Should I give you something else to be unhappy about?"

"No, Master. I was simply clearing my throat," Taz choked.

"Now it appears your throat may need some additional clearing," Dravon chuckled. The room quickly became quiet as he slammed Taz back to the ground.

"I've noticed an increase in the recapture of subjects we keep too close to their place of origin. Your laziness in not moving subjects is just one example of your inefficiency. From this moment forward, all captured subjects must be moved to a new location within the region shortly after their recruitment. Is that understood?"

"I've already been doing that," Sez replied, standing near the front of the group.

Dravon glanced at his prize student and then continued. "It appears that at least one of you has some intelligence. Has anyone else had the same ingenuity?"

The rest of the demons looked at each other in silence, with an occasional angry glance at Sez.

"Just as I thought. Well, now you imbeciles should be able to raise your numbers," Dravon bellowed.

"Yes, Master," they all responded quietly.

"In three days of human time, I want reports from the liaisons with the divisions of child abuse, juvenile crime, and technology on further suggestions for recruitment growth."

A demon in the back cried out, "That's not enough time."

"Who said that?" Dravon roared.

The demons divided from front to back, revealing a lone demon, now shaking with fear.

"Perhaps in your case, I should make it two days," Dravon replied menacingly.

"No, Master. I will be sure to complete whatever task you desire within three days."

Dravon stared angrily at him for several moments before turning his attention back to the group.

"I have a way to increase our efficiency," Sez again proclaimed from the front.

"And what is that?" Dravon inquired with a suspicious look.

"I have motivated my human to maximize the number of connected hours per day, swelling our recruiting rate dramatically."

"Is that so, Sez? Did you hear that everyone?" Dravon asked. "Another excellent idea from Sez. Listen up! I want everyone to maximize the connected presence of their human to see what the cumulative effect will be. Now go! Back to work!"

It didn't take long for Sez to return to his human prize, Derrick. The abuse and neglect Derrick suffered during childhood had made him very pliable to manipulation. Also, Derrick was willing to take advantage of the naïve girls other demons brought his way. He required almost no training in his chat skills, quickly learning not to push his subjects too hard during the recruiting process. Derrick was the most successful recruiter Sez had enlisted in decades.

If only he could have ten Derricks!

*****

Heather awakened with a start, relieved to see that she was alone in the bed. Her last customer must have left after she fell asleep. He was a regular, a lawyer from another town. Thankfully, he always left a large tip, allowing her to earn her required $750 for the night. Heather felt relief wash over her as she realized she wouldn't have to endure a beating today. She stood and began putting on her clothes, listening for sounds from either adjacent motel room. When she heard nothing, she concluded the other two girls must have fallen asleep as well. Heather looked at the clock and saw it was just after 7 AM. Melanie would be up soon, knocking on their doors.

After using the bathroom, she thought about showering but decided to wait until she was back at the house. She was hungry and tired, but thankful that none of the customers from the night before had been abusive.

Heather glanced at the motel phone and briefly wondered about calling her mother. Then she remembered that Daddy had told the managers to report any outgoing calls. Daddy would surely find out if she tried to call someone and then he would beat her.

Initially, she had felt funny calling Derrick, Daddy, since he wasn't old enough to be her father. But the slap Bobbi received when she kept forgetting, had etched the label deep into Heather's mind.

If she did find a way to talk to her mother, would she believe her? Heather almost couldn't believe what had happened the past couple weeks herself. Every night she was trapped in this same motel room, forced to allow multiple men take advantage of her. Daddy arranged everything, down to the amount of time they could spend with her. She blocked the revolting images from her mind. The only thing that kept her from going crazy was that she knew she wasn't alone. Terri and Bobbi were in the rooms on either side of her, forced to endure the same nightly abuse as Heather, all to make money for Derrick and Melanie.

Heather sat on the chair, waiting for Melanie to knock. Every night was the same. Melanie would drive the three of them from the house to the motel around 7 PM. Melanie, or Auntie, would stay in the car watching the rooms, making sure no one tried to run away. Terri had tried to run soon after Heather arrived, but Melanie caught her and brought her back. When they returned to the house the following morning, she told Daddy all about it. Heather had never seen him so angry and mean. He began beating Terri across her back and legs, forcing both her and Bobbi to watch. Even thinking about it now caused Heather to shake with fear. Ever since that day, Heather had put all thought of running away out of her mind.

She had accepted her fate, willing herself to get through each night, hoping none of the customers would hit her. That was the only good thing about Daddy. Once she had been hit a few times by a construction worker, and Daddy swore he'd never be allowed back. Heather hadn't seen him since. Some customers had become regulars, coming every 3 or 4 nights. At first, they had seemed a little surprised by her young appearance, but it never stopped them from wanting sex.

Heather had learned to go to another place in her mind during sex so that she could survive the ordeal. She was surprised to find out that both Terri and Bobbi did the same thing. Of course, the pot that Melanie gave them also helped.

Heather heard the familiar three knocks on the motel room doors and walked out of the room into the fresh morning air. Melanie was waiting outside.

"How much did you get last night?"

"At least $800," Heather said as she handed the wad of cash over to Melanie.

"You've been doing really good lately," Melanie noted as she tucked the cash into her purse. "I might even let you spend a little more time with the other girls, now that you've settled in."

"I'd like that," Heather replied, with the first glimmer of hope she'd had in many days.

Terri and Bobbi came out of their rooms and handed their night's earnings to Melanie.

"Excellent, ladies. It looks like there won't be any beatings today. Let's go home and get some rest."

Melanie unlocked the car doors and slid into the driver's seat as the three girls climbed into the back seat of the sedan. After the short drive to the house, the girls went upstairs to shower since Derrick was still asleep in his bedroom.

"Go ahead and wait in Bobbi's room with her while Terri showers," Melanie said to Heather. "Like I promised, you don't have to wait alone in your room anymore."

Heather grabbed some things out of her room and quickly walked into Bobbi's room where Bobbi was sitting on her bed, staring out the window.

"I keep thinking that some night the police are going to come and save us," Heather said quietly so that no one else could hear her.

"You might as well put that thought out of your head. I have a regular customer who is a cop, and he told me

Derrick gives him free access," Bobbi answered. "Part of his reward for not reporting what's going on."

"Really?" Heather responded dejectedly. "How are we ever going to get out of this mess?"

"I've been doing this for four months now, and I still haven't figured a way out. If Melanie isn't watching us, Derrick is."

"How have you been able to put up with this for all that time?" Heather asked as she sat down on the bed next to Bobbi.

"Just like I told you the other night on the way to the hotel. I go to my safe place in my mind, and ignore what's happening to me."

Heather was silent for a couple of minutes before turning to Bobbi, "How did you meet Derrick?"

"Through Lookbook. I was bitching about my mom, and he just started chatting with me, being understanding and all."

Heather felt a stab of guilt as Bobbi continued.

"My mom was into guys in a big way. She never went more than a week without a boyfriend, and couldn't care less what happened to me."

"I kinda know what you mean," Heather replied.

"Well, I got pretty tired of my mom always chasing guys, and I went online to vent. I was pretty lonely, so when Derrick, or SBC-"

"Yeah, he used that with me too," Heather interrupted.

"So, when he wanted to spend time chatting with me, I was all in. We switched to Instachat, and one thing led to another, and here I am."

"You're what, seventeen?" Heather asked.

"I'll turn seventeen next month," Bobbi replied, her eyes suddenly filling with tears.

"Why don't you go next," Heather replied as Terri came out of the bathroom. "I can wait."

"Thanks, Heather. You're OK."

"What's got into her?" Terri asked as she walked by, drying her hair.

"Nothing. We were talking about how we're stuck here, and Bobbi remembered her birthday."

"That's stupid. Daddy will get her something for her birthday. All she has to do is tell him. Daddy's here to look out for us."

"So why did you run before?"

"I was mad about giving all the money to Daddy. When I was working on my own, I used to make good money, and I loved spending it," Terri replied.

"You used to do this on your own?" Heather asked in shock.

"Well, you have to do something to survive, and being in the game gets you more money than anything else. I guess you've never had to live on the street."

"No, I haven't," Heather replied, feeling somewhat guilty about how much she took for granted in her own home. "How'd you end up on the street?"

"My mom kicked me out. I guess I was cramping her style. Anyway, I had no place to go and needed to stay warm. Some guy offered me his place for the night, as long as I slept with him."

"And you did it?" Heather exclaimed.

"Girl...what choice did I have? You got no business-"

"I'm sorry. You're right. I've never had to live on the street. I can't imagine what it would be like."

"It weren't all that bad. I stayed warm, ate well, and got some pretty fine clothes too. Then Daddy found me."

"How?"

"He was out cruising one-night several months back and saw me on the street talking to a john in a car. He came up and told me he could help me up my game so I could triple what I was making in a night. So I went with him, and now I'm glad I did."

"I thought you were mad because he keeps all the money?"

"I was at first. But now I don't mind because Daddy tells me he loves me and cares for me. I ain't ever had anyone care for me before."

"Man. And I thought I had it bad," Heather replied quietly.

"Look! I don't need you feeling sorry for me or anything. I do just fine…OK?"

"I didn't mean anything. I just-"

"Leave it…OK? I did what I had to do, and that's that."

Bobbi soon came out of the bathroom, giving Heather her turn. After Heather finished her shower and was walking into her bedroom, Derrick called from downstairs.

"My fine ladies! Daddy wants to talk, so come on down."

The three girls shuffled down the stairs, still drying their hair. When they came into the living room, they found Derrick in his usual position, sitting in his favorite chair working on his laptop. After a few moments, Derrick looked up at the three girls.

"Since you've all been doin' so well this past couple of weeks, Daddy wants to reward you."

The girls looked at each other and then back at Derrick.

"Auntie Melanie is going to take all of you shopping after you've had a chance to sleep."

"Really! Can we buy anything we want?" Terri asked.

"As long as it's sexy since you'll be shopping for customers," Derrick answered.

The girls' excitement quickly faded.

"And, since you've all been so good, you can each buy an outfit for yourselves," Derrick added.

All three girls looked up at Derrick, feeling surprisingly excited.

"And I have another surprise for you," Derrick announced.

"What's that?" Terri asked, feeling more hopeful.

"I'm planning to take you all to a bowl game real soon."

"But what if we don't want to go to a bowl game?" Heather asked.

"But you want to make your Daddy happy, don't you?" Derrick replied with a serious tone. "After all, Daddy loves you and takes care of you. That's why Auntie's taking you shopping."

"I'm glad you love us, Daddy," Terri spoke up, lightening the mood. "If it'd make you happy to take us to some game, I'll go."

"That's my girl! It will make me very happy, especially with all of you providing entertainment to some of the sports fans," Derrick exclaimed with a grin.

*****

Taron looked down on the scene, watching Heather's response to the news, as he floated near the ceiling with Tem next to him. He saw Heather's face drop, and her posture slump slightly. Dult looked up and smiled wickedly at Taron from his safe proximity to Sez. Dult belonged to Sez's gang of demons and had attached himself to Heather shortly after her arrival.

Taron and Dult had had their share of encounters since Heather's arrival as Taron repeatedly thwarted Dult's efforts to drive Heather into the pit of despair through her ongoing suffering. Taron knew this latest news would provide a new opening for Dult, so he returned Dult's smile with a resolute stare.

Tem meanwhile watched his charge Bobbi for her reaction to the news. She seemed entirely passive throughout the conversation.

"Do you believe she's completely given up?" Taron asked Tem.

"These four months of human time have been extremely challenging for her. In spite of my efforts, she is slowly descending into despair. She has not prayed for at least three months, and her passive response tells me she is losing all hope."

Corel flew in through the house's roof, joining the two angels and placing a hand on each of their shoulders.

"I bring you both a message from Solen, my friends. But first, what are the latest developments here?"

They backed through the walls of the house to a safe distance outside that would prevent a demon from overhearing their conversation.

"Sez has successfully suggested to Derrick that he take the girls to the bowl game two hours away," Taron replied. "He is letting them do some shopping today in a cruel attempt to convey his care for them."

"How are the girls holding up?"

"Bobbi seems to have lost all hope and has ceased to respond to any positive news," Tem answered. "Since Terri doesn't have an assigned angel, she has now fully come under Derrick's control, believing that he actually loves her."

"The Spirit has patiently waited for Terri to request assistance, but her stubbornness has prevented it so far," Corel responded. "And what about Heather?"

"I've managed to keep Dult from causing her to descend into despair, but it appears she has taken this latest news quite hard."

"If they only knew this development will lead to their eventual release," Corel said.

"How has Heather's mother responded to her absence?" Taron inquired.

"Her mother remains unconcerned, convinced she has returned to live with her father, thanks to the influence of Skulty. Heather's friend Sue continues to be very worried, but in spite of Sue's repeated request that Nancy notify the police, Nancy has failed to report Heather's absence to any officials."

"I'm not surprised that Skulty's powers of distraction have effectively prevented Nancy from realizing the true fate of her daughter," Taron replied. "And what news do you bring from Solen?"

"Now that we have identified the demon controlling Abigail, we are very close to disrupting his influence over her. Solen is hoping to time our intervention so that Hope House will be open and ready for Heather after she is released from this bondage. Unfortunately, since Bobbi is from another region, she won't be able to take advantage of Hope House. Neither will Terri since she is considered an adult and does not qualify for their services."

"Derrick is planning to take the girls to the bowl game next weekend. Have all the preparations been completed in that city?" Taron asked.

"Yes. Solen and I both know the city leader well, and he assured me that they would be ready to act on our arrival."

"That's excellent news, Corel," Taron commented. "I will be relieved when Heather begins to receive the specialized services Hope House will provide."

"More importantly, we know that the abuse these girls are enduring will soon come to an end," Tem added. "Perhaps in due time, I can help make the authorities in Bobbi's region aware of the work of Hope House."

"More homes like Hope House are desperately needed, as well as homes for young adults like Terri," Corel added. "It remains part of the Lord's future plans."

As the three angels gazed off in the distance, they could make out the towering figure of Prince Valden.

"It is not yet his time," Corel noted. "For now, we must focus on Travoz, and the demonic horde under Dravon."

"I look forward to the day when our Lord returns, and the world is made new and free from all evil," Taron replied.

"As do we all my friend! For the Lord and His glory!"

Chapter 10

Pride's Power

Abigail sat in her office, reflecting on her lunch with Charlotte earlier that month. Initially, she had been very pleased that Charlotte was considering her offer to transition to the role of executive director of Hope House. But there had been a few occasions since that conversation when Abigail wasn't so sure she was doing the right thing. Now, as Abigail once again sat thinking about removing Eric from his position as ED, she reminded herself that Eric had started Hope House and had worked very hard to make it a reality. And the organization did seem to be progressing toward its goal of serving young survivors of sex trafficking.

Was it wise to replace Eric at this critical moment? But if they kept Eric in his current role, what would she do about Charlotte? If Abigail rescinded the offer to Charlotte to lead Hope House, she'd never be able to recruit her in the future.

Abigail heard the familiar locking of the doors and realized that it was already time for the bank to close. Her assistant manager stuck her head in the door.

"All the doors are locked, and we've secured all the drawers and the vault. We're all heading home. Is there anything else you need me to do?"

"No. I'm just finishing up a couple of things before I leave myself. Have a good evening!"

"You too."

After her staff left, Abigail got up and closed the blinds covering the windows in her corner office. She returned to her desk computer and pulled up the accounting report for the day. Abigail hesitated for several minutes, and after sighing heavily, she proceeded with her task. Abigail took her keys and opened the multiple locks on the vault, spending just a couple of minutes inside before relocking it.

Abigail returned to her office, trying to recollect her thoughts. What had she been thinking? Oh yes, Hope House. How could she forget that expertise was necessary in the world of social work? And since Eric didn't have that expertise, he could potentially lead Hope House into a massive blunder. If that happened, it would bring shame to the whole organization, including her as the board chair. No, Hope House would be much better off having Charlotte as ED with her social work background and leadership experience.

It made perfect sense to recruit Charlotte to lead the organization.

*****

Solen and Corel floated far above the city awaiting the arrival of Aland, whose large form approached from below.

"Welcome, my friend," Solen said as he smiled warmly at the impressive Watcher. "We just received your summons. I hope you have good news regarding Travoz."

"The Lord has graciously enabled," Aland responded. "Travoz's arrogance and pride have seduced him to leave Abigail periodically, believing it wouldn't jeopardize his plan. He was absent for some time this afternoon, allowing me to observe Abigail closely. I believe I have the answer you need for defeating Travoz."

"Excellent news," Corel exclaimed. "What did you discover?"

"This is the first time I've been able to observe Abigail at the end of a workday. She did something unusual at her computer after everyone else left the bank. As the manager of the bank, she has access to all the accounting files, including the reports sent to the regional manager. Today she accessed that file and decreased the reported total intake by five thousand dollars."

"That's certainly unusual," Solen replied thoughtfully. "There's only one explanation for doing that in secret. She must be embezzling."

"I've only been able to witness it this one time, but if it's happened before, then I would suggest you are right Solen," Aland responded.

"Were you able to observe her remove any money?" Corel asked.

"Travoz returned just as she was going to unlock the vault, shielding my view. But I question whether she had any legitimate reason to unlock the vault after closing."

"If she has been embezzling, this sin would explain how Travoz gained access to Abigail," Corel observed. "No wonder she fell under his power so quickly."

"Yes, by engaging in this sin habit, Abigail would have grieved the Spirit, thus providing an opening for Travoz," Aland responded.

"Were you able to discern any reason for this sin?" Solen asked.

"I haven't been able to confirm whether this is related, but Abigail does have a granddaughter with cystic fibrosis."

"I'm very familiar with that condition," Corel interjected. "It's a chronic illness caused by a genetic abnormality. Cystic fibrosis is usually associated with frequent hospitalizations and high medical bills."

"So, if Abigail's daughter and son-in-law are struggling to pay these medical bills for some reason, it makes sense that Abigail might try to help out of compassion," Solen replied as he thought through the implications of this news. "Aland, you previously mentioned that our efforts to overcome Travoz's control over Abigail would be enhanced if we coordinated the attack with a humbling of Abigail, is that correct?"

"That is correct."

"While we don't want to humiliate Abigail completely, for her sake we can't allow this habit to continue, especially with the ongoing presence of Travoz."

"I agree, Solen," Corel responded. "What do you suggest?"

"If the bank discovers this sin of Abigail's and her superiors confront her, we will have the opening we need. Corel, I want you to go to the bank's main office and find a way to implement an unannounced audit of Abigail's bank branch."

"When would you like this unannounced audit to occur?" Corel asked.

"See if you can have it timed for next Thursday afternoon, so hopefully most employees will be gone by the time they discover the discrepancy in the records."

"Great idea, Solen. I should be able to find a believer within the bank leadership that has that authority."

"Good. I'll revisit the angelic nexus to make sure we're prompting the saints to engage in both prayer and fasting to maximize our ability to defeat Travoz. Aland, this has been most helpful. Do you mind continuing to watch Abigail and Travoz until we complete this mission?"

"Not at all. The work of Hope House is too important to allow it to fall into the wrong hands."

"For the Lord, and His glory!"

*****

Eric and Melinda walked into the coffee shop and found a table near the window. Eric pulled off his coat and put it on the back of the chair as Melinda sat down.

"What can I get you?" Eric asked.

"A Chai latte would be great. Thanks."

Eric returned shortly with drinks in hand, sitting down across from Melinda.

"Thanks for agreeing to meet with me outside the office," Eric started. "There's been a lot of tension lately, and I thought it would be best to meet somewhere else."

"No problem. I'm kinda glad to get out of there myself."

"No doubt," Eric chuckled. "Oh, and thanks as well for taking up the extra load of preparations to open the house. My meetings with potential donors have kept me too busy to help you as much as I had hoped. Plus, I'm putting in extra time to get ready for the next board meeting."

"Sure. I know we won't be able to stay open very long without the money to pay staff, plus I kinda like getting paid myself," Melinda answered with a smile.

"Since we've finished hiring the new staff for the house, I wanted to find out how the training is progressing?"

"Pretty well. Marge finally got her last training module to me yesterday, more than a week late."

"I've decided to ignore her passive-aggressive attitude this past couple of weeks since I have more pressing matters to accomplish. At least Marge completed her portion of the curriculum," Eric noted.

"Marge's efforts have been helpful. She's training the new staff on trauma-informed care today, allowing me to catch up on some other things."

"When will the training be completed?"

"The state requires at least 50 hours of training, so we should be done by the end of next week."

"That's great. Do you think these new staff will truly be ready when we open the house?"

"It's hard to tell. Right now, everything is theoretical to them. The real test will come when we have a girl begin acting out at the house. I'll make sure I'm close by and available for the first couple of weeks."

"I'm so thankful to have you on the team, Melinda. Your expertise as a trauma counselor is invaluable as we move forward."

"It's an honor, Eric. The work of Hope House is critical, and right now, these girls don't have any other place to go. I hope we quickly learn from our mistakes since this is such a new field in social work."

"The Lord will protect us, I'm sure," Eric responded. "How about the other preparations to open the house?"

"That's part of what I'm planning to get done today. If all goes well, everything should be ready to open by the end of next week, or at the latest, the beginning of the following week."

"That's perfect...our upcoming board meeting is next Friday, and I was thinking of setting an opening date at that meeting. If things go as planned, we could even make a public announcement that day, or over the weekend."

"That's exciting, Eric!"

"Well, let's both be praying that everything goes well at that board meeting."

"Don't worry. That's been my prayer for the past couple of weeks."

"Thanks, Melinda. I appreciate it. Listen, I know you've got a lot to get done today, and I've got to run as well. Let me know if you need anything from me."

"Sure! And thanks for the latte!"

Eric rubbed his hands together to generate some warmth as he walked into the Red Lantern restaurant the following Monday morning. He spotted Jason already sitting in a booth, sipping his coffee.

"Good morning, brother," Eric said as he sat down. "You're here early this morning."

"I just happened to wake up a little earlier than usual, that's all. Good to see you, Eric."

The waitress came right over, carrying a cup of coffee.

"I thought you might want this," she said, smiling. "Shall I put in the usual Hearty Farmers breakfast for you this morning?"

"Sounds like a plan, though one of these days, I'm going to need to start exercising to get rid of these extra pounds," Eric answered with a quick laugh as he patted his stomach.

"I'll just have my usual oatmeal," Jason told the waitress before she walked away.

"Always the healthy one, aren't you? When I get the house open, and this stress dies down, I may have to switch to oatmeal myself."

"Why wait? You could begin your new diet plan today. Should I call her back?"

"I'm too hungry this morning. Maybe next week."

"Speaking of stress, how is your response to the board coming?"

"I was able to finish it over the weekend. Now I have to work on putting everything in God's hands, as you've so consistently been reminding me these past several weeks," Eric said jokingly.

"Glad to be of service," Jason chuckled. "But I do recognize that putting Hope House in God's hands is the tough part, especially when it's something you've worked so hard to develop."

"So, any suggestions to help me?"

"Just remind yourself of God's truths."

"Such as…?"

"What we've talked about previously, that your identity or your worth comes from being God's son. Worth always comes from being, never doing."

"I remember that, and I also remember that if I'm truly deriving my sense of identity from God, I'll have a sense of peace because my only desire is God's will, correct?"

"You've been paying attention," Jason replied, mocking surprise. "How's that been going for you?"

"I find that I can link my identity to the Lord early in the morning, especially when I take the time to do my devotions. But it seems that by mid-morning, I've somehow switched to being ED of Hope House rather than God's son. I have to admit; it's been frustrating."

"I've been working to cement my own identity to the Lord for years, and I still have my struggles," Jason responded. "Every time someone from the church tells me how wonderful a job I'm doing as their pastor, the old struggle leaps up."

"You just need someone like me to remind you of your faults."

"That role has been more than adequately filled by Heidi," Jason laughed. "But seriously, it takes time to develop the habit, and a lifetime to perfect it."

"Great. The last thing I need now is another lifetime struggle."

"It will be difficult for you, especially since you care so much about what happens with Hope House. After all, you birthed the organization."

"And if God has planned that I no longer lead Hope House?"

"Then only your worldly job description changes, not your identity as God's son. Remember that true faith or trust in God is the currency of God's Kingdom," Jason replied.

"I'm not sure I'm following you."

"Christians often fall into the trap of believing their accomplishments in this life are what truly matters. Don't get me wrong; what we do is important. But it's faith that actually pleases Jesus. Do you remember the story of the centurion who wanted Jesus to heal his servant?"

"Yeah."

"In that story, the centurion believed Jesus could heal his servant without traveling the two days distance to his home. Do you remember what Jesus said about that?"

"Not exactly."

"Jesus announced to His disciples that He had not witnessed such faith in all of Israel. It is one of the few times in the New Testament that Jesus was amazed."

"So, you're saying that the way to impress Jesus is through our faith, not through our works?"

"That's another way of putting it," Jason grinned. "My point is that Jesus will be most pleased if, through this trial, you can maintain the faith that Jesus is accomplishing His will, no matter what happens. That's the reason you have to keep reminding yourself of these truths because by meditating on them, you transfer the truths from your head to your heart."

"And how long does that take?"

"Normally months, and often years."

"But I only have five days."

"Yes, but another truth is that God knows that. Remember, you have His Holy Spirit living within you. God, with His Spirit, will help you get through this."

The waitress brought their plates, and Eric sat thinking for a few moments after Jason prayed.

"And what about the spiritual warfare side that you've mentioned before. Are there actual angels and demons involved in what's happening to Hope House, and how does that work?"

"Yes, there probably are actual angels and demons involved," Jason chuckled. "But exactly how it all works is under debate. What we do know is that since the fall, God has allowed Satan to exert his influence and essentially rule this world. We see the results of this rule played out in the division and conquest of Israel recorded in the Old Testament. And the New Testament brings greater clarity about Satan's rule."

Jason pulled out his Bible and began looking for a passage.

"The New Testament first mentions Satan's rule in the temptation of Jesus recorded in both Matthew and Luke. Luke's account put's it this way in Luke chapter four, verses five to seven:

> 'The devil led him up to a high place and showed him in an instant all the kingdoms of the world. And he [the devil] said to him, 'I will give you all their authority and splendor, for it has been given to me, and I can give it to anyone I want to. So if you worship me, it will all be yours."

Of course, Jesus didn't worship Satan, so the kingdoms of the world remained under Satan's authority. Paul reinforces Satan's rule in his letter to the Ephesians."

Jason flipped through several pages. "Here, let me read it from Ephesians chapter two, verses one and two:

> 'As for you, you were dead in your transgressions and sins, in which you used to live when you followed the ways of this world and of the ruler of the kingdom of the air, the spirit who is now at work in those who are disobedient.'"

"Is the kingdom of the air the same as the world?" Eric asked.

"Most commentators believe it is."

"So, does Satan get to have his way in this world for the time being?"

"Not completely. When Jesus came and lived among us, He introduced God's kingdom into this world. When He died on the cross for our sins, Jesus defeated Satan. Jesus will eventually return and completely reclaim the world as His kingdom, but until then, He commands us as Christians to redeem portions of the world from Satan's control. That's what you are doing with Hope House."

"But I'm still not clear how all this works in the spiritual realm."

"You're not alone, brother," Jason agreed. "There is much we don't understand. But at least we have the big picture. Satan has some authority in this world, but the Second Coming of our Lord will completely eliminate Satan's authority. Until then, we as Christians are called to redeem as much of the world as we can, using His power."

"So, in the meantime, I'm supposed to simply trust that the Lord will do with Hope House as He desires, right?"

"Yes, and don't forget the prayerful attitude. You can pray for the Spirit to help you turn Hope House over to Him. And you can also pray that whatever evil force has brought this attack upon Hope House will be soundly defeated."

"Thanks, Jason. I can do that."

*****

"Jason's mentoring is providing the wisdom Eric needs for the upcoming battles," Riel said to Solen from their usual spot near the ceiling of the Red Lantern.

"I agree, but Eric's timeframe to apply that wisdom has been greatly shortened by the enemy's plan. If Eric becomes resistant to the Spirit and fails to trust in the Lord, his relationship with the board could easily deteriorate, causing unforeseen difficulties with Hope House," Solen noted.

"He is slowly becoming aware of the reality of this spiritual realm."

"Yes, and the more aware he becomes, the better equipped he will be to continue to lead Hope House."

"How are preparations proceeding to deal with the dark force influencing Abigail?"

"Aland has identified the being as Travoz, a fallen Watcher from Europe. It appears he was recruited into this region for this assignment in part because he would be unknown to us."

"Have we learned how to separate him from Abigail?"

"Fortunately, Aland has also been very helpful in providing a strategy to free Abigail, which we are now beginning to put into place. Lord willing, the separation will occur this coming Thursday, one day before the next board meeting."

"The Lord's timing is always perfect."

"I agree, Riel. However, I'm concerned there might be an unexpected attack on Eric within the next several days. I don't dare discount the possibility that our enemy has a secondary plan against Eric to supplement their strategy with Abigail."

"For Eric's sake, I hope that's not the case since he's already having difficulty staying focused on his work. But the enemy loves to strike when their target is weak, so I'll be sure to stay alert as I continue to remind him of our Lord's many truths."

"For the Lord and His glory!"

*****

The following Thursday, Abigail walked out of her office, stopping briefly at the desk of her assistant manager to let her know she was going out for lunch. She decided to walk on this sun-filled day since the restaurant was only five blocks away. The board meeting was tomorrow morning, so she was hopeful that Charlotte would give her an affirmative answer regarding the offer to be ED of Hope House. If Charlotte agreed to assume this new responsibility and could repeat her success with The United Way, it would significantly raise the standing of Hope House within the community.

Abigail chuckled to herself as she thought of the reaction the other city leaders would have when they learned that Charlotte was leaving The United Way to come and lead Abigail's new little organization. They would be surprised at first, but eventually, they would understand. She remembered their comments when she first told them about joining the board of Hope House. Some were surprised she would involve herself in a religious organization. Others had patronized her by saying it was nice for her to get involved in the fight against child sex trafficking, right before changing the subject.

Joining the board of Hope House was a means for Abigail to show her true leadership abilities outside the bank. And when she and Charlotte made Hope House into a thriving success, they would see her differently. Abigail couldn't help feeling excited as she thought about working more closely with Charlotte. They would be a great team together. Abigail would bring her banking and financial expertise, while Charlotte would add her social work and leadership expertise. Yes, it was almost a match made in heaven.

Abigail walked into the restaurant and spotted Charlotte at a table near the window.

"I hope I'm not late," Abigail said as she grasped Charlotte's hand.

"Not at all; you're right on time."

"I couldn't help myself. I had to walk on this beautiful day."

"Oh, I'm jealous. My morning meetings didn't give me time to walk."

"I guess one of the advantages of being in banking is fewer meetings. So, what are you going to have, Charlotte?"

"I like their taco salad; it's my favorite here."

"Me too! Then it's settled. I'll order for us since this is my treat."

"Why thank you, Abigail. That's generous of you."

"Oh, it's my pleasure," Abigail said as she called over the waitress and gave her their orders.

"Now, I hope you've had enough time to think over my offer?" Abigail asked as she took a drink of water.

"Actually, it didn't take much time, Abigail. I've been thinking about embracing a new project, and I believe this would fit me perfectly. So, I would be honored to accept the position of Executive Director of Hope House, of course, once the matter with the current ED is worked out."

"I'm so thrilled, Charlotte! You've made my day! We're very fortunate to have you join us, and I know that you'll enjoy the challenge of working in this new, developing field."

"That's very gracious of you. You're right; this is a whole new field of rehabilitation. I've been doing some reading since our last lunch together, and I was shocked to see how few well-researched articles there are in the social work literature relating specifically to child sex trafficking."

"That's just one of the many ways you can make a tremendous impact. I'd love to see Hope House become a model for other homes around the state, and eventually, around the country. With you at the helm, I can easily see that happening."

"Well, I don't know about that," Charlotte replied with a chuckle. "But it sure sounds exciting."

"Our next board meeting is tomorrow morning. As I mentioned briefly before, I've convinced the rest of the board members of the wisdom of replacing our current ED, except for the one member who is blind to his faults. I will introduce the motion at the end of the meeting tomorrow, and at the worst, the motion will pass with one vote against it. At best, it will be unanimous."

Charlotte smiled after taking a sip of water. "I will wait to hear back from you before I put in my notice at The United Way. Remember, I promised them a four-week warning of any change in my status. However, I will creatively find some time to begin the transition into the leadership of Hope House."

"I'm sure we're going to need all the time you can give us. We may have to delay the opening of the house, but that's a small price to pay for getting the leadership we need," Abigail replied. "I will plan to call you around noon tomorrow."

"Very good. I'll look forward to it," Charlotte said as their salads arrived. "Now, let's do some planning…"

Abigail left the restaurant feeling elated. Everything seemed to be going according to her plan. Even the situation with her granddaughter was getting resolved since her son-in-law would qualify for health insurance next month. Abigail believed this latest installment of cash would be enough to cover her granddaughter's care until that time. Then she could begin paying it all back. Abigail had never meant to keep all this money. It was a loan after all, just not an official one.

Abigail walked into the bank and was surprised to find three strangers in her office.

"Just who are you?" she asked.

"Hello, Mrs. Wilson," an older man answered. "My name is Charles Porter, and this is Barbara Snell and Cindy Foster. We're examiners from the home office, and we're here to do a quick spot audit. It shouldn't take more than a couple of hours, and we'll soon be out of your way."

Eric pulled into the parking lot of the Villa Milan, surprised that the large parking lot was nearly full. He drove around for some time before eventually finding an empty spot. He'd never been here before, but he'd heard it was a great place to have fundraisers, which was why he had come today. Two women had approached him six months ago after one of his community presentations. They told him they were survivors of trafficking and wanted to help Hope House get open. They asked his permission to organize a fundraiser.

Eric felt a little concerned that he hadn't checked into the background of the women in some way or at least asked them more questions about what they had in mind. They had offered to take care of everything, and now the date for the fundraiser had arrived. All he knew was that he was supposed to say a few words about the work of Hope House and enjoy the lunch.

When he walked into the restaurant, he was shocked at the number of people gathered inside, filling the large room. There had to be close to 500 people. He was very thankful he had dressed up, if only slightly. He looked around the room and recognized several leaders from the community, though he didn't know them personally.

Carol, one of the luncheon organizers, spotted Eric, and walked over to greet him.

"Eric, I'm so glad you were able to make it."

"Wow, are you kidding? This turnout is amazing!" Eric exclaimed. "I thought this was going to be a group of 30-40 people, not several hundred."

"When Beth and I decided to organize this fundraiser, we wanted to make a real difference. Our goal today is to raise two hundred fifty thousand dollars for Hope House since this is a significant personal cause for us. Eric, you are a true pioneer by starting this organization."

"Well, I don't know about that. But I can tell you that I'm a little overwhelmed by this response. Two hundred fifty thousand dollars! I had no idea."

"It's our contribution to what you are doing. We have a seat reserved for you upfront. After the restaurant serves lunch and the guests have had a chance to eat, we'd like to have you speak for about 5-10 minutes about the mission and vision of Hope House."

Carol led Eric toward the VIP table, introducing him to several community leaders along the way. When they reached the table, Eric saw that he was sitting next to the Mayor, who had already arrived.

"Mayor Baker, I want to introduce Eric Stone, the Founder of Hope House," Carol said.

"Eric, it's a pleasure to meet you in person finally. I've been hearing about your great work for some time," the Mayor said as he stood and shook Eric's hand.

"Why thank you, Mayor, it's an honor to meet you. I'm not sure what you've heard, but I'm just trying to do my part to help these girls."

"I think you're doing a little more than just your part," the Mayor said with a smile. "It's my understanding that you've succeeded in raising awareness about child sex trafficking throughout the vast majority of the churches and schools in our city. We owe you a great debt for bringing this despicable crime to light."

At that moment, Beth spoke into the microphone, welcoming everyone and asking that they all take their seats so that the program could get started. Eric sat down, looking around his table. In addition to the Mayor, there were several members of the city council, as well as Carol and Beth. Before today, Eric had never met any of these people. Now he was eating lunch at a VIP table with them.

Throughout the lunch, Eric answered questions about the work of Hope House and received several congratulations when he shared that the house was very close to opening. The more Eric interacted with the others at his table, the more he felt that he deserved to be there. They were right; he had been the one to bring sex trafficking to everyone's attention. Hadn't he worked tirelessly these past five years without so much as a thank you from anyone? Maybe Carol was right; perhaps he was a pioneer. He couldn't help feeling more and more proud as he looked around the room with the realization that all these people were gathered together because of something he had started.

Beth walked up to the podium to begin the program. She shared how she had first become aware of Eric's work when he spoke at her church a couple of years ago. She knew about child sex trafficking, but until she heard Eric, she didn't know anyone who was doing anything about it. Beth shared her deep heartfelt concern about what the girls endured in sex trafficking, coming to tears several times during her talk. She concluded by recognizing the ground-breaking work Eric had accomplished.

When Beth finished, Carol came up to share as well. She related how she had also learned about Eric's work through one of his many community presentations. Carol went on to talk about the need for specialized residential facilities, just like what Eric was creating. Carol seemed to know a great deal about the issue, telling everyone that there were only a handful of homes similar to Hope House around the country. She finished her talk by reminding everyone that their city was very fortunate to have a program like Hope House.

As both Beth and Carol spoke, Eric felt a growing sense of purpose and worth from his work at Hope House. Finally, he was receiving the recognition he deserved for all the hard work he had done. He was being featured today because of that work. He was sitting at the table with these other significant people because he had been the one to start Hope House. He had to admit; it felt terrific.

Carol concluded her portion of the program by introducing Eric as the Founder and visionary behind Hope House, a pioneering residential treatment program that would change the lives of the girls who came to live there. As Eric walked up to the podium, he received loud applause along with a standing ovation. Yes, this felt amazing.

*****

A dark flash came up through the floor just beneath Eric, surprising Riel. In a split second, it attached itself to the base of Eric's skull and looked up at Riel in triumph. Riel recognized the snake-like form; a demon that specialized in pride. It was Riel's least favorite type of demon because once attached; it was almost impossible to remove as long as the host continued to welcome thoughts of pride.

Riel realized this was not a random attack. Extensive planning and coordination with human events was required to provide an opening for a demon of pride to attach itself to a believer, especially one who was guarded by an angel.

"Lord, remind Eric that all of these accolades are because of your empowering," Riel prayed fervently, as he pulled out his sword in case other demons tried to take advantage of the situation. As Eric got up to speak, the size of the demon grew, feeding off the pride now being experienced by Eric.

Riel stayed close to Eric to prevent any further attacks, recognizing that only a significant humbling episode would weaken the grip of this demon.

"Holy Spirit, help Eric remember that none of this would have happened, except through You and Your enabling. And Jesus, turn his eyes from himself, toward You!"

Chapter 11

Derrick's Defeat

Heather was sleeping deeply, dreaming about hanging out with friends after basketball practice, when she suddenly felt someone shaking her awake.

"Time to get up," Melanie declared in a loud voice.

"What time is it?" Heather asked groggily.

"Like I said, time to get up."

"But I still feel tired."

"You'll have plenty of time to sleep later. Right now, there's things we got to do."

"Like what?"

"Just get dressed and go downstairs; you'll find out," Melanie answered harshly as she went to wake up Terri and Bobbi.

Heather climbed out of bed and made her way to the bathroom ahead of the others.

After cleaning up and brushing her teeth, Heather returned to her room and changed into her regular clothes, noticing they badly needed washing. She brushed her hair, pulling it back into a ponytail, and walked downstairs to find Derrick working on his laptop, as usual.

"How's my girl?" Derrick asked in an upbeat mood as he looked up.

"I'm OK..."

"Just OK, huh? Well, cheer up. You're all in for a big day today."

"What kind of big day? Are we going to have to start working early?"

"You'll see. You're all going to get spoiled again today. I'll tell you all about it when the others come down."

Heather sat down on the couch, rubbing her eyes, still trying to wake up. She'd fully transitioned to sleeping during the day since she worked all night, every night. For Heather and the other girls, it was the equivalent of two in the morning. Even Melanie was usually sleeping at this time.

Terri and Bobbi eventually made their way downstairs, both half awake and yawning. After they joined Heather on the couch, Derrick set his laptop on the table next to his chair and stood up.

"Remember a while back I promised to take you to a bowl game?" Derrick started.

The girls slowly nodded.

"Well, the day has come. We're leaving in a few hours and should be there by tonight. But before we leave, I've got a couple of surprises for you."

The girls didn't say anything but kept their attention focused on Derrick.

"Daddy always takes good care of his girls, right?"

All three silently nodded their heads 'yes'.

"Well today, Daddy is going to take extra special care of his girls. After you grab something to eat, Daddy's going to take you to get checked out, and then we're going shopping."

"What do you mean, checked out?" Terri asked.

"I mean checked out to make sure you don't have any diseases or such."

"I don't understand, Daddy," Bobbi replied.

"Me either," Heather chimed in.

"Well, sometimes men carry diseases, and I just want to make sure my girls are clean," Derrick answered.

"What'll we have to do? It ain't goin to hurt, is it?" Terri asked, becoming alarmed.

"Now don't get all bothered about it," Derrick replied sternly. "I'm taking you to a clinic where they'll run some tests to make sure you're all OK, that's all."

"But I don't want to go to no clinic," Bobbi whimpered with tears in her eyes.

"You ain't got no choice," Derrick replied with growing anger. "You're going to make Daddy mad, and that's a mistake. Besides, after we get done at the clinic, Daddy's taking you all shopping, cause' Daddy's just trying to take good care of his girls, right?"

The three girls sat quietly.

"Right?" Derrick said louder.

"I guess so," Bobbi stammered, while the other two nodded their heads slightly.

"That's right! Now the doc will take good care of you, and it'll be over before you know it. Then you'll get to buy whatever you want," Derrick replied, softening his voice once again.

"Really?" Terri asked. "We can buy another outfit like we did before?"

"Yep, plus some things Auntie will pick out for you. Now go grab something to eat; we're leaving in thirty minutes," Derrick said in a tone that stopped any further argument.

Derrick pulled up to the door of the urgent care clinic and turned to the girls in the back seat.

"Now, Auntie's going in with you to make sure you all behave. You follow her lead, just like always," Derrick said threateningly. "I'll be waiting out here, and if I hear about anybody pulling a crazy stunt, there'll be hell to pay!"

"Yes, Daddy," they replied in unison.

As they walked into the clinic, Melanie whispered loud enough for all of them to hear, "Now, let me do all the talking."

Melanie walked up to the window at the reception desk, while the girls followed.

"How much does it cost to get checked out for infections?"

"What kind of infections?" the woman at the window asked.

"You know, the kind women sometimes get from having sex."

"Are you symptomatic?"

"What does that mean?"

"Are you having some problem, like pain?"

"Oh, it ain't me. These are my little sisters, and they're...well, they're worried they may have caught something from their boyfriends."

The woman behind the window looked at the three girls and turned to Melanie.

"How old are your sisters?"

"Oh, the youngest is 18. She don't look it, but she is. This one's 20, and the oldest is 22," Melanie responded, pointing to Terri last.

"Do you have any insurance?"

"No, we'll just pay with cash."

"Do you have any identification?"

Melanie thought for a minute before responding. "I got my driver's license, but I must have left theirs at home. Can't you see them without it?"

The woman turned to an older woman working on a computer nearby, before coming back to the window. "Since you're paying with cash, it's not necessary. We can use your ID."

"So, how much will it cost?"

The woman again turned to the older woman before responding. "A complete sexually transmitted infection evaluation, including blood work, will cost approximately $250 per person."

"We have to have blood taken?" Bobbi whined, before getting a stern look from Melanie.

Melanie turned back to the window, and after some hesitation, replied, "That'll be fine."

"Here are some forms for each of the patients to fill out, and once you've completed that, we'll call you back when we're ready."

Melanie took the clipboards from the woman and brought the three girls over to a group of chairs in the corner of the waiting area, away from everyone else.

"Now you can each put down your first name, but I want you to use Wilson for your last name, got it?" Melanie whispered. "And put your ages just like I told you."

Each of the girls took the clipboards and started filling out the forms.

"What should we use as our address?" Terri asked quietly.

Melanie gave them the number and street to use as they all copied the address. When the three girls had completed and signed the forms, Melanie took them to the window before returning to wait.

Ninety minutes later, Melanie and the three girls walked out of the clinic and over to the car where Derrick was waiting.

"What's Klamidya, Daddy?" Bobbi asked as she got into the back seat. "I asked Melanie, and she told me to ask you."

"See, I told you it was important for you girls to get checked out. It's just a little infection you can sometimes get from guys. They gave you some medicine, didn't they?"

"Yeah, I've got some pills to take for a week."

"Did they find anything with you two?" Derrick asked, looking at both Heather and Terri as they got into the car.

"No," they both said quietly.

"They took some blood and won't have the results back for a couple of days," Terri added. "They said they'd call Auntie if anything shows up."

"Any problems?" Derrick asked Melanie as she joined him in the front seat.

"No, except it cost a little more than we expected."

"How much?"

After hearing the total, Derrick replied, "We'll make up for it tonight." Derrick then pulled out of the clinic parking lot, heading toward the mall. "OK, girls. Like I said because you've been working so hard to keep Daddy happy, now you get to go shopping!"

Several hours later, Derrick pulled into the parking lot of a motel and sent Melanie into the office to retrieve the key cards for their rooms. Heather sat up, realizing she had fallen asleep during the drive. She looked over at the other two, still sleeping, surrounded by their shopping loot. Scanning through the car window, Heather recognized the similarity of this motel to the one they used back home, except this one was maybe a little newer. The motel had two stories of rooms, each one with an outside door so customers could enter and leave the rooms without going through a lobby. And just like back home, there was only one stairway from the second floor to the parking lot.

Derrick started checking his smartphone, and as Melanie walked up to the car, he suddenly began yelling, "Damn it! DAMN it! DAMN IT!"

"What's wrong?" Melanie asked, turning to check on the girls.

"This new app, PlentyofFish, screwed up and didn't post my listings for tonight. DAMN IT! That means we won't have any customers and I'll lose tonight's take."

Melanie sat quietly for a couple of minutes while Derrick continued swearing, finally throwing his phone down.

"Maybe it's not so bad," Melanie started. "The girls have been working every night after all, and giving them a night off could help them better serve the customers tomorrow night, right?"

"That wasn't in my plan Mel, especially after spending all that money today. Damn it!" Derrick sat fuming while Melanie waited. Heather sat quietly as the other two girls rubbed the sleep out of their eyes, having been awakened by all the yelling.

"I'm going to get the girls settled into their rooms," Melanie announced.

"Let's put them together to save some money since we won't have customers tonight," Derrick replied.

"It don't matter, Hon. It's too late to get our money back now. We might as well let them have their own rooms to rest for tomorrow night."

"You're always taking their side and looking out for them, damn it! What about the money we're losing?"

"Hon, you know I love you, and the girls'll make up for it. You'll see."

"Damn right! I want those girls working hard tomorrow night you hear? And I don't want to hear no bitching!"

Melanie got the girls and their bags out of the car and took them to their rooms.

"Daddy's in a bad mood now, so nobody get any ideas about leaving, or you'll get a beating you'll never forget," Melanie warned. "Remember, Daddy and I will be in the end room, right by the stairs, so ain't no one getting by our room without us knowing it."

The girls each went quietly into their rooms, relieved and thankful to have a night to spend alone in a bed. Heather opened her shopping bags, laying the negligées off to the side, and pulled out the sweater top and jeans she had bought. As she laid them out on the bed, she was surprised at how thankful she was to be able to buy an outfit. Now Heather had two outfits she could wear, in addition to the clothes she had brought with her several weeks ago when she left her house.

After taking a shower to clean up, Heather tried on her new outfit for the second time before getting into bed. Within a short time, she was sound asleep.

*****

Taron turned to Falden high above the hotel.

"Your help in our operation is greatly appreciated. Canceling Derrick's new listings was a brilliant move. Now Heather and the other girls can have the reprieve they so desperately need."

"Derrick doesn't have the same protection in our city as in Springfield, so it was easy to cancel his listings," Falden responded. "Several of our larger churches are now engaged in the fight against sexual exploitation since they learned about its existence two years ago. During major sporting events like this bowl game, they have prayer teams praying around the clock."

"I've felt that prayer since arriving," Taron noted.

"It's enabled the angelic nexus here to convince city officials to establish a specialized task force, and more importantly, to shield the significance of the task force from the demonic overlords."

"Sez's arrogance has also been quite helpful," Taron chuckled. "He has no clue what he's just stumbled into."

"Yes, and I suggest we keep it that way as long as possible. We don't want him alarming Derrick to our plan."

"We also don't want Derrick's response to turn violent," Taron added. "That means we'll need to neutralize Sez's influence at just the right moment."

"Our city nexus leader has promised Solen that he will make sure Sez is properly handled," Falden answered. "He's also working closely with Solen to coordinate your intervention."

"Who is your city leader?" Taron asked.

"His name is Ethron," Corel answered as he joined the other two angels. "I worked with him when the first settlers came to this state over two hundred years ago. He's an excellent strategist and a strong warrior."

"I will share your arrival and kind words with him," Falden replied.

"Please do. I have a great affection for Ethron. Taron, what is the condition of the girls?"

"Heather's periodic prayers have allowed me to pour strength and resilience into her while also preventing Dult from eliminating all her hope. She does miss her home and friends terribly."

"What about the other two girls," Falden inquired.

"The older girl, Terri, has given herself into the control of one of Sez's associates, limiting my ability to help her. She will need a great deal of care once we free her from Derrick's control. However, I've also been able to assist the other girl, Bobbi. Her intermittent cries for help have allowed me to instill peace into her, strengthening her will to survive."

"Well, tonight they can all rest, and soon they'll be free," Falden said. "Tomorrow I will make sure the task force members take special notice of Derrick's listings. Fortunately for us, they have become passionate about rescuing young girls."

"For the Lord and His glory!"

*****

Heather spent most of the next day watching TV with the other two girls, feeling somewhat relaxed for the first time in several weeks. It helped to be awake and alert again during daylight. Bobbi had been quiet most of the day, choosing instead to watch cartoons on the cartoon channel. Heather couldn't quite understand her fascination with cartoons, especially since she was older than Heather. Terri had tried to change the channel a couple of times, but Bobbi had pleaded with her to change it back. Terri had relented, confirming Heather's suspicion that Terri was becoming protective of Bobbi, acting as if she was her older sister.

Melanie however, had been unusually uptight throughout the day, probably because Derrick was still in a bad mood. Heather was learning that Derrick hated losing money even more than spending it.

Melanie came into Heather's room, carrying a couple of pizza boxes.

"Daddy wants to get started early tonight, to make up for last night. He's got lots of customers lined up, so I got you some food. You've got 30 minutes to eat and get into your new things. Oh, and by the way, tonight's quota is $1000, not $750."

"What?!" they all cried.

"Why's Daddy punishing us?" Terri asked.

"Daddy's not punishing anybody. It's business," Melanie answered sternly. "Now I don't want no complaining, ya hear? Daddy's been really good to you this past couple of days, so you need to show him how much you appreciate it."

Terri looked over at both Heather and Bobbi, frowning as she stood up. Bobbi didn't say anything, but Heather saw a deep sadness slowly creep across both of their faces as they grabbed some pizza and went to their separate rooms.

Heather felt herself deflate as she sat looking blankly at the TV, ignoring the cartoon. Up until yesterday, she had separated herself from what was happening to her. It was the only way Heather could survive mentally. She had just let the men do things to her while she went off to another place in her mind. But last night and today had been different. The extra time Heather had to think gave her more opportunity to realize her predicament. Today, Heather kept trying to think about something else, but the realization of her situation kept pressing in. In thirty minutes, another strange man was going to come into the room and use her for his pleasure.

Heather started to cry, but then she had a thought to pray.

"Lord, I know I kinda got myself into this mess, but I really need your help right now to get through tonight. And please show me how I can get away from Derrick and Melanie, so I don't have to do this anymore."

Heather sat quietly, trying to think of something else to pray when she sensed a growing peace and strength come over her. In spite of her seemingly impossible situation, she strangely knew she was going to be OK. Heather wiped the tears from her cheeks, grabbed a piece of pizza, and went into the bathroom to change into a new negligée. This one had a wrap that made her feel slightly more covered, even though it was sheer. She turned off the TV and sat quietly on the bed, waiting for the inevitable knock on the door.

*****

Taron stood towering over both Kul and Dult as he alternated pointing his sword at each of their necks.

"It only takes a little prayer to change who's in control. Now, why don't you both skulk off somewhere and leave this poor girl alone?"

Dult picked himself up and grunted as he flew out of the motel room in the opposite direction of Sez's room while Kul quickly followed him. Taron watched them both fly away before passing down through the floor and moving underground to gain some distance from the motel. It was vital for him to keep the presence of his fellow angels hidden at this critical moment.

"Heather is stable, and should be able to handle the potential shock of what is to come," Taron replied as he joined Falden, Corel, and Ethron, far above the motel.

"Excellent," Corel said before turning to Ethron. "Solen wanted me to tell you that he is very appreciative of all your help and cooperation."

"He's a great warrior and has been an inspiration to me for many generations," Ethron answered. "Plus, it's good to see you again, old friend."

"I was pleased when Solen gave me this assignment, knowing I would have the chance to work alongside you again," Corel answered. "I must tell you, Falden has been quite helpful alerting the task force to Derrick's presence."

"We've been fortunate that several of their top leaders are devoted followers of Jesus, thus greatly enhancing our ability to influence them," Ethron answered.

"Yes, once I led them to Derrick's listings, they quickly realized that he might be exploiting young girls," Falden interjected. "Their passion and experience have enabled them to quickly organize a sting operation."

"I'll just be happy and relieved when we finally free Heather from Derrick's control," Taron declared.

"It will happen soon, I assure you," Ethron answered. "I understand this Sez who is currently controlling Derrick only possesses the strength of a low to mid level demon, but just in case, I've assigned three angels to make sure he doesn't disrupt the arrest."

"Our reconnaissance assures us that, while he has some ability to leverage technology, his warrior abilities are only average," Corel replied.

"We'll be able to confirm his warrior ability, or lack thereof, very soon," Ethron said, as they continued to watch the scene below unfold.

*****

Heather sat on the bed, considering her change in mood. There was no question about it. She was now feeling hopeful, in spite of her unchanged circumstances. Was she losing her mind? She knew Derrick would never let her go as long as she was making all this money. But, somehow, she knew that she would be OK. Heather shook her head in wonder just as a knock came at the door. She sighed as she got up and opened the door, standing behind it as much as possible. A tall man in his 30's walked in.

"My, you're a young thing," the man said. "What's your name?"

"You can call me Dream Girl," Heather answered.

The man walked around the room, looking briefly into the bathroom.

"So, this is my first time doing anything like this. How does it work?"

"You tell me what you'd like, and after we're finished, I'd appreciate you leaving me a gift to cover costs," Heather answered, careful to use the language Melanie had taught her.

"And when I tell you what I want, you'll tell me the size of the gift I should leave?"

"Yeah, that works."

"And how old are you?"

"I'm 18, though most people tell me I don't look it," Heather lied.

"So, let's say I want you to take off that sexy outfit and lay on the bed naked, what kind of gift would that take?"

"$75 if you just look at me, $150 if you touch me, and $250 if you have sex with me."

"Jake, did you get all that?"

"Who's Jake?" Heather asked suddenly, alarmed and unsure of what was happening.

"Never mind young lady," the man said with a new commanding voice. "Go cover yourself up, and sit on the bed, please."

Heather did as she was told, looking questioningly at the stranger as he continued to speak to someone outside the room.

"Jake, where are we with the other two girls? I see. OK, I'll wait to hear back from you."

*****

Sez looked up just in time to see three angels rapidly descend on him with swords drawn. He quickly turned to pull out his sword, but the angels expertly placed their sword tips at his neck, immobilizing him.

"I wouldn't bother trying anything Sez," one of the angels admonished. "We have permission to send you to the pit if necessary. Now move away from the man."

Sez released his grip on Derrick and slowly moved outside the room with the angels. He looked up to see an enormous angel along with several smaller angels, floating just above the motel. Additional angels were escorting demons at sword-point from the rooms belonging to both Terri and Bobbi.

*****

Heather sat quietly on the bed as the man carefully inspected the room, opening drawers, and rechecking the bathroom. He appeared to be listening through an earpiece and put a finger to his lips motioning Heather to be quiet. After about five minutes, he came over to Heather and pulled something out of his pocket.

"I'm Detective Marker. I'm a vice officer for the city, and this is my badge. I need you to continue to cooperate with me. We're making some arrests right now, and we'll soon be taking you downtown."

At first, Heather felt relieved. Perhaps her ordeal was over. Then she realized she might have to go to jail because of what she had been doing. She began to shake all over, trying not to cry.

"Can I at least get dressed?" Heather asked, on the verge of tears.

The officer put his finger to his lips again and seemed to be listening.

"Good. So the guy clammed up right away, huh? What about his bottom? OK, well we'll have plenty of time to talk to them all downtown. Thanks, Jake."

The officer turned to Heather.

"Yes, go ahead and get dressed in the bathroom. Then we'll put you with the other girls."

"You're arresting Terri and Bobbi too?" Heather said without thinking.

"So, that's the names of the other two girls, huh? And what's your real name?"

After a long pause, she finally said, "Heather."

"OK, Heather. Go and get dressed. We'll be leaving soon."

When Heather came out of the bathroom, a woman wearing a police uniform was standing in the motel room doorway next to the detective.

"Hi Heather, I'm Officer Turner. I'll be taking you downtown for processing. Since we're transporting you, I need to put these handcuffs on you, so please turn around."

"Am I going to jail?"

"You'll be spending the next several days locked up until we sort everything out. Then a judge will decide what happens to you."

After the officer handcuffed Heather, they came out onto the outdoor walkway where both Terri and Bobbi were standing handcuffed with another female officer next to them. They looked at Heather; she could see that Bobbi had been crying, but Terri had a determined look on her face. Heather looked further down the walkway to see Derrick and Melanie walk out of their room in handcuffs. Derrick looked angry and was yelling at the officers that he hadn't done anything wrong. Melanie tried to push against the officer that was leading her toward the stairs. Another officer came out carrying Derrick's laptop. Heather watched as they were both placed into the back seat of separate police cars. Terri and Bobbi were placed into the back of a third car, while Heather rode alone in the final vehicle.

When they reached the police station, they were each placed in separate rooms after the intake person completed the booking. Heather sat waiting for what seemed like an eternity. She was thankful they had taken the uncomfortable handcuffs off, allowing her to sit alone. The room was small, cold, and sterile. It only contained a metal desk and three similar chairs, one of which Heather was using. As she looked around the room, she saw a camera in the upper corner, just above the door. The room had no windows, leaving Heather with very little to look at except the cement block walls.

Finally, the woman who had called herself Officer Turner came into the room carrying a file. She sat down at the desk, and after briefly looking through the papers, she looked up at Heather.

"So, Heather, how old are you?"

"As I said earlier, 18, though I look younger," Heather replied hesitantly.

"Look, I know that this guy Derrick, and his bottom, Melanie, told you to lie to us about your age, but that's only going to hurt you. If you really are 18, which I doubt, then you'll be arrested for soliciting since you're an adult. But if you happen to be younger than 18, it will go a lot easier on you. Do you understand?"

Heather sat for a few minutes, thinking about whether or not she should tell the truth about her age. Derrick had been clear. If the police ever arrested any of the girls, Derrick had consistently told them that they must lie about their age and he would help them get out. If they didn't lie, Derrick threatened that he would find them and beat them. However, that was when Derrick was staying home, letting Melanie watch over them. But tonight, Derrick had also been arrested. It didn't seem like Derrick would be able to help her, and he certainly couldn't beat her. Maybe she was better off telling them the truth.

"I'm actually 15," Heather said finally.

"I thought so. And what's your last name, Heather?"

"Wallace."

"And where are you from?"

"Brookview."

"Are your parents still in Brookview?"

"My mom lives there with my stepdad."

"Wanna tell me how you ended up with Derrick?"

Heather spent the next several minutes briefly telling the officer how Derrick and Melanie had tricked her to come and stay at their house. She didn't mention Ted's assaults; instead, she just said that things were not good at home.

Officer Turner jotted down some notes on a piece of paper before looking up again at Heather.

"This is very helpful, Heather. Look, here's what's going to happen. In a little while, we'll be transferring you to a juvenile facility. Before then, I'm going to have a social worker talk with you. The more you tell her, the more we can help you. And don't try lying to her; she picks up on that real quick, OK?"

Heather slowly nodded her head, still trying to comprehend all that was happening to her.

"Heather, thanks for telling me the truth about your age and about what happened to you. By chance, do you want to tell me the ages of the other two girls while you're at it?"

"I'd rather not…"

"I thought that might be the case, but that's OK; we'll find out eventually. We always do."

*****

"Thankfully, you successfully influenced Heather to tell the truth," Corel noted as he turned to Taron. "If she had lied about her age, it would have delayed our plans."

"Heather's periodic short prayers made the difference, allowing me to dislodge Dult and Kul. Now that Dult is gone, Sez's lies through Derrick no longer have the same power," Taron responded.

"I'll get word back to Solen that everything is progressing according to plan, while you continue to support Heather," Corel replied.

"For the Lord, and His glory!"

Chapter 12

Travoz's Travails

Abigail sat at the extra desk in the bank lobby, periodically glancing at the auditors in her office. Her anxiety had kept her from getting much accomplished throughout the afternoon, though she had made a valiant attempt to look busy. What really occupied Abigail's thoughts was formulating a legitimate explanation for the missing money, assuming the auditors would discover her recent forbidden activities. However, closing time was rapidly approaching, and Abigail still lacked any credible justification if the auditors questioned her.

Abigail had noted a change in the demeanor of the examiners about mid-afternoon when they took on a new seriousness as one of them repeatedly pointed at the computer screen. Unable to keep away, Abigail had briefly entered the office to ask if she could get them some coffee or tea, but they brusquely rebuffed her. It was now almost closing time, and Abigail stiffened as she saw one of the auditors approach her.

"Mrs. Wilson, when the last customer leaves, we'd like you to dismiss your staff after they've locked up. But we need you to please stay behind for some questions."

Abigail's heart sank; she had to come up with an explanation.

About fifteen minutes later, when everyone had left the bank, the auditors called Abigail into her office. The person Abigail had concluded was the lead auditor, Charles Porter, was sitting at her desk, while the two younger women sat in the remaining chairs along the wall of the office. Porter had an abundance of grey hair, while the two women appeared to be in their mid to late thirty's.

"Please come in Mrs. Wilson, and have a seat," Porter instructed.

Abigail sat down in the remaining chair directly in front of the desk, trying to calm herself by taking a deep breath and clasping her hands together.

"Mrs. Wilson, as you know, the bank periodically does spot audits on all our branch offices around the region," Porter began. "Usually, nothing abnormal shows up, and we can certify a clean audit."

Abigail felt her palms become moist as her breathing quickened and her muscles tensed.

"However, unfortunately, that is not the case today. You see, we've found some irregularities that we need to ask you about."

"Why are you starting with me, and not one of my employees?" Abigail asked.

"First of all, as the bank manager, you are given the oversight of your employees, and they are your responsibility, are they not?"

"Yes, they are."

"And secondly, the irregularities seem to be occurring in association with your specific login."

Abigail's throat tightened.

"What irregularities exactly are you referring to?"

"As I observe your response, Mrs. Wilson, I think you know. But in answer to your question, we've found, not just irregularities, but a particular pattern of irregularities that makes us very suspicious."

"Such as?" Abigail retorted as she tried to sound confident.

"Such as a pattern of you logging in regularly after the bank closes and making a change in the total intake for the day," Porter said as he watched Abigail. "I see by your surprised look that you weren't aware that we were able to monitor changes in the daily total. It's a security measure we put in place several years ago to protect the bank from employees who might say, begin to think they could make unauthorized and self-serving changes to the total."

Abigail swallowed hard.

"Is there anything you wish to tell us, Mrs. Wilson?" Porter asked as he clasped his hands together on her desktop.

Abigail was quiet for several moments, realizing she had been exposed and caught. As her mind reeled with the ramifications of what was happening, her confidence collapsed, and Abigail began to cry.

*****

Travoz felt his hold on Abigail weaken just as he looked up to see five angels rapidly approaching him, led by another Watcher. Travoz released his grip on Abigail and tried to assume a defensive stance, but not before the other Watcher seized him from behind, and the angels began engaging Travoz's entourage of demons.

"Greetings, Travoz. Aren't you a little far from your normal haunt?" Aland asked as he firmly grasped Travoz's arms, preventing him from drawing his sword.

Initially, the demons with Travoz tried to fight off the angels, but Solen, Corel, and the others quickly overpowered them, sending them scurrying out of the bank, leaving Travoz alone and spitting curses.

Holding Travoz's arms very tightly, Aland whispered into the fallen Watcher's ear. "That was easier than I expected; perhaps time has weakened you."

Travoz grunted and struggled against Aland, unable to loosen his arms. Solen put his sword beneath Travoz's chin.

"It's been several centuries since I've done this to a fallen Watcher," Solen replied.

"You don't have the power to defeat me, angel" Travoz snapped.

"But I do," Aland answered as he moved Travoz away from Abigail and out of the bank. "I have to admit, I don't often encounter fallen Watchers, so this feels quite gratifying. You are a disgrace to our kind. If it were up to me, I'd throw you into the pit. But the Lord has other plans for you, so you've been granted a brief reprieve."

Travoz continued to struggle, trying unsuccessfully to free himself from Aland, as the angelic group took him high into the air above the city.

"This isn't my choice, but, unlike you, I follow my Lord's instruction. Now leave this region," Aland commanded as he released Travoz. "The Lord has granted me the privilege of escorting you to the pit if you should choose to disobey. There's nothing that would please me more than having one less fallen Watcher to deal with."

Travoz gave Aland and the other angels a wrathful look as he conceded defeat and flew off toward Europe, cursing the angelic group.

"I thought you were going to accompany him at least part of the way across the ocean," Solen replied.

"There is one final mission we need him to unwittingly accomplish before he leaves," Aland declared. "I believe he will undertake that critical task as soon as he exceeds my visual limits, and by completing it, he will create a fault line within the demonic strongholds over this region."

"I see," Solen responded. "Thank you again, my friend. Your assistance has been critical in our efforts here."

"My pleasure Solen. As always, for the Lord and His glory!"

*****

The auditors waited patiently for several minutes while Abigail collected herself, grabbing tissues from her desk and wiping away the tears mixed with mascara.

"I'm so sorry. I meant to pay it all back. It's just my granddaughter. She's been sick a lot. And the bills..."

"I'm glad you no longer deny your actions, Mrs. Wilson," Porter replied unsympathetically. "However, your rationalizations are of no consequence to us. We hear all kinds of excuses in our line of work. We will report our findings to our legal department, and they will decide if and what charges to bring against you. Regardless, you will be required to repay the amount you have embezzled, with interest of course."

Hearing the word embezzled startled Abigail. She had never thought of her actions as embezzling; it was merely an unauthorized loan.

"Mrs. Wilson, you have ten minutes to gather your personal belongings and turn in your keys before we escort you from the bank," Porter declared firmly. "Oh, and by the way, I wouldn't try taking any sudden trips. It will only make things worse for you; besides, we have the means to find you."

Eric walked in the door of his home, feeling on top of the world!

"Evening Hon! How's my beautiful bride?" Eric asked as he walked into the kitchen.

"My, you're in a good mood. What brought this on?" Maggie asked as she opened the oven door to look inside.

"Remember that luncheon a couple of women wanted to set up?"

"Not offhand."

"You know, about six months ago a couple of women asked if they could set up a fundraising luncheon for Hope House."

"Vaguely. You haven't mentioned it recently."

"I almost forgot about it, till it came up on my calendar. Anyway, you wouldn't believe how many people were there; almost five hundred!" Eric exclaimed as he sat down at the kitchen table.

"Really! That's wonderful! Too bad I wasn't there to enjoy it with you," Maggie smiled, sitting down across from him.

"I mean, they did an incredible job. And best of all, these two women raised over two hundred fifty thousand dollars!"

"You're kidding! Wow! That must have been some luncheon!"

"Yeah. The ladies don't have the final numbers yet, but it was astounding. And it felt amazing to finally get some recognition for all the work I've done."

"You mean all the work that the Lord has done through you."

"Of course. And Hon, I sat at the VIP table with the mayor! He not only knew who I was, but he also thanked me for being the one who raised awareness of child sex trafficking here in the city. Several city council members were there too. It was just what I needed to get ready for our board meeting in the morning."

"What do you mean?"

"I plan to tell Abigail and her groupies all about this luncheon and remind them that none of this would have happened without me."

"You mean without the Lord using you, right?"

"Yes, yes. Tomorrow, I plan to remind the board that there's no way they can replace me as Executive Director. If they try, the organization is doomed to fail."

Maggie eyed Eric with a growing concern.

"You seem to be a little full of yourself tonight," Maggie gently chided.

"Now, don't go trying to bring me down. I deserve a little credit, don't I? I'm going upstairs to change. What's for dinner?"

"Maybe I should warm up some humble pie?" Maggie suggested.

"Very funny."

Throughout dinner, Eric continued to talk about his various conversations with the guests at the luncheon, recounting all their kind words and praise to him. Maggie listened for some time before reaching her limit.

"So now, Superman, I suppose you're ready to go national with you're amazing talents and ability."

"What'd you say that for?" Eric asked. "I'm just saying that it's true. Much of the awareness of child sex trafficking in this city is because of me and my efforts."

"I think you forget one crucial thing."

"I know what you're going to say. Yes, of course, the Lord helped me. But that's the whole point. He chose me to do this, right?"

"Sounds like the Lord couldn't have done it without you," Maggie replied snarkily.

"That's not what I meant."

"Sure sounds that way."

"Fine. You think what you want to think, but I beg to differ."

Eric's phone buzzed, and he saw that Cheryl was calling.

"Hi, Cheryl. I'm glad you called. I was just about to call you tonight," Eric said as he stood up from the table, giving Maggie a quick smirk before he walked into the living room.

"Really? What about?" Cheryl asked.

"I wanted to go over some preliminaries with you about the board meeting tomorrow. I've decided to meet Abigail and her cronies head-on."

"But Eric-"

"I've been thinking long and hard about this, Cheryl, and I've made up my mind. How dare they think they know better than me how to run Hope House."

"Eric, that's why-"

"I'm sure you'll agree with me, Cheryl," Eric continued without listening. "You've always been a great support to me, and I want you to know I appreciate it."

"Yes, Eric, but-" Cheryl said more loudly.

"I think confronting Abigail and her co-conspirators right at the beginning of the meeting will put them in their place. They need to recognize that I'm the one that made Hope House what it is, and I won't tolerate a rebellion."

"ERIC!" Cheryl shouted.

"What? Don't you agree?" Eric asked, shaken by Cheryl's shout into the phone.

"Eric! You're not listening. That's why I called. I just got off the phone with Janet. Abigail called her earlier."

"OK. Why is everyone on the board calling each other, and no one is calling me?"

"Eric, I'm calling you right now. What's got into you?"

"Nothing. Go ahead."

"It seems that Abigail was fired from the bank today. She didn't give Janet many details, but she's resigning from the board of Hope House."

Eric took several moments to process the news.

"Eric? Are you still there?"

"Yeah. I'm just surprised, that's all. And you don't know why the bank fired Abigail?"

"No, but she did tell Janet that she's in some financial trouble and could even possibly lose her house."

"I can't imagine Abigail getting herself into that position financially. Her pride must have somehow brought all this about."

"Not necessarily," Cheryl responded, still surprised at Eric's attitude. "Janet shared that Abigail recently took out a second mortgage on her house to help pay some of her granddaughter's medical bills."

"I didn't know she had a sick granddaughter," Eric replied, beginning to soften.

"I didn't either until tonight. I understand that Abigail's granddaughter has some chronic illness and has had several hospitalizations."

"That's too bad," Eric replied as he felt his whole demeanor change. Suddenly he felt guilty for all his negative thoughts toward Abigail, realizing it could easily have been someone in his own family with the illness.

"Listen, Cheryl; I'm sorry for what I said earlier."

"I know you didn't mean it. But you sure didn't sound like yourself."

Eric thought back to his conversation with Maggie during dinner, realizing that he hadn't been himself. "Sorry, Lord," Eric prayed silently.

*****

Riel's sword flashed, knocking the slithering demon off Eric's neck and back, just as its grip on Eric loosened.

"Your brief tenure is over," Riel announced, pointing his sword at the demon. "Now why don't you go and find some pigs to bother?"

The demon coiled on the floor next to Eric, looking up at Riel. "He was an easy target," the demon hissed. "That was so much fun, I think I'll hang around for a while."

"I don't think he will be as easy a target next time," Riel countered. "You've helped him learn a valuable lesson, and I plan to use it for his edification. Now go! I'm tired of your presence."

After the demon slithered off, Riel placed his hands around Eric's head.

*****

"No, I didn't mean it, Cheryl. I don't know what came over me," Eric replied as he sat down in a nearby chair. "I was honored at a luncheon today, and I guess I got a little full of myself. Please forgive me."

"Of course you're forgiven, Eric. But we should also be praying for Abigail. She has been so helpful to you with Hope House, and now she's no doubt going through a tough time."

"Absolutely. Let me pray now. Lord, we bring Abigail before You and pray that You will comfort her during this difficult time. We do pray, Lord, that You will somehow intervene so that she will not lose her home. Show us what we can do to come alongside Abigail and help her during this difficult trial. Above all, Lord, we pray that Your will be done. As always, we pray in Your Son's precious name. Amen."

"Amen. Eric, I also called to let you know that Abigail told Janet that she no longer questions your ability to lead Hope House. I'm not sure why Abigail's undergone this sudden change of mind, but it probably has something to do with being let go from the bank. Regardless, she asked Janet to call several board members to communicate her renewed support for you."

"Well, that's good news at least. Since Janet is the Vice-Chair, I assume she'll be taking Abigail's place as Board Chair."

"Janet told me that she doesn't have the time to take on the responsibilities of Board Chair at this point. That's another reason she called me. She asked me if I would take the position."

"Really! That's quite a turn around from last month!"

"Yeah, I was shocked. Surprisingly, Abigail recommended me to Janet."

"Are you considering accepting the position?" Eric asked.

"I'm open to it, especially after what's happened recently, but the rest of the board will need to be fully supportive."

"That's wonderful news. Praise the Lord! I can't believe how quickly everything has changed. Thank you, Cheryl, for your willingness to take this on. It means a lot to me."

"Please remember, I'm only doing this if the rest of the board fully supports it. And, of course, I'm also doing it for the Lord."

"Absolutely."

*****

Solen joined Riel near the ceiling above Eric.

"The word of our intervention is filtering out. How's Eric taking the news?" Solen asked.

"Since Eric no longer has a spirit of pride, he seems genuinely concerned for Abigail."

"Spirit of pride? I somehow missed that development."

"Eric became conceited during a luncheon earlier today, allowing a pride demon to latch on. I believe it was part of a coordinated effort on the part of the enemy to disgrace Eric. I've been busy trying to minimize the damage Eric could cause since then, so I haven't been able to get word to you."

"Since I don't see the demon, I assume you've resolved the problem."

"A little humbling from Cheryl created the opportunity I needed to dispatch the demon. I hope and pray that this has corrected Eric's view of himself so that he will not be so easily self-elevated in the future."

"Our Lord never misses an opportunity to continue to shape His sons and daughters into His image," Solen replied. "I came to let you know that in response to the prayer of Eric and Cheryl, the Lord has asked that I send Adren to comfort and support Abigail."

"And what is the news about the first client of Hope House?"

"Things are progressing nicely on that front as well," Solen smiled.

"For the Lord and His glory!"

*****

Eric had just finished making the coffee for the board meeting when Cheryl came into the office.

"Good morning, Eric."

"Morning, Cheryl. I'm glad you got here early. I wanted to apologize again for my outburst last evening. I don't know what came over me."

"Eric, it's all water under the bridge. You've been under a lot of pressure this past month, and I'm glad that the Lord seems to have turned things around."

"Yeah, but the pressure is no excuse for the way I was acting. I'm just thankful that our Lord is a forgiving God."

"Believe me; I am as well since I've made my share of mistakes. I hope and pray that we don't run into any other surprises during the meeting this morning."

"Me too. Why don't we pray before the others arrive?" Eric suggested.

"Great idea. I'll start. Lord, we first of all, thank You for Your work behind the scenes allowing me to be considered as the next possible Board Chair this morning. We do lift Abigail up to You again and pray that You will comfort her during this difficult time. We pray that she will be able to keep her house and that through this trial, she will draw closer to You. Lord, we also pray for this upcoming board meeting. Inhabit our thoughts and words. May Your will be done this morning."

Before Eric could pray, the door opened, and several board members came in.

"Welcome, everybody," Eric said, looking up. "I've got some coffee brewing, and muffins on the table."

After subdued greetings, they all grabbed some coffee and found their usual places around the table. Cheryl slowly made her way to the head of the table as Janet came and sat down next to her.

Cheryl leaned over, whispering, "Janet, would you start the meeting by summarizing what happened last evening?"

"Sure… I'd be happy to."

Cheryl called the meeting to order, and after opening with prayer, turned to Janet.

"Since not all of you are aware of some recent events, I've asked
Janet to start the meeting by updating everyone."

"Thanks, Cheryl. Well, as many of you know, Abigail and I are good friends. Last evening, she called to tell me that she's resigning from the board of Hope House. I'm not at liberty to go into all the details, but there have been some significant life events that will prevent her from carrying out her responsibilities. Also, she wanted me to relay to you that she no longer has any reservations about Eric leading the organization. She regrets her previous statements and hopes all of you will give your full support to him moving forward."

Eric observed different reactions around the table. Some board members appeared to already know about this development, while others expressed surprise.

"She couldn't even come to the meeting and tell us herself?" Steve asked.

"No, she felt it would be best if she just spoke through me," Janet answered. "And with what I know, I agree."

After a short period of silence, Janet continued.

"As you all remember, I agreed to be Vice-Chair of the board. However, I didn't expect to have to assume the role of Board Chair this quickly. Because I'm not currently able to devote the time and effort necessary to chair this board, I've asked Cheryl to assume the position since she's been on the board from the beginning."

"However, I am not willing to assume the chair role without the complete support of the entire board," Cheryl interjected. "Is there anyone else that would like to accept this role?"

Eric looked around the table, expecting someone to say something, but they all remained quiet.

"OK. If no one else desires to assume the role of Board Chair, I am willing to do so, if there is a motion, second, and a unanimous vote in agreement," Cheryl replied.

"I move to nominate Cheryl as Board Chair," Janet stated.

"I second the motion," Tom added.

"Is there any further discussion?" Janet asked.

"Not hearing any, all in favor of the motion signify by saying aye."

Several ayes echoed around the table.

"Any opposed, signify by the same sign."

Silence.

"OK. The vote appears unanimous, so with that, I'll turn the meeting over to our new chair, Cheryl."

"Thank you, Janet. It's a difficult time for Abigail, and I hope everyone will keep her in your prayers. Eric, can you update the board regarding our progress toward opening?"

"Absolutely. We have now hired all the personnel necessary to staff the house, and they should finish their training today. We should also complete the programming piece by the end of the day since it is in the final stages of development."

"What other barriers remain before we open Hope House?" Janet asked.

"We only need to run a few errands, like buying fresh food."

"Wow! I didn't realize we were this close to opening," Cheryl exclaimed.

"We haven't done any publicity regarding our progress because of what came up at the last meeting," Eric answered. He looked around the table to see several brightening faces. Eric recognized a complete change in board attitude from the month before.

"That's exciting," Steve replied. "We need to set an opening date and get an announcement out to all our donors."

"When is the earliest you believe we can reasonably be ready to open Eric?" Cheryl inquired.

Having previously thought through his answer, Eric responded, "I think the earliest we could open would be next Wednesday, especially if we only take one girl."

"Ruth, you have some connections with the media, don't you?" Cheryl asked.

"Yes, I'm always putting advertisements in the newspaper for my realty. Why?"

"Do you think you could get The Brookview Times to write an article about Hope House opening?"

"I can sure try. I'll call my contacts at the paper today."

"Remember, we need to make sure they will keep the location of the house undisclosed," Eric added.

"Thanks for the reminder," Ruth replied. "If they agree to do a story, I'll make sure they are aware of that."

"What about one of the TV stations? Does anyone have a connection there?" Cheryl asked.

"One of the executives of a local station goes to our church,"
Janet answered.

"Do you feel comfortable asking him if he would set up a taped interview with Eric or one of his staff?"

"The executive is actually a she," Janet chuckled. "Anyway, she keeps telling us that she wants to use her position for the Lord, so here's her chance."

The level of excitement around the table continued to grow as others came up with ideas of how to leverage contacts into getting the word out about the opening of Hope House. Before long, a plan was in place and the date set for the official opening of Hope House the following Wednesday.

*****

Travoz was beside himself with rage as he stood yelling at Benzal, spittle flying out of his mouth each time he screamed.

"You lied and tricked me into this fiasco! You told me this was too insignificant for the Enemy to get involved.

How could you miss that they had another Watcher assigned to that woman, you fool!"

"I thought you told me that another Watcher couldn't stop you," Benzal yelled back.

"If I knew a Watcher was involved, I could have prevented his interference. But you assured me there was no high-level surveillance around this woman. This debacle is all your fault!"

"Don't blame me for your incompetence," Benzal yelled back, rising from his chair and looking directly into Travoz's bloodshot eyes. "You bragged about your powers, and instead you've endangered our whole operation against this group. I should have known better than to trust a foreigner."

Travoz grabbed the hilt of his sword, considering the strength and size of his opponent.

"You think you can somehow beat me in my stronghold?" Benzal laughed scornfully. "You are indeed a fool. Even if you happen to beat me in battle, you would still have to face my loyal horde that vastly outnumbers you."

"Who says they are loyal?"

Just then, a small messenger arrived.

"Master, Prince Valden commands your presence. He also asks that you bring the foreign Watcher."

Benzal looked first at the messenger, and then at Travoz still holding the hilt of his sword, trying to come up with a means to avoid a confrontation with Prince Valden. Unable to come up with an alternative, he turned back to the messenger.

"Very well. When does the prince want to see us?"

"Immediately, Master."

Travoz smiled with wicked malice as he recognized Benzal's predicament.

"I would be honored to speak with the regional prince," Travoz intoned.

"Don't be so sure, Travoz. You will not be able to fool Prince Valden easily in your attempts to hide incompetence."

"As I'm sure we'll find out," Travoz smiled, as they both flew to the regional headquarters. When they arrived, they found Prince Valden towering over several of his lieutenants, yelling and cursing at the group.

"This should be good," Travoz smirked.

After ranting and cursing for several minutes, Valden finally dismissed the lieutenants and turned his attention to Benzal and Travoz, beckoning them to come nearer.

"So, this is the renowned foreign Watcher," Valden started, closely eyeing Travoz.

"Yes, my name is Travoz and-"

"I hear you failed spectacularly," Valden interrupted, scowling at Travoz.

"He did fail, and I want-" Benzal started.

"SILENCE!" Valden roared. "I'll get to you soon enough, Benzal."

Travoz stiffened himself for a possible blow from the regional prince, knowing the propensity of his own prince to strike when angry.

"Tell me EXACTLY what happened," Valden commanded as he turned back to Travoz. "I know that my foolish captain here thought it wise to bring you into my region to help disrupt this weak fledgling group, and yet somehow you've failed."

"Everything was proceeding according to my well-conceived plan, Prince Valden. But Benzal failed to inform me that the opposition in this city was also using a Watcher. Further, a small army of warrior angels, which, your captain failed to account for, accompanied this Watcher. I can't be held responsible for his incompetence."

"I'll decide who's responsible for this fiasco!" Valden yelled, before turning to Benzal with obvious malice. "And now...what have you got to say Benzal?"

"Travoz assured me that he could complete this small, insignificant assignment without any assistance from me. Therefore, I should not be held accountable for his arrogance and incompetence."

Valden quickly grabbed both of the mighty demons by the neck with his massive arms, raising them to his eye level.

"You're both fools since you've both failed to recognize I've had my spies watching this whole pitiful episode," Valden replied, speaking slowly, turning first to Travoz. "You are a pathetic Watcher who failed to account for, not only for the Enemy's surveillance, but also my own."

Valden slowly squeezed Travoz's neck as he continued to speak.

"Instead of dealing with you myself, I'm sending my best warrior to escort you from my presence and my region. He will also carry a report of my extreme displeasure of your abysmal failure to your prince. I happen to know how he deals with failure. My prize warrior will make sure you find your way home," Valden commanded as he released the fallen Watcher from his grip.

Travoz massaged his disjointed neck, just as a giant warrior approached him. Soon they both were flying in an arc toward Europe.

Valden then focused his attention on Benzal, continuing to hold him for several moments.

"You are ultimately responsible for this fiasco. You should have backed up the efforts of the foreigner since you knew the Enemy called this ragtag group. Did you think He would leave them unprotected? Your incompetence has caused me to consider whether I made a mistake promoting you to this position. But because I rarely, if ever, make mistakes, I will give you one more chance to destroy this group. Fail...and it will bring your downfall. Now leave. I'm sick of looking at you."

As soon as Valden released Benzal, he flew quickly out of the regional headquarters, determined to do whatever was necessary to reestablish favor with his Prince. And the only way he could do that was by destroying Hope House.

Benzal flew to his headquarters and commanded Dravon to come to him at once. Within a short time, Dravon appeared, looking apprehensive.

"I'm assigning you a new task," Benzal ordered. "You are to focus solely on the disruption and destruction of this new organization, Hope House. I want you to use all available means and demonic resources to achieve this goal."

"Does that include infliction of illness?"

"Didn't I just say 'ALL AVAILABLE MEANS'?" Benzal retorted angrily.

"Yes, Master. I assume this will take priority over our other ongoing projects."

"It doesn't need to take priority over our other schemes because I've given you everything you need to take this group down. Begin immediately, and the next time I see you, all I want to hear about is the astounding devastation that you have wreaked on this horrific Hope House. Understood?"

"Yes, Master."

Chapter 13

Heather's Help

Heather stared blankly out of the window of the van as it drove down the road, periodically glancing at her ankles and wrists, enclosed in metal cuffs. The authorities had treated Heather like a criminal ever since her arrest, keeping her in cuffs every time they removed her from her jail cell. Heather had expected to go home within a short time of being released from Derrick and Melanie's control. Instead, she'd transitioned from one form of captivity to another, this one sanctioned by the state. On the evening of her "rescue", she was taken to a juvenile detention center and locked up with other juveniles arrested for a variety of crimes. While she hated having her picture taken as if she was a criminal, the most humiliating thing was the cavity searches. That's when the anger started.

It helped that she'd been put in the same cell as Bobbi, allowing them to support each other through the strange and frightening situation. But as time went on over the weekend, Heather's anger had grown from intermittent flare-ups at the injustice of their treatment, to a continuous, pulsing, red-hot furnace within her. It was slowly replacing all other emotions, giving her a forged steel demeanor. None of this was her fault, except for her stupid mistake of running away from home. Even in that, she'd had little choice. And yet, here she was, treated like she was a common criminal.

How dare these people regard her and Bobbi with scorn, without any sympathy whatsoever? They had no clue what they had been through, and they didn't care. It just added fuel to her anger.

Even the judge this morning had looked at her as if she was a piece of trash. As soon as he found out she was from Brookview, he quickly gave orders to have her transferred out of his jurisdiction back to her home city. Yep, just taking out the trash.

The van pulled into the courthouse jail complex in Brookview, and parked outside a door with a big orange sign that read 'Receiving'.

Great. They even have a special door for receiving trash, Heather thought. A man in a guard uniform walked up to the driver's window.

"What do you have today, Ben?" the guard asked.

"Some young prostitute we arrested late last week. Our judge found out she's from Brookview and sent her over. Here are the papers."

"The guard glanced at the papers and looked through the window back at Heather. "OK. I guess we'll have to make room for her even though we pretty much got a full house in there."

Now I'm being placed into a trash compactor, Heather thought, feeding the anger even more.

"Alright, young lady; time to get out," the guard yelled after coming around and opening the door of the van.

Heather struggled to her feet and shuffled to the door the best she could with her ankles joined by a chain. Getting out of the van and onto the ground was going to be tricky, particularly since she wasn't used to ankle cuffs.

"Come on! I ain't got all day," the guard said as Heather fought against the chains to get down the steps.

"I'm doing the best I can," Heather declared, releasing some anger.

"Listen, Sweetheart. We don't take no back talk here, understand?" the guard responded threateningly.

Heather stood on the ground looking at the guard, fury pouring out of her eyes. The guard looked back at her for a moment before turning and roughly escorting her through the door of the jail complex.

Inside the door was a small room with a bench welded to the metal floor off to the right side. A large metal door was on the left, and a thick window took up most of the wall facing Heather. A woman sat behind the window and spoke through a microphone.

"Who's this, Jake?"

"A prostitute that just got transferred in. Here's the paperwork."

The woman pushed a metal box out from under the window, and the guard placed the papers inside. The woman took and reviewed them, looking up periodically at Heather standing shackled in her bright orange jumpsuit.

"You know we're about full. We'll have to put her in with Bertie," the woman said as she pressed a button to unlock the door. Once inside, they took off the ankle and wrist cuffs while she stood in front of another window.

Fortunately, Heather didn't have to go through another cavity search. Once her papers were processed, the guard led her back a hallway to the last cell. Inside was a girl about Heather's age, covered with tattoos, sitting on the lower bunk. Derrick had made Heather and the other girls get tattoos on the back of their necks with his street name: Wizard. But she hadn't seen anyone with that many tattoos and piercings.

"Hey, Bertie. Got a roommate for ya," the guard said jokingly.

"F--- you!" Bertie responded loudly, eyeing Heather closely. Bertie remained sitting on the bed while Heather came into the cell, just before the door slammed loudly behind her.

"OK Bitch. As you can see, I got the bottom bunk, which leaves the top for you. And don't give me no sh--," Bertie declared.

Six weeks ago, Heather would have been scared to death. Now, her anger only made her feel stronger and more in control.

"I'd rather have the upper; it's what I'd want anyway," Heather lied as she climbed into the top bunk. After about an hour of silence, Heather decided to broach some conversation.

"So what got you in here?"

"Why do you care?"

"Just trying to make conversation; not much else to do."

"Well, why don't you tell me first, since you're the new bitch."

"I got caught in a prostitution sting."

"A whore, huh?"

"I ain't no whore," Heather yelled as she jumped down from the bunk and faced Bertie, glaring at her. "I was forced into it."

"Take it easy! I didn't mean anything. But you got some spunk. I like that. I've had to turn a few tricks myself."

Heather looked at Bertie for a few minutes before responding. "So you know how much it stinks."

"Sure do. I had to do it to get my drugs. I do know some guys are worse than others."

"So, is that why you're in here...drugs?" Heather asked as she climbed back into the upper bunk.

"Mostly. I've been selling smack and crystal off and on to get by."

"You worked by yourself?"

"Naw. I was part of a gang here in Brookview."

"I didn't know we had gangs here," Heather said without thinking.

"Where'd you grow up?"

"Here, just never had to deal with gangs."

"A protected prissy, huh?"

"Does it look like it?" Heather snarled.

After some time, Bertie started in again. "So how'd you end up in the life?"

Heather told Bertie about Ted and his assaults that led to her running away. When she mentioned how Derrick and Melanie had tricked her using YourOn, Bertie piped in. "I've heard of that. I saw some guys using it where I was staying, recruiting girls into the gang."

"Yeah, well, it worked on me, and I heard it worked on other girls in the Juvie I just came from."

"Don't I know. There are some real bad pervs out there."

*****

Taron and Corel hovered far above the juvenile detention center, watching the demon on Bertie's shoulder talk with Raxen, the new demon Heather had inherited from the previous juvenile detention unit.

"It was wise for Solen to suggest that I allow a demon of anger to influence Heather temporarily," Taron noted. "The anger has been beneficial in helping Heather assert herself forcefully with the other prisoners."

"Solen wouldn't have suggested that unless he was confident in your ability to prevent other demons from becoming attached to Heather," Corel related as he looked down at the host of demons inhabiting the unit below. "She doesn't need any influences other than anger right now."

"Even though her anger has provided some protection for Heather, it has also strengthened Raxen's influence over her," Taron observed. "But I'm most concerned about her growing false sense of power. She's beginning to believe she can control her future, opening the door to pride."

"Solen feels the benefits of anger presently outweigh the risks, even though it does make her more susceptible to other demonic influences. This anger is feeding off the shame surrounding the circumstances of her arrest. That shame will prove to be the key factor leading to her restoration."

"I understand the juvenile judge in this city is a believer," Taron replied.

"Yes, and our network made sure he recently attended a meeting detailing the state's new Safe Harbor Law. It successfully changed his understanding of child prostitution so that he no longer perceives these children as criminals."

"Seeing Heather as a victim rather than a criminal will completely alter his attitude toward her," Taron observed. "Is he aware of the work of Hope House?"

"We've utilized his connection with one of the board members to make sure he knows not only about the work of Hope House, but also that they are opening soon."

"If everything continues as planned, Heather won't have to stay in this facility for more than a few days. I rather enjoyed my frequent little encounters with the demonic horde at the last detention center, and I'm looking forward to some more sword practice here," Taron proclaimed.

"We certainly wouldn't want your warrior skills to soften," Corel replied with a chuckle, eyeing the vast array of demons below.

"When have you ever seen my sword skills soften?"

"Never, and it doesn't look like they will anytime soon!"

"For the Lord and His glory!"

*****

Heather shuffled into the courtroom, with wrists and ankles in cuffs once again. She sat down at the table on the right side of the courtroom designated for defendants. Next to her sat a court-appointed attorney. On the other side of the room was the prosecutor's table, with a young woman sitting alone. In the middle of the courtroom, an elevated chair sat empty. It had a small wooden barrier in front of it and access to the chair on either side.

In the back of the courtroom, there were three rows of benches for visitors. When Heather looked back at the benches, she was surprised to see her mother sitting in the last row, staring at her. She had not spoken to her mother since leaving home several weeks ago. Heather assumed the social worker who visited her in the juvenile detention center yesterday evening must have told her mother about the hearing. Heather felt a pang of guilt as she saw her mother, but anger quickly replaced it. If she had only believed Heather about Ted, none of this would have happened. Heather turned away to look at the elevated judge's bench at the front of the courtroom. She steeled herself for the hearing, not sure what was going to happen.

Everyone in the courtroom stood at the command of the bailiff as Judge Parker entered through a door in the front wall. He was dressed in the usual black robe, emphasizing the slight graying at his temples. Heather watched him closely as he made his way to his chair and sat down, wondering if he would be kinder than the judge who transferred her here. Heather saw him looking at her, and when their eyes met briefly, Heather thought she saw some warmth, which helped her relax as everyone sat back down.

"In the case of 'State vs. Wallace', what charge are you bringing?" the judge asked, looking at the woman sitting at the table across from Heather.

The woman stood and faced the judge. "Your Honor, the state has provided evidence that Ms. Wallace was engaged in soliciting, along with two other women," the prosecutor replied. "Because this is her first arrest, the prosecution is open to the imposition of a fine along with the minimum jail term."

Turning to the side where Heather was sitting, the judge asked, "And what does the defense have to say?"

The woman sitting next to Heather stood up. "Your Honor, I have briefly reviewed the evidence, and since it appears to show overwhelmingly that the defendant was engaged in prostitution, the defense will accept the prosecution's offer."

Heather looked up at her, wondering if she was going to have any say about all of this. She didn't have any money, and she was pretty sure her mother wasn't going to pay anything. Besides, she certainly didn't want to go back to jail.

"And where would she be placed after release from her jail sentence?" the judge asked.

"Your Honor, I just received this case late yesterday, and I haven't had a chance to research her home situation. However, I understand that the defendant's mother is here with us today."

The judge looked toward the back of the courtroom.

"Would the defendant's mother please stand?"

Heather turned to watch her mother slowly rise to her feet, her face reddening.

"Please come forward and join your daughter at the defendant's table," the judge requested.

Heather watched as her mother came forward frowning and sat down at the table next to her.

"I understand from the statement the defendant provided our social worker that she claims to have been assaulted by your husband, is that correct?" the judge asked.

Heather's mom turned to Heather, giving her an angry look. "Yes, Your Honor, my daughter has made that claim, but I don't believe her. She tends to make things up."

"Is that right?" the judge responded. "In my experience, young girls rarely make up stories about being assaulted in their home. At the very least, you should have reported the allegation to child protective services so that they could investigate the allegation." The judge was quiet for a moment, continuing to look back and forth between Heather and her mother. "The fact that this young woman left home after the second alleged assault persuades me to believe that she was likely telling the truth. Furthermore, I understand that you never filed a missing person report even though your daughter has been out of the home for several weeks."

Heather's mother started to say something, but the judge stopped her.

"I find your complacency regarding the care of your daughter rather disturbing."

Turning back to the prosecutor's table, the judge asked, "What about the possibility of enrolling Ms. Wallace into a treatment program as outlined in the new safe harbor legislation?"

"Your Honor, our office is not yet familiar with that legislation, though we've heard of it."

"I just attended a meeting detailing the legislation myself. It creates a diversion possibility for minors found engaging in solicitation." The judge turned to the table where Heather was sitting. "Is the defense aware of this new legislation?"

"No, Your Honor."

The judge then looked directly at Heather. "Young lady, I know that it seems I've been ignoring you this whole time, but there were certain issues that needed to be brought out before hearing from you. Now, as you just heard me tell your mother, I'm inclined to believe your reports of repeated assaults at home. Am I correct in assuming that you would rather not return home until that matter is cleared up?"

Heather nodded her head yes and spoke quietly, "Yes, sir."

"Would you be willing to go into a new program designed to help girls who have been through what you've been through?"

"Yes, sir."

"Good. I hereby order both the prosecution and the defense to investigate whether the defendant meets the requirements of the state's new Safe Harbor Law and report back at another hearing in 24 hours. I also order

Child Protective Services to investigate the defendant's charges of assault by the stepfather. The defendant is remanded back to juvenile detention until after the hearing tomorrow. This hearing is adjourned."

Heather's mother turned and walked out of the courtroom without speaking a word to her. Heather sat watching her mother leave, feeling abandoned and alone. Initially, she felt like crying, but then anger replaced her sadness, growing slowly until it became rage.

*****

Skulty massaged Nancy's head and whispered into her ear just before she stood and walked out of the courtroom. His glance back at Heather revealed he had accomplished his goal as he saw Raxen grow in power like a parasite, feeding off of Heather's rage. Raxen continued passing his talons through Heather's head as he looked up to give the angels above him a repugnant, triumphant smile.

Near the ceiling, two heavenly beings radiated the light of holiness into the spiritual realm encompassing the courtroom.

"I know Solen wants me to allow Raxen to generate anger within Heather, but it's never easy to be passive during such turmoil, since it implies weakness," Taron replied.

"From what I understand, you've been anything but passive since Heather arrived in Brookview," Corel noted. "I just learned that Dravon also assigned Dazon to harass Heather, now that he's no longer needed to manipulate Charlotte to be ED of Hope House."

"Dazon has been quite persistent in his efforts to get to Heather, but I've managed to dissuade him so far."

"I've dealt with Dazon in the past, and I can attest that he won't give up until he finds the opening he needs."

"Which is why I'm keeping such a close watch on her," Taron remarked.

"Solen has assigned you a very delicate undertaking. You must protect Heather from overwhelming demonic influence while at the same time, convincing the dark forces that their ongoing efforts are successful."

"Solen correctly recognizes that if the enemy believes their efforts regarding Heather are still proceeding successfully, they will focus their attention on the staff of Hope House, who are all in a better position to endure the attacks," Taron replied. "How are Eric and his new staff holding up under the increased assault?"

"So far, Eric has been relatively unaffected since his battle with pride. But his staff have come under a varied assortment of attacks. While they had been warned repeatedly about increased warfare by other similar Heaven-called organizations, they still lacked preparation for this level of withering assault. We have protected them from the most serious incursions, but Solen felt that allowing them to experience some new hardships will prevent them from underestimating the enemy's commitment to protecting this stronghold in the future."

"Why has Eric been spared? Has Solen placed extra protection around him?"

"The enemy's attempt to fill him with pride was premature and has backfired against them. Since his humbling, he hasn't needed any extra protection. But he is mystified by the intensity of the attack on his staff, due to his inexperience in warfare."

"He and his team are now getting an advanced course in spiritual warfare," Taron responded with a chuckle. "May they take these lessons to heart!"

"Yes, as James, the brother of our Lord, wrote almost two thousand years ago, may they learn to consider these painful trials as a source of joy."

"For the Lord and His glory!"

*****

"Thanks for changing our normal meeting time," Jason said as he sat down across the table from Eric.

"No problem! Even pastors need time away," Eric said, smiling. "How was your long weekend away?"

"It was very restful, just what Heidi and I needed. We went to see her parents out east, and since they love their grandkids, it gave Heidi and me several opportunities for dates with just the two of us. But enough of me; catch me up with things at Hope House."

"Jason, you wouldn't believe what's been happening."

"You might be surprised," Jason replied with a smile.

"Well, first of all, everything completely turned around less than twenty-four hours before our board meeting last week. It was like a miracle!"

"What do you mean?"

"Remember how during the meeting last month, Abigail, our board chair, challenged my ability to lead the organization?"

"Of course, we talked a great deal about it."

"Last Thursday evening, she suddenly resigned from the board."

"Really? Do you know why?"

"It turns out that she's been dealing with several personal issues, including a sick granddaughter. I learned last week that she's been helping her daughter with the medical bills. But the most significant development is that she lost her job at the bank.

"It sounds like she's going through a terrible ordeal."

"Yeah. I felt a little guilty about all the judgmental thoughts I've had about Abigail this past month."

"And so the board was less inclined to question your ability without her leadership?"

"Even better than that! For reasons I still don't understand, Abigail completely reversed herself and sent word to the board that she fully supports me. The board has now completely dropped any question of my competence."

"That's wonderful, Eric. It sure seems like the Lord has been at work on your behalf."

"Thankfully, though I know some of my actions didn't help," Eric admitted as he looked down at the table.

"What do you mean?"

"Let's just say that just before I found out about Abigail, I got a little full of myself."

"What brought that on?"

"I was honored last Thursday at a luncheon raising money for Hope House, and, with all the accolades, I began to personally take too much credit for the success of Hope House."

"That's easy to do; we're all susceptible to that."

"Yeah, but I got it into my thick head that I was the one who was mainly responsible for the accomplishments of Hope House, and said some stupid things."

"Not that I've ever done that," Jason said with a chuckle. "So what brought you back to reality?"

"Some pointed and humbling remarks from Maggie and one of my board members. It's embarrassing to think back on some of the stupid things I said."

"We've all been there, brother. Hopefully, the lesson will serve you well in the future."

"It better. The board has set the opening of the house for today, so I have to leave a little early."

"Wow! A lot has happened since I left. I didn't realize you were so close to opening!"

"We almost had to delay our opening due to staff illness and family emergencies, but enough staff members have recovered so that we're continuing with our planned opening today."

"Haven't you hired extra staff to cover for illness?"

"Absolutely. But I never thought we'd lose almost 80% of our employees to both illness and family emergencies at the same time."

"You don't see the connection, do you?" Jason asked.

"What do you mean?"

"Eric, remember how we've talked at some length about how there is always far more going on around us than what we perceive? We've talked several times about the whole issue of spiritual warfare. That's what's going on!"

"You mean spiritual warfare can also cause someone to become sick?"

"Absolutely! While not every medical problem is related to demonic activity, there are many examples in the New Testament of people having physical diseases connected to demons."

"I never put those two things together. But now that you bring it up, it sure seems strange that all these ailments and emergencies came up just as we're about to open."

"No doubt the enemy was also involved in your brush with pride last week. I will notify the church's prayer chain of your opening as soon as I get back to the office. But before you go, let me pray for you now."

"Absolutely…"

"Lord, I lift Eric and his staff to You and pray that you will provide an extra layer of protection around them as they move to open Hope House today. May those who are sick experience recovery, and may those who've had family emergencies experience the freedom to work as necessary at Hope House. Lord, I also pray for the girls who will be coming to Hope House. May your Spirit begin the process of opening their hearts to the Gospel of Jesus Christ, so that they can come to know You during their time at the house. We ask all this in the name of Jesus. Amen."

*****

Solen, Corel, and Riel briefly continued lifting their hands in prayer and praise, as the spiritual illumination around them increased until the prayer concluded. Afterward, Solen turned to the other two heavenly beings.

"The activation of the prayer chain will allow me to dispatch additional warriors to lessen the intensity of the enemy's assaults. However, the Spirit does not want to completely stop the attack so that the spiritual edification of the staff may continue. We only need to free up enough workers to make sure the house opens today."

Solen looked at Riel, giving him a knowing smile. "What do you think, Riel? Would you like a little assistance protecting Eric?"

"You know I love a challenge and could easily handle up to five of the demons I've been seeing. But you also know that I will always submit to your authority," Riel responded.

"I have every faith in your ability," Solen chuckled. "But I don't want to risk underestimating Benzal at this critical juncture. I think it's best to have Joft assist you for the time being, with Corel backing up both of you as necessary. Between the three of you, Eric should be well protected."

"Any change of plans regarding Heather and Dazon's ongoing attempts to harass her?" Corel asked.

"I'm confident that Taron will be able to keep Dazon away from her, while he continues allowing Raxen to enhance Heather's anger. The Spirit has instructed that we not interfere any further at this time. Hope House will soon welcome Heather as their first client."

"Taron is very much looking forward to that moment," Corel added.

"I know that it has been difficult for Taron to witness all of Heather's suffering," Solen noted. "But he will soon be able to rejoice in Heather's new birth. Has the message of Hope House's opening been delivered to the judge?"

"Jehos prompted his friend on the board to contact him. He should be receiving the news any minute now," Corel answered.

"Excellent."

"How is Abigail doing after her great humbling last week?" Riel asked.

"Adren has been encouraging and ministering to her, protecting her from any additional attacks from the enemy," Corel responded. "I understand that she's revealed the truth of her financial predicament to her daughter."

"Solen, do you have any sense of the Lord's plan for Abigail?" Riel asked.

"The Spirit has revealed that Abigail will renew her faith in the Lord and draw closer to her daughter, eventually moving in with her to help care for her granddaughter."

"That would allow her to sell her home and recover some assets from the property," Corel interjected.

"Yes. When the judge learned about the granddaughter's medical condition, she decided not to sentence Abigail to any jail time since it was her first criminal offense. Abigail only has to pay back the money she stole with interest and will be on parole for the next five years," Solen declared.

"Once again, the Lord has redeemed a potentially evil situation for His glory!" Riel proclaimed.

"Yes, and as Abigail draws closer to the Lord during this difficult time, she will be able to share her renewed faith with her daughter, who has been in a long season of questioning," Corel replied.

"May Abigail's sacrifice and dependence on the Lord have its intended effect on her daughter's heart," Riel prayed.

"Amen! For the Lord and His glory!"

*****

Heather sat down after Judge Parker entered the courtroom and used the gavel to call the hearing to order. She searched for her mother in the back of the courtroom, catching sight of her just as she sat down again in the last row of guest benches. The same attorney from yesterday was sitting at Heather's right side, while across the room, the same young female attorney was seated at the prosecutor's table.

Today, however, a middle-aged woman was sitting in the elevated chair in the middle of the courtroom. She initially looked through several papers on her lap, and then glanced over at Heather, looking intently at her. Not knowing who she was, Heather avoided her gaze.

Judge Parker finished looking at the computer screen on his left, before moving files around on his desk as if he was looking for something. He motioned to one of his aides to come near and whispered something to her. She then left through a door at the front of the courtroom.

"In the matter of 'State vs. Wallace', both the prosecution and the defense were to investigate the requirements of the new Safe Harbor Law. Related to that new statute, I have just learned that a new residential treatment facility specializing in the rehabilitation of child sex trafficking victims is opening today. The name of this facility is Hope House."

Turning to the woman at the prosecutor's table, the judge continued. "Has the prosecution had the opportunity to investigate this new statute?"

"Yes, Your Honor."

"Does the prosecution agree that the defendant meets the legal requirements of this new statute?"

"Yes, Your Honor, taking into account the defendant's age as well as the circumstances surrounding her arrest, the prosecution believes the defendant does meet the requirements of the Safe Harbor Statute."

"Does the prosecution have any objection to the court holding charges of soliciting in abeyance and remanding the defendant into the custody of Hope House?"

"No, Your Honor, as long as this new facility is duly licensed by the state to care for minors."

"It is my understanding that they have just received their state license to operate a rehabilitative facility for minors."

"The prosecution then has no objection then to the court remanding the defendant to the facility."

Directing his attention to the woman sitting in the elevated chair in the middle of the courtroom, Judge Parker asked, "What is the guardian ad litem's position on this matter?"

"Your honor, having reviewed the statute, I believe placement at this new facility will be in the best interest of the defendant," the woman answered, looking over once again at Heather.

"So, we have agreement with both the prosecution and the court's GAL," the judge replied as he turned to Heather's side of the courtroom. "Has the defense also reviewed the new statute?"

"Yes, Your Honor," the woman on Heather's right replied.

"Do you also agree that the defendant meets the requirements of the statute?"

"I do, Your Honor. I also agree that placing the defendant at this new facility would be in her best interest."

The judge then focused his attention on Heather. "Young lady, given your mother's lack of concern about your whereabouts the past several weeks, and her failure to report your alleged assaults, I have significant apprehension about sending you back into that home. In addition, I want the allegations of assault fully investigated before placing you back with your mother."

Heather swallowed hard and glanced back at her mother, who was staring stone-faced at her.

The judge continued. "Therefore, I only see two options for you. I could sentence you to serve jail time for solicitation, but I frankly don't believe you are the criminal here. I believe you are the victim. As a victim, you need treatment, and it seems almost providential that just as you come to court today, a new facility designed to help you recover from the trauma you've endured is opening. Are you still in agreement with trying out this new treatment program?"

"Yes, Your Honor," Heather replied hesitatingly, not at all excited about the option of spending more time in the detention center.

"I think you are very fortunate that this option is now available because, without it, I would have little choice but to send you to jail."

The woman Judge Parker had spoken to previously, returned and handed a paper to the judge.

"This is a form that will enable your transfer from the juvenile detention center to this new facility. You need to understand that if you fail to follow the program at this facility, or if you choose to run away from this home, you will be in contempt of court. That means not only that you could be sentenced to serve time in juvenile jail, but also, that your sentence could be extended depending on the circumstances. Do you understand, Heather?"

This was the first time the judge had used her name, and Heather nodded her head yes, simply understanding she'd better not mess up at this new house.

"Do you have any questions, Heather?"

Heather shook her head no and again glanced back at her mother, who continued to sit expressionless in the back of the courtroom.

"Very well. I, therefore, remand the defendant over to the care of Hope House today. I will schedule a follow-up hearing in 30 days to evaluate your progress. This hearing is adjourned," the judge said, striking his gavel just before walking out of the courtroom.

Heather stood and turned to look at her mother, whose back was to her as she walked out of the courtroom. Couldn't she even say goodbye? Fine, Heather thought with anger welling up within her. I don't need you either.

Chapter 14

Hope Begins

"I just got a call from juvenile court, Eric," Melinda announced as Eric walked through the front door of the Hope House. "They have a client they want us to interview."

"Already! That sure didn't take very long."

"I was a little surprised myself when I got the call, but it shows how much we are needed," Melinda replied.

"Don't forget the TV crew is going to be here within the hour for that interview," Eric reminded her. "How are all the final preparations going?"

"Come in and see for yourself."

Eric walked into the kitchen to the right of the entry and on into the dining area beyond. A dining table large enough for ten people took up most of the space. Off to the side of the dining room was a single bedroom. Eric stepped into the doorway to see a bed made up with a pink comforter and a teddy bear resting on the pillow. A new dresser stood next to the far wall, just to the left of the closet. On top of the dresser sat an open makeup bag containing a hairbrush and mirror. Next to the makeup bag was a small basket of other goodies. On the right side of the bedroom stood a door leading into an adjoining bathroom.

"This room looks perfect," Eric said with a smile. "I'll make sure the TV crew gets a shot of it. This is the bedroom you plan to use if we end up taking this girl from juvenile court today, right?"

"Yes, I'd rather have the girls initially stay in here since it's much closer to the center of activity. After they've stabilized and we've had a chance to get to know them, we'll move them into one of the other five bedrooms on the upper and lower levels."

Eric peeked into the bathroom to see towels hanging by the shower and soap on the counter along with bottles of shampoo and conditioner.

"How long do you think it will take for the staff to be able to handle our limit of 6 girls?"

"We'll need to add clients slowly over the next six to nine months, watching how things go. Each time we add a new girl, we're adding a whole new personality to those already here. When those personalities are traumatized, they become very delicate. If we increase the number of clients too quickly, we could increase the chances of having one or more run away."

"It's coming to fruition after all these years," Eric mused as he continued to walk through the house. "Hard to imagine that this was once just an idea the Lord planted in my head."

"Eric, you remember Tavia from our interviews," Melinda said as a young woman walked into the living room.

"Yes, hello, Tavia. Are you going to be on duty if we end up accepting this girl today?"

"I haven't had a chance to tell her yet," Melinda interjected. "I just got a call from the juvenile court about a potential client. I'm going over shortly to interview her to see if she would be a good fit for our program."

"That's exciting! I've been praying that we would get someone right away."

"How many staff do you plan to have on duty for this girl?" Eric asked.

"Since it's only one client, one staff per shift will be plenty. I don't think we'll need to add a second staff person until we have three girls, as long as they are fairly stable. Tavia, I might need you to stay until six or so if that's OK. If we end up accepting this girl, I'll need to get the evening and night shift covered. With everyone out sick or on personal leave, I'd hoped I would have a few days to make those arrangements."

"I'm fine staying until whenever," Tavia replied.

"Thanks. That will help tremendously. Well, I'm going to head over to the juvenile court to interview this girl. I'll let you know as soon as I can if we're going to accept her."

"I'll try to make sure the TV crew doesn't hang around too long, in case she needs to come soon," Eric replied, turning back to Tavia. "Remind me again of your background, Tavia."

"I just graduated last spring from college with a psych degree. I learned about child sex trafficking in my junior year, and I've been passionate about doing something to help these girls ever since. I'm thrilled to be a part of what you are doing here, Mr. Stone."

"Please, call me Eric. Mr. Stone takes me back to my teaching days," Eric said with a chuckle. "So what have you been doing so far today?"

"I've just been cleaning the bedrooms, making sure everything is ready. We went grocery shopping this morning to get some fresh food items like milk and eggs, just in case we had someone come today. Good thing we went!"

"I like the teddy bear touch the Soroptimists added to their bedroom decorations," Eric replied as he started walking upstairs. "Did you know that they donated all the bedroom furniture and put it all together themselves?"

"Yes, Melinda told me. They did a great job. I especially like their idea of painting each bedroom a different color. My favorite is the pink bedroom next to the dining room."

"Good thing they came up with that idea; I know I never would have," Eric said chuckling as he walked past the two upstairs bedrooms and bathroom. "If it had been up to me, everything would have been painted with the same drab, earthy tone."

They turned to go back down to the main level, and then around the corner to the lower section of the split-level home.

"Do you know which bedroom Melinda plans to use after the client becomes stabilized?"

"She mentioned the green room downstairs since its windows are more difficult to climb through."

"Hard to imagine why these girls would want to run from a nice, safe house like this," Eric sighed. "I know it's related to all the trauma they've endured, but common sense would tell me they would want to stay. Even though I've been raising awareness of this problem for five years, I still have a hard time wrapping my mind around the damage done to these girls."

After passing by three more bedrooms and two bathrooms, they finally ended up at the doorway of a small office.

"I haven't seen Melinda's counseling room since she moved her furniture in. It looks warm and cozy," Eric observed.

"Yeah, I almost feel like going in and taking a nap in the client's big chair."

"Hopefully, not while you're on duty," Eric kidded, as the doorbell rang. "That's probably the TV crew. I'm glad they were able to come today before we get our first girl, while the house still looks picture perfect."

"Yeah, I'm sure that won't last long."

Eric and Tavia walked upstairs and opened the front door. An attractive woman in her 30's was standing on the porch along with an older man carrying a large camera bag.

"Good afternoon. Welcome to Hope House. I'm Eric Stone, the Founder, and this is Tavia, one of our new staff," Eric said as he welcomed them into the house.

"I'm Shelly Moore from TV 9 news, and this is Walt Connor. We're here to interview you about your work."

"Thank you for coming and featuring us," Eric replied.

"We were very excited to hear about the opening of Hope House," Shelly said as they walked into the kitchen. "Sex trafficking is an issue grabbing a lot of national attention, so we were thrilled to learn about your organization and the possibility of developing a local story. Most people, including myself, were not aware this is happening right here in our city."

"Well, your timing is perfect. My director just left to interview our first potential resident. Where would you like to set up for the interview?"

Shelly and Walt walked through the kitchen and dining area and then went into the living room.

"What do you think, Walt? This area seems roomy enough with plenty of light."

"This room should work fine after I set up some additional lights," Walt answered.

"We'd like to get some shots of the other rooms, including bedrooms if that's alright. We can use that for background in the piece," Shelly replied.

"Sure, whatever you need," Eric answered. "I just want to confirm that our location will remain undisclosed, so I'd prefer not getting any video shots of the outside of the house."

"Oh, we understand. We've run into that before when we've featured homes for domestic violence victims, so it's not a problem."

Walt started setting up his camera and a few lights while Tavia went to finish straightening up the bedrooms.

"Have you interviewed with us before?" Shelly asked.

"Not with your station. I did have an interview about a year ago with one of the other stations after a large public awareness event we sponsored."

"Good. The more experienced you are, the more relaxed you'll appear. Now all you have to do is keep looking at me, not at the camera. I'll simply be asking you some questions about how you started Hope House, about sex trafficking, and what you hope to accomplish here."

"Sounds good."

After setting up several light stands, Walt fitted Eric with a microphone and turned on the lights. During this time, Eric prayed silently for the Spirit to give him a humble attitude as well as the right words to use during the interview.

Standing next to the camera, Shelly held a microphone in her hand and began questioning Eric.

"Could you start by telling us your name and your role here with Hope House?"

"Sure. My name is Eric Stone, and I'm the Founder and Executive Director of Hope House."

"I understand Mr. Stone, that today is a big day for Hope House."

"Yes, after five-plus years of preparation, we are finally opening the doors of Hope House, and might admit our first residential client today."

"I'm sure that's very exciting for you and your staff. Could you tell our audience a little bit about the specialized work you plan to do here?"

"Hope House is a specialized residential treatment center for young girls who have been victimized by child sex trafficking. In addition to providing food, clothing, and housing, our clients will be able to attend an online school and also receive specialized individual and group therapy."

"Could you help our viewers better understand child sex trafficking?"

"Sure. Child sex trafficking is when any minor, defined as a child under the age of 18, is placed into any form of sexual exploitation, such as stripping, production of pornography, or more commonly, prostitution."

"But is that type of thing widespread here in the U.S.?"

"It's more common than most people imagine. Conservative estimates for the number of children within the U.S. entrapped in some form of child sex trafficking are in the tens of thousands, with more liberal estimates ranging into the hundreds of thousands."

"Those numbers are surprisingly high."

"Yes. Most people believe child sex trafficking only happens in countries in SE Asia. While it certainly is occurring in many other parts of the world, it's also found right here in the United States in all our major cities."

"What happens to those victims once they are released from that exploitation?"

"Unfortunately, many of them are kept in juvenile detention facilities because authorities either view these victims as criminals or have very few alternatives available to help them. Hope House is the first residential treatment facility in the state to specialize in caring for victims of child sex trafficking."

"How many facilities are there like this across the country?"

"It's hard to know exactly, but through my limited national networking, I would estimate that there are fewer than thirty facilities similar to Hope House."

"And what prompted you to take on a massive project like this?"

Feeling the empowering of the Spirit, Eric decided to dive in. "It was a calling from the Lord that came while I was a teacher."

Shelly got an uncomfortable look on her face, but Eric continued.

"I've been a Christian for almost twenty years, but I never knew something as horrific as child sex trafficking was happening here, and when I began to investigate it, I learned that there was little being done to help these girls and boys when they leave the trafficking scenario. That's when the Lord gave me a calling to start Hope House."

"Well, we certainly wish you and Hope House the best in this new endeavor, Mr. Stone," Shelly replied, trying to conclude the interview quickly.

"Thank you. We'll need all the prayers and best wishes we can get."

*****

Riel stood next to Eric, shining brightly and glaring at the three demons near Shelly who had been sent by Benzal to distort the interview. Eric's prayer and submission to the Spirit were all Riel needed to protect Eric and secure his opportunity to share about the Lord. Joft and Corel floated overhead guarding against additional demonic involvement, confident that Riel was more than capable of handling the three demons. As the interview concluded, the threesome flew off, presumably back to Benzal's headquarters.

"Benzal's not going to be pleased when he finds out how miserably they failed," Joft chuckled as Riel floated up to join them.

"After he takes his anger out on them, he'll no doubt double his efforts against the rest of the Hope House team," Corel noted. "Thankfully, the prayer chain has responded well, strengthening our efforts to support the staff of Hope House."

"While we can protect the staff from a demonic attack, they are still susceptible to their spiritual misconceptions and lack of spiritual warfare experience," Joft noted.

"Not to mention that their increased head knowledge has made them susceptible to overconfidence," Corel replied. "Solen has instructed the heavenly cohort to keep reminding the staff to rely on the Spirit's empowering. As long as they remain dependent on the Spirit, we will be able to protect them from discouragement and failure."

"They will need that protection once Heather begins to release the rage and anger trapped within her," Riel said.

"Very true, Riel. Even though the staff are trained extensively in trauma, many of them still believe that simply being nice to the girls will move them toward healing," Corel replied. "The next few weeks will test their ability to love these girls in ways they never imagined."

"Lord, may Eric and the staff remain open to the Spirit's leading as they experience firsthand from Heather the rage and bitterness that can result from human sinfulness," Joft prayed.

"For the Lord and His glory!"

*****

Heather looked around the bedroom as she tossed her backpack onto the bed. She didn't like pink all that much, but it was a whole lot better than the drab gray of the cell in juvenile detention.

"Heather, this is Tavia. She is one of our residential staff and will be staying with you until later this evening," Melinda announced from the bedroom doorway.

"Hi, Heather! Welcome to Hope House."

"Hi…" Heather responded quietly.

"Tavia, why don't you show Heather around the house while I get her records put away."

Heather followed Tavia around the house, feeling a strange mixture of emotions. She was relieved to be away from Derrick and Melanie, as well as that horrible detention unit. But who were these people? What did they want from her? Why had they gone to the trouble of creating this house? There must be a catch somewhere.

Heather found it difficult to trust anyone after her experience with Derrick and Melanie. Besides, something about this place didn't make sense. These people had to be getting something from all their work.

What Heather truly wanted was to go home; at least the home she had two years ago right after the divorce. A home with just her mother, and without Ted. How long would she have to stay in this place? The questions kept racing around in her mind as she and Tavia walked through the house.

The house was warm and inviting all right, but it wasn't home. Heather pictured her mother cooking in the kitchen, awakening a deep sadness within her. Did her mom miss her? Had her mother ever really loved her? The pain of that thought caused Heather to shift her thinking back to what Tavia was saying.

"And this is our counseling room."

"Counseling room? I don't need any counseling. I'm just fine," Heather responded emphatically.

Melinda was inside the room at her desk and turned toward the two, standing in the doorway.

"Heather, you've been through a great deal of trauma since you left home. That's what I'm going to help you work through."

"I thought only crazy people needed counseling. Are you saying I'm crazy?"

"Of course not. It will be much better for you if we help you process what you've been through rather than ignoring it. But we'll get to that soon enough. For now, all you need to do is relax and get comfortable in your new home."

"How long will I have to stay here?"

"Well, at least 30 days, and possibly longer than that."

"It takes that long to have counseling?"

Melinda chucked. "Oh, it takes much longer than that. But let's take it one step at a time. I know you want to go home, but as you heard in court, certain things need to be investigated and possibly changed before you can go home."

Yeah, Heather thought to herself. All they need to do is put Ted in jail, and then I'll be able to go home. Since they're now checking him out, it shouldn't take that long. I may even be able to leave before the thirty days are up.

The next morning after breakfast, Karen, the daytime staff person, gave Heather a Bible and suggested that she spend some time reading it. She called it devotions. Heather thought back to the warm memories of attending church with her mother. They had Bibles in the pews of the church, though Heather hadn't spent much time reading one. Heather decided to start reading at the beginning of the New Testament so she could learn more about this Jesus. She still had some concerns in the back of her mind that this home might be part of some religious cult, but she knew it wouldn't hurt to read the Bible, and it might even help her figure out these people.

Heather's school records had not yet arrived, so she couldn't start school. That meant she was able to spend the rest of the morning doing what she wanted, at least within the restrictive rules of Hope House.

She couldn't watch TV or even get on the Internet. All she could do was watch previously screened movies. Most of them were boring, but she managed to find a few that she liked. What she mostly missed was getting online to connect with friends. It had been weeks since she'd had any communication with Sue. Just a quick FaceTime or chat with Sue would let her know Heather was OK. She could even catch up on all the news about her other friends at school.

Heather couldn't understand it. They'd told her they didn't want her getting on the Internet at all for now. It had something to do with her safety. At first, Heather got angry and walked into her bedroom, slamming the door. But after stewing on her bed for a while, she remembered her gullibility using You'reOn with Derrick, so she let it drop and watched a movie instead.

In the afternoon of her first full day at the house, Heather had a session with Melinda. They mostly talked about Heather's home life and her mother. Melinda asked about the divorce, and most of her questions had to do with how Heather felt about things. The attacks by Ted never came up.

Over the next several days, Heather got used to the routine in the house. Wake up at 7, take a shower, make the bed, and then have breakfast. After cleaning up from breakfast, she'd spend time reading in her new Bible. Since she couldn't start the online school, Heather had a lot of free time. Fortunately, Cindy, one of the house staff, gave her a small iPod to use to listen to music.

After living in the house for a week, Heather moved to a downstairs bedroom to allow a new girl, Angelica, to move into Heather's original bedroom. Angelica was African American and the same age as Heather. She also lived in Brookview but went to a different school, so Heather didn't know her.

At first, she seemed nice enough, keeping to herself and not saying much. But as the days continued to pass, Angelica became more comfortable in the house and started to boss Heather around. Initially, Heather let it slide. But one afternoon, Angelica stopped the DVD player right in the middle of a movie Heather was watching, and put in a rap video instead. Heather lost it.

"Hey! What are you doing? I was watching that!" Heather yelled.

"Not anymore, bitch! Now it's my turn," Angelica said with a sly smile.

"You'd better put my DVD back in, or else!"

"Or else what, you little white bitch?"

"Don't call me a bitch!" Heather yelled as she stood up, facing Angelica.

Tavia rushed into the room to investigate the yelling, followed by Melinda.

"What's going on?" Tavia asked as she saw Heather and Angelica face off with each other, fists balled, and only inches separating their faces. Tavia quickly got between the two of them, pushing them apart.

"OK. What started all this?" Tavia asked, looking at Heather.

"I was minding my own business, watching a movie, and she came in and stopped it."

"Is that true?" Tavia asked, turning to Angelica.

"She's been hogging the DVD all day, and it's my turn to watch what I want to watch," Angelica stormed.

"OK...OK, let's all cool down, shall we?" Melinda directed as she came up alongside Tavia to separate the girls further. "Maybe it's time we went outside and got some exercise."

Heather stared at Angelica, feeling a murderous rage she had never experienced before. It made her feel powerful as if she could do almost anything. Angelica looked back at Heather, trying to make a smirk, but Heather saw the doubt in her eyes, realizing that Angelica was scared. It was another confirmation for Heather that anger could help her get and keep what she wanted. All she had to do was get angry enough, and she could make it happen.

"Let's go outside and walk around, preferably in different areas so you can both cool down," Melinda directed.

*****

Jehos and Taron stood next to each other three feet off the floor, facing opposite directions, each with their swords drawn. Jehos had his sword pointed at Dazon, who was now attached to Angelica, while Taron challenged an enlarged Raxen who was drawing power from Heather's rage. Both Raxen and Dazon smiled at each other as they continued passing their talons through their respective host's heads, pleased with their success at almost bringing the girls to blows. As the girls separated, both angels resheathed their swords, maintaining a close watch on the demons as they floated up through the ceiling.

"Dazon's success in finding an opening with Angelica will complicate both Heather and Angelica's progress in the home," Jehos observed.

"His attachment appears strong," Taron noted. "Are you aware of any faith background with Angelica?"

"Solen told me that her maternal grandmother was a faithful follower of Jesus and strongly influenced Angelica until her entrance into heaven. Since that time, Angelica has not displayed any regard for her grandmother's church or beliefs, turning instead to drugs."

"I don't believe we'll be able to dislodge Dazon from Angelica until she repents from that path," Taron declared.

"I agree; fortunately, she is in a place that will help encourage that decision."

"In the meantime, Heather is feeding off the rage stirred up by Raxen, making it more difficult to remove him. The Spirit has given permission for his expulsion as soon as I have an opening. But that is becoming more difficult as Heather becomes more self-reliant."

"It's a strategy the enemy has been using for centuries," Jehos replied. "Take the pain of suffering, turn it into anger, and direct it toward others or our Lord whenever possible."

"Instead of looking at suffering as James has instructed," Taron rejoined. "If they could see the world from our perspective, they would understand why James calls believers to rejoice while suffering."

"And they would understand our jealousy as heavenly beings. We cannot be shaped more into the likeness of our Lord as they can. Suffering is the tool He uses, as vividly displayed in the lives of the great Apostles."

"Their refusal to grasp that concept allows the enemy instead to use suffering to fuel anger and harden their hearts."

"But our Lord is never outmaneuvered when it comes to those He knows will eventually choose Him. Rage and anger will never satisfy their need for love."

"My favorite opening to disrupt the enemy is when they finally come to that realization," Taron announced. "Anger may leave them feeling powerful, but it also leaves them feeling empty, ready to turn to the Lord."

"There's nothing like the celebration over a new lamb coming to the Shepherd!" Jehos proclaimed.

"Absolutely! And I look forward to that celebration with Heather. In the meantime, I keep praying that her heart will not completely close to the Lord."

"I join you in that prayer asking the Spirit to prompt her to realize her need of Jesus and reach out to Him in prayer."

"Yes. Those brief, precious moments of prayer have allowed me to remind Heather of our Lord's love and affection for her."

"Reminders that she desperately needs at this time in her life."

"For the Lord and His glory!"

*****

"Good morning, brother," Eric announced as he sat down across from Jason.

"Good morning, Eric. How are you holding up with all the new activity at Hope House?"

"Pretty well. We've now got two girls, and I think the staff members are beginning to get their feet under them," Eric answered as the waitress brought a cup of coffee. "I'm just a little concerned that things may be going a little too well if you know what I mean."

"There is always that concern," Jason chuckled. "But just because you've endured a significant attack doesn't mean that another one is coming right away. There is another possibility. It could be that everything is going well at Hope House because of all the prayers of the saints."

"Well, I sure hope that's the case. We could use six to twelve months of relative calm."

"Do the girls seem to be adjusting well?" Jason asked.

"There have been the expected bumps in the road. Anger issues and some acting out, but nothing we didn't anticipate."

"That's good news. I'll make sure to remind the prayer chain to keep Hope House at the forefront of their prayers."

"Thanks. And please pass along our appreciation to all your prayer warriors. All of us at Hope House are very thankful for the support."

"It's part of our responsibility as brothers and sisters in the Lord, but I will certainly pass on your thanks."

"Speaking of getting six to twelve months of relative calm, I did want to ask your thoughts about something, if I could, Jason."

"Absolutely. That's why we're meeting each Monday. What's on your mind?"

"Well, remember several weeks ago we talked about how I might be making Hope House into an idol?"

"Yes. I think I was the one who suggested that it might be occurring, to your dismay," Jason added with a smile.

"You were right, of course, but it's been a more difficult problem to deal with than I imagined. How do you maintain an eternal perspective all through the day?"

"Great question, Eric," Jason responded after they had given their breakfast orders. "I assume you are spending time in the Bible every day."

"Yes. I happen to be reading through the book of Acts right now."

"And I also assume you're taking time each day to pray."

"Yes, but lately I've been increasingly distracted as I try to pray."

"Have you ever tried praying Scripture?"

"No. I've never even heard of that. What Scripture do you use?"

"The Psalms are full of prayers that can help us focus our minds on the Lord. If you've never prayed Scripture before, I'd recommend a book by Dr. Ken Boa. It's called *Handbook to Prayer: Praying Scripture back to God*. It contains three months worth of daily prayers to God that can help you get your prayer time started."

"Thanks, Jason," Eric replied as he put a note in his smartphone. "Any other ideas?"

"Have you ever read John Eldredge's book *Waking the Dead*?"

"Doesn't sound familiar."

"It's a good read and would be encouraging to you because, in it, Eldredge writes extensively about spiritual warfare. He has a daily prayer for freedom in the appendix, which takes about 7-8 minutes to read through."

"Is it a Scriptural prayer as well?"

"It's all based on Scripture, and you'll find Scripture within it. But it's different than Boa's approach. It's a prayer that affirms many of the important Christian doctrines. I don't do it every day, but occasionally, when my mind is unusually distracted, and I'm having trouble getting my prayers started, I'll read through it aloud."

"You have trouble getting prayers started?" Eric asked with some surprise.

"We all do, brother," Jason replied with a chuckle. "Even pastors are not immune to struggle in prayer. I suspect that it's often related to warfare in the spiritual realm, though not always. That's why I read the prayer aloud because I believe that demonic forces hate to hear us repeat the many truths found in the prayer."

"Then, I'll need to get that book, as well," Eric said as he reached for his phone.

"I think it would be helpful for you to read various Christian books as often as you can to remind yourself of the many Biblical truths about who we are as believers in Christ. I know I find it helpful to remind me of even the basic things, like the Lord is in control, even when it doesn't seem that way."

"I have trouble imagining that you need reminders of those basic truths."

"We live in a world that is constantly telling us things completely opposed to the Word of God, so we all need to recognize how that influence is impacting us."

"I know. I'm trying to remind myself that the Lord's plan for Hope House may be very different than whatever I hope to accomplish."

"Exactly. And whatever happens, it won't be you that accomplishes it; it will be the Lord using you."

"I meant that."

"I know you did. Just a friendly reminder," Jason said with a smile. "Remember, His priority will be the girls coming to faith in Him. That's foundational because, without His presence in their lives, they have little hope for true healing."

"Preach it, brother!" Eric said, smiling as the food arrived. "How about if I pray before we eat?"

*****

"How right Jason is about how much the demons hate to hear the truths of Scripture spoken aloud," Corel replied, floating above their table, along with Riel and Joft.

"No doubt his wisdom has been gained in part through the influence of Solen," Joft noted.

"Yes, though I'm sure his daily study of Scripture has also had its impact. By the way, Joft, thanks for the suggestion to prompt Eric to ask that question," Riel replied.

"Thankfully, his spirit remains receptive," Joft answered.

"The more tools we can give him, the better he will be able to stand his ground against future attacks," Corel observed.

"For the Lord, and His glory!"

Chapter 15

The Celebration

Heather sat at the dining table, finishing her bowl of cereal when Melinda walked into the kitchen.

"Heather, when you're finished with breakfast, could you please come downstairs to my office? There are a few things we need to talk about."

"OK," Heather replied, wondering what she had done wrong.

After rinsing her bowl and putting it into the dishwasher, Heather walked down to Melinda's office.

"What did I do now?" Heather asked as she stood in the doorway.

"Do you think you've done something wrong every time someone wants to talk with you?" Melinda asked.

"Seems that way lately."

"Well, you haven't done anything wrong this time. I need to talk to you about some developments in your home investigation."

"Developments?" Heather hesitantly inquired as she walked into the room and sat down.

"Child Protective Services called me yesterday afternoon. They've completed their initial investigation of Ted and your home."

"Are they going to send him to jail?"

"No, not exactly. While the social workers at Child Protective Services believe what you told them about Ted, they haven't been able to corroborate anything."

"What does that mean?"

"It means they haven't found any evidence to support your story. Ted agreed to allow the caseworker examine his computer, and she didn't find any child pornography on it, or any other type of pornography for that matter."

"That's impossible. Ted must have tons on his laptop," Heather replied angrily.

"That may have been true, but Ted must have removed it somehow."

"How would he know to remove it?"

"Well, that's just it. The caseworker suspects your mother warned him about the investigation since she was in the courtroom when the judge ordered it."

Heather looked down at the floor, confused.

"Did my mother tell the caseworker about the second attack?"

"The caseworker only mentioned that your mom told her that you've been telling a lot of lies about Ted. They interviewed Ted as well, and of course, he completely denies that he's done anything wrong. So your mother seems to be supporting Ted's side of the story. With a clean preliminary search of his computer, the authorities don't have any reason to arrest Ted."

Heather sat, continuing to stare at the floor for several minutes, before looking up.

"So, what happens now?"

"The judge issued a court order yesterday for Ted's computer to be examined by a court-appointed expert. Unfortunately, that will take some time."

"So, where does that leave me?"

"Well, as the judge said in court, you're supposed to stay here until Child Protective Services completes the investigation. The professional examination of the computer may take as long as ten days."

"Will I be able to see my mother during that time?"

"Well, that's the other reason I wanted to talk to you. Your mother is upset because of the investigation and your allegations. She's told the caseworkers that she would rather not visit you for the time being," Melinda explained carefully.

Heather sat, staring again at the floor. She had told the caseworker about Ted's assaults so that her mother could learn the truth about him. But now her mother didn't want to see her?

"Did she say why she didn't want to see me?" Heather asked slowly, on the verge of tears.

"Just that she's still annoyed about your allegations against Ted."

"But they're true!"

"I believe that; we all believe that. But at this point, your mother still believes Ted's side of the story."

"It isn't fair," Heather suddenly yelled, jumping out of her chair. "I'm the one who has to suffer while he gets what he wants."

"I agree with you, Heather; it isn't fair. But once the expert completes the thorough examination of Ted's computer, the truth will come out, I'm sure."

"In the meantime, I'm stuck here with you guys and not able to be with my friends. I can't even FaceTime or message them. That stinks," Heather wailed as she sat down again.

"At least you are safe here, Heather."

"Yeah, safe and bored out of my mind. I'd give anything to be with my friends. Could you at least let me FaceTime with Sue?"

"That's a little unusual, but I tell you what. I'll call your caseworker to check if we can make an exception since you aren't getting any family visits. Maybe I can arrange a periodic FaceTime with Sue. Would that help?"

"Yeah, that would help a lot."

After a few more moments of silence, Heather looked up at Melinda. "So why are all of you being so nice? Do you get paid extra for that?"

Melinda chuckled, "Heather, we're all doing this out of a calling from the Lord."

"I've heard that a lot here lately, but I have no clue what that means."

"All of us who work here are Christians. It means we have given our lives over to Jesus Christ."

"So, is He kinda like your master or something?"

"Not in the way you're probably thinking. We all try to live our lives in a way that pleases Him."

"I still don't understand."

"Hopefully, in time, you will. But think of it this way, Jesus is the most important person in each of our lives, and because of what He has done for us, we want to live lives that honor Him."

"You mean the death on the cross thing? I've been reading about it in my Bible."

"That's exactly what I mean. We believe that Jesus is God and created everything we can see, feel, hear, and touch. We also believe that Jesus gave Himself as a sacrifice to pay for our sins-"

"But I'm not the one who's sinned!" Heather interrupted.

"You may not have sinned in the same way Ted has, but do you believe you've never done anything you shouldn't have?"

"Well...I've done some things I'm not proud of," Heather replied.

"The Bible tells us that everyone has sinned, but the good news is that Jesus' death on the cross has paid the price for us to get right with God."

"Still, I'm not the one who needs to get right with God."

"I know that you feel that way right now, but don't forget you've made your own mistakes."

Beginning to feel a little uncomfortable, Heather asked, "Is there anything else you needed to talk to me about?"

"No, not now. But we can continue this conversation about Jesus anytime you want."

"I'm fine for now; thanks."

*****

"Heather is slowly beginning to recognize the strength of her mother's allegiance to Ted," Jehos noted.

"Yes, and the pain of that realization is softening her heart, rather than increasing her anger," Taron responded, looking down at Raxen who was still hanging onto Heather.

"I see the unconditional love from the staff is loosening Raxen's grip on Heather considerably," Jehos observed.

"It's also rewarding to see that he's returned to his normal stunted size."

"Heather's daily Bible reading these past three weeks, along with the prayers of the saints have also had an impact. Unfortunately, I don't see any evidence of Angelica's heart softening."

"No, she has been more resistant to the faith atmosphere within the house, allowing Dazon to implant his lies at will," Jehos replied.

"Dazon may be winning the battle for Angelica's mind, but I doubt Raxen has the wits to recognize whether he's winning or losing," Taron chuckled. "I sense it won't be long now before Heather turns her heart toward the Lord in child-like faith to find the joy and peace she so desperately needs. Then I'll have my opportunity to send Raxen whimpering back to Dravon."

"From what I've observed, she simply needs to maintain her questioning attitude with the staff as they interact throughout the day, and her heart will be ready."

"Along with some prayer on her part," Taron noted.

"And then...let the celebration begin!"

"For the Lord and His glory!"

*****

Judge Parker struck the gavel after taking his seat behind his elevated bench.

"This court is in session to review 'State vs. Wallace.'"

Heather sat back down in the same chair she had been in thirty days before on the right side of the courtroom. Her court-appointed attorney was again on her right, and another woman she didn't know sat on her left. The same prosecuting attorney was on the opposite side of the courtroom shuffling through some papers. The large chair in the center of the courtroom held the woman who had been at the previous hearing. Heather turned to the back of the courtroom to see if her mother was there, but couldn't find her.

Judge Parker turned to Heather's side of the courtroom, looking at the woman sitting to the left of Heather.

"Ms. Cummings, I understand you have completed your investigation into the defendant's home situation, is that correct?"

"Yes, Your Honor. We've interviewed the defendant's mother and step-father, and completed our examination of the step-father's computer."

"And what did you find?"

"The step-father, Ted, has completely denied all allegations of assault on repeated occasions. The defendant's mother has not provided any corroborating evidence to support the alleged assaults and has consistently sided with her husband. The initial examination of the computer failed to find any evidence of child pornography. However, our computer expert was able to undelete several files on the step-father's computer consistent with child pornography."

"And what was the response of the defendant's step-father when confronted with this evidence?"

"Your Honor, he completely denied any knowledge of the material and accused our computer expert of planting the evidence on the computer."

"And the defendant's mother?"

"She initially appeared upset when she learned about the evidence, but she didn't challenge her husband's account."

"So what conclusion have you reached regarding the validity of the defendant's accusations?"

"Your Honor, we have referred the evidence concerning possession of child pornography to the prosecutor's office. Regarding the alleged assaults, since we have been unable to find any corroborating evidence, we will not be referring any charges of sexual assault for prosecution. However, we believe it is very likely that the assaults did take place."

"Is the defendant's mother here in the courtroom?" Judge Parker asked loudly, looking to the back of the courtroom. Everyone turned around to see if anyone came forward, but no one did. Heather looked again and failed to find her mother.

"Was she informed of the hearing this morning?"

"Repeatedly, Your Honor," Heather's attorney answered.

"Was a subpoena issued?"

"Due to her presence at the previous hearing, we didn't feel it was necessary, Your Honor."

Judge Parker glanced at Heather and then looked down at his desk, making some notes.

"I am deeply disturbed by the lack of protective action on the part of the defendant's mother. Her lack of presence at this important hearing only adds to my concern. Furthermore, her inability or unwillingness to corroborate the assault allegations has convinced this court that the defendant's home remains unsafe for the defendant at this time. I, therefore, recommend that the defendant continue in her current placement for an additional ninety days, at which time another review hearing will take place. Is this acceptable to the prosecution?"

"Yes, Your Honor, we have no objection."

"Is this acceptable to the court's GAL?"

"Yes, Your Honor," the woman in the middle chair responded.

"Very well. We will review the defendant's progress and her situation in ninety days," the judge declared as he struck the gavel, before getting up and walking out of the courtroom.

Heather sat in the chair on the verge of tears. She had hoped Ted would be arrested by now and that her mother would realize how wrong she had been. She never dreamed she would have to remain at Hope House for another three months. Why didn't her mother come to the hearing? Didn't she want to see her only daughter?

"Don't worry Heather," her attorney said, turning toward Heather. "It looks like Ted will end up getting arrested soon and should get a sentence that will include jail time."

"But where was my mom?"

"I'm not sure. We were expecting her to come."

The woman from Child Protective Services on Heather's left jumped into the conversation. "Heather, your mother seems determined to support Ted in spite of all the evidence we found on the computer. I'm not all that surprised she didn't come today. I'm so sorry, Heather."

Heather stood and walked slowly toward the door at the back of the courtroom where Melinda was standing, trying to grasp everything that had just happened. They had found child porn on Ted's laptop, and the authorities should arrest him soon. But in spite of that, her mother still believed Ted, rather than her own daughter. How could that be? She understood her father was rarely there for her since he was an abusive drunk. He couldn't be there for anybody. But why had her mother turned against her, refusing even to visit her? Was she really that worthless?

"Are you alright, Heather?" Melinda asked as she put her arm around her.

Heather didn't respond but just kept walking out of the courtroom and down the hall with Melinda.

During the ride back to Hope House, Melinda decided to let Heather have some time to think. When they arrived back at the house, Heather still hadn't spoken a word.

Melinda and Heather walked into the house to find Eric standing in the kitchen talking with Angelica.

"Who are you?" Heather asked, surprised to find a man in the Hope House.

"Hi, Heather; I'm Eric. I'm the one who started Hope House."

"You know my name?"

"Sure, I've known you were here since you arrived. I've just waited to come and visit until now so you and Angelica could get settled. How did the hearing go?"

"I'd rather not talk about it."

"Sure, I understand," Eric responded, glancing at Melinda who shook her head slightly. "Well, I was just about to tell Angelica the story of how Hope House got started. Do you want to join us?"

"I guess…"

Eric led them both over to the dining table and sat down, while Melinda slipped away to her office to make some notes.

"I used to be a teacher here in town until about six years ago."

"What did you teach?" Angelica asked.

"High school history."

"Boring. Too bad it wasn't math so you could help me with my homework."

"Sorry, I'm not very good at math. But let me know if you ever need help with history."

"What made you stop teaching?" Angelica inquired.

"Well, about six years ago, I attended a school event where I learned about what you girls experienced before coming to Hope House. I was shocked that something that horrible happened here. I also learned that a home like this was critical to helping you recover from that experience. Within a short time, the Lord called me to start Hope House."

"You heard God's voice?" Angelica asked incredulously.

"Not an audible voice; it was something I just sensed within me."

"You must be some kinda religious freak or something," Angelica said with a smirk.

"No Angelica, just a follower of Jesus."

"What does that mean?"

"It means that I've given my life to Jesus, and I try to live as He wants me to live."

"And He told you to start Hope House?"

"Yes, in His unique way."

"Why would he do that?" Angelica asked as Heather continued to sit quietly, periodically looking off in the distance.

"Because God has a special love for young people, especially those who have suffered."

"Why doesn't God simply stop the suffering?" Heather suddenly asked with intensity.

"That's a great question, Heather, and I'm afraid I don't have a real good answer for you. There are rare times when God does intervene against suffering and abuse, but there are many times when He doesn't stop it. It may be that He wants us to stop the suffering. Regardless, what I can tell you is that He hates abuse and wants to heal those who experience it."

"Seems like it would be better to prevent suffering, rather than helping someone get better afterward," Heather said flatly.

"I agree; from our perspective, that makes sense. But God has a completely different perspective, and wants more than just keeping us safe."

"What could be better than keeping people safe?" Angelica asked.

"Having everyone come to know Him as the loving God He is. God has allowed us to have free will, which means we can choose to do something outside of God's will. That's when people hurt themselves and others."

Both girls sat quietly for a few moments before Eric continued.

"Have either of you expressed a commitment to Jesus?"

"No. I don't even know what that means," Angelica replied while Heather just shook her head.

"It's responding to the Gospel or the good news of Jesus Christ."

"I've heard about the good news in the church my grandmother used to take me to, but I never really understood it," Angelica said.

"Well, to understand the good news, you first have to understand the bad news."

"I don't need any more bad news," Heather interrupted.

"You've had plenty; both of you have in fact. You may have read about the bad news in Paul's letter to the Romans, where he tells us that all have sinned and fall short of the glory of God."

"Yeah, Melinda said something about that the other day," Heather continued.

"It means that our selfishness has separated us from God. But God couldn't allow that to continue, so He sent His Son, Jesus, to remove that separation through His death on the cross. John tells us that God loved us so much that He sent His Son to die for us."

Heather perked up a little and asked, "You mean God didn't abandon us?"

"Not at all; in fact, just the opposite. God loves us so much He sacrificed someone very dear to Him, His only Son so that we could have a relationship with God."

"God wants to have a relationship with us?" Heather asked with surprise.

"Absolutely. Jesus is waiting for us to turn to Him and ask Him for that relationship."

"Does it mean that I'll have to go to church every Sunday?" Angelica questioned.

Eric chuckled, "No, you won't have to go to church every Sunday, but rather you'll want to go to church every Sunday. More importantly, God will want you to live the life He has planned out for you."

"God has a life planned out for me?" Heather inquired with increasing interest.

"Yes, the best life you could imagine."

"Well, it wouldn't take much to make it better than the life I have right now," Heather replied with frustration. "But I still don't see why God doesn't just prevent bad things in the first place."

"I know it's hard to understand. Just remember, God asked me to start Hope House because He knew you girls would need it. This house represents God's love for you in a genuine way. If you ever want to have that special relationship with God, you can talk with any of the staff or with me.

"Thanks," Angelica responded, while Heather sat quietly thinking.

Later that afternoon, Heather sat in her room, thinking back to what had happened in the court session earlier that day. She still couldn't understand why her mom didn't come to the hearing. And why didn't her mother at least want to visit her? Heather thought back to the last time she saw her mother at the previous court session a month ago. Her mother had been angry because Heather had told the authorities about Ted's assaults. But why would she be angry? They had happened, and it had forced Heather to leave the house. How could her mother be so blind to the truth?

A thought kept recurring on the periphery of Heather's mind. Everything pointed to the fact that her mother supported Ted more than Heather. Even finding child pornography on his computer had failed to convince her mother of Ted's guilt. For reasons too painful to contemplate, Heather's mom was abandoning Heather for Ted. Heather had tried hard to push the thought away, but everything that had happened today made it too difficult to ignore, especially now that she was alone.

The thought kept growing until it overwhelmed her like a wave crashing over her. Heather began crying uncontrollably, burying her face in the covers of her bed. After Heather had cried for several minutes, Tavia appeared at her door.

"Are you alright, Heather?"

Heather didn't respond, and Tavia came over and sat on the bed next to her, putting her arm around Heather, sitting for some time while Heather continued to cry.

"I know you were hoping to go home," Tavia said as Heather slowed her crying.

"I just wanted it to be the way it used to be."

"What do you mean Heather?"

"I just wanted it to be my mom and me, but she didn't even come today."

"I'm so sorry. I know that must have hurt not having your mother there."

"I just wanted her to believe me, but she's choosing to believe Ted over me."

Tavia sat quietly next to Heather and continued to rub her shoulder. After a few minutes, Heather wiped and blew her nose.

"I guess I'm on my own now."

"Heather, you're never completely on your own."

"Sure, I am. My mother has made her choice, and my father is a drunk. Who else is there?"

"Don't forget that you have a Heavenly Father, One who will never abandon you."

Heather thought back to some of the things Eric and Melinda had talked about earlier.

"Does God still love me, even with all the things I've done?"

"Look around, Heather. Hope House is the house He created for you. Do you think He would have done that if He didn't love you?"

"But this house isn't just for me. Angelica is here too, and there will eventually be other girls."

"Yes, but never forget that you are one of those girls. Not only that, you were our first girl."

"But I've never done anything that would make God love me."

Tavia chuckled, "None of us can ever do anything to make God love us. He simply does. And what's more, God sent His Son Jesus to die for us, so that we can spend eternity with Him. That's called Grace."

"So does everyone spend eternity with Him?"

"Only those who have accepted His love and given their lives back to Him."

"What do you mean, accept His love?"

"Jesus died on the cross for us some 2000 years ago. For many, it's simply a historical fact. But those who truly believe that Jesus was God's Son accept His death as payment for their sins. A payment that opens the door to a relationship with God."

After sitting quietly for a few minutes, Heather asked, "To have a relationship with God, I only need to believe that Jesus died for my sins?"

"Believe in your head, and also with your heart."

"What does that mean?"

"That you not only believe Jesus died for you as simply a fact, but that you place your trust in Him as your Savior."

"And what does that mean?"

"Someone who only believes in their head that Jesus died for them will continue to live their lives in whatever way they want. But someone who also places their trust in Jesus will want to live a life that is pleasing to God."

"I don't want to be alone."

"And you don't have to be alone. There's an additional gift that God gives us when we turn our life over to Him."

"Additional gift?"

"He sends the Holy Spirit to live within us."

"I've never heard of that before."

"I can show you all about that later, but the most important thing you have to do is decide whether you want to trust in Jesus."

"I do want to trust in Jesus, but I don't know how."

"It's easy; all you have to do is pray along with me.

'Jesus, I believe that you are God's only Son and that you died for me on the cross to take away my sin. I now trust that your death has opened my relationship with the

Father, and I give my life over to You. Thank you for all You've done for me, and help me to lead a life that is pleasing to You by giving me Your Holy Spirit. Amen.'"

After Heather prayed aloud the prayer offered by Tavia, she sat quietly waiting. A sense of peace came over her along with a strong feeling that she was no longer alone. She felt like giggling for the first time in months, and couldn't help but smile.

"Thanks, Tavia, I feel a lot better now. I feel…light, not nearly as heavy. I also don't feel alone. I want to learn more about this Holy Spirit."

"There will be lots of things we can talk about in the days ahead," Tavia said as she gave Heather a big hug. "For now, I'm just thrilled to have you as my sister in Christ!"

"Sister??"

"Oh, that's another gift I forgot to mention. But you'll learn about that soon enough!"

*****

The room exploded with light and sound as innumerable angels sang praise to the Lamb who gave His life for His sheep. Corel, Jehos, and Solen participated in the incredible celebration as Taron flew up to join them. He had effectively detached Raxen from his hold on Heather, and dispatched him from the room, expecting him to stay as far from Dravon as possible.

Adding another name to the Book of Life always brought festivity to heaven as the angels gazed up at the throne where the Lamb was visible. There was an unmistakable smile on His face as He looked down at the celebration.

As the angels continued to worship, Taron could see the new light of the Holy Spirit dwelling within Heather.

"This never gets old, does it?" Taron replied, turning to Solen.

"Not for a couple of thousand years, at least," Solen chuckled as he continued raising his arms in praise to the Lord.

"While Heather will continue to have struggles, she will no longer be alone," Corel announced. "She is now part of the Bride of Christ, and the enemy better beware!"

"For the Lord and His glory!!!"

Chapter 16

Finding Freedom

Eric sat pensively in the booth at the Red Lantern, nursing a cup of coffee while looking out the window as the morning sun began to light up the day.

"You look deep in thought," Jason commented as he sat down.

"Good morning to you, too!" Eric responded with a chuckle. "Just reflecting on the past five months since we opened Hope House."

"Hard to believe it's already been that long. Anything you want to share?"

Eric laughed, "It's hard to know where to start. You've been through a lot of it with me thanks to our weekly meetings, so you know we've had our ups and downs. I was thinking things were finally smoothing out until this past weekend."

"Oh, what happened?"

"We added a fourth girl about a couple of weeks ago, but she ran away Friday night."

"How did that happen? I thought you had them locked in the house?"

"It takes a special license to operate a lockdown facility. We may eventually work toward that goal, but until then, we monitor the girls closely and try to make the home as hospitable as possible, so they want to stay. However, if they want to leave, they can eventually find a way past our limited security measures."

"It must be hard to see these girls reject all that you are trying to do for them."

"The tragic thing is that last night our staff found an advertisement for her on the Internet, so she's fallen back in with a trafficker."

"What can you do now?"

"We've reported it to the new local human trafficking task force, and they'll hopefully find her soon. But she'll probably not be sent back to Hope House since we're not a lockdown facility and she's shown a predisposition to run."

"How did the staff react?"

"They were devastated. All of the staff, including myself, are questioning what else we could have done to help this client. We had all become very fond of her. The staff members understand that traumatized clients frequently run away. But it's never easy when you care for the client and know that they are often running toward danger. The good news is that this is the first AWOL we've had in five months."

"So, with this setback aside, you're pleased overall with how things are going?"

"Yes. Before you came in, I was thinking back on how much has changed since the blowup with the board five months ago. I can't thank you enough for all the support and advice you gave me through that difficult time."

"My pleasure," Jason replied. "I've enjoyed getting to know you better, and besides, I should thank you for opening my eyes to the horrible reality of human trafficking. If it weren't for meeting with you, I would hardly know a thing about it. Now that you mention it, how are things going with your board?"

"Cheryl has done a great job as Board Chair. She's been very supportive of all our work and has even recruited two new board members."

"Whatever happened to the previous Board Chair that got into trouble in her job...what was her name?"

"Abigail. She ended up not going to jail since it was her first offense. Instead, she was sentenced to pay a hefty fine on top of the money and interest she owes the bank. I recently heard from one of our other board members that she's now working as a realtor to pay back all that money."

"So, no more upheavals from the board?"

"Not so far, and I doubt anything like that will happen again with Cheryl as Chair."

"It sounds like the Lord has answered our prayers for the protection of Hope House and its leadership."

"I'd have to say that five to six months ago, I wasn't all that sure about the power of prayer; but now I am a true believer! In the early stages of setting up Hope House, I tried to do pretty much everything without first seeking the Lord's direction and empowering. But thanks to your help, I'm trusting and resting more in the Lord."

"So, what's ahead for you and Hope House?"

"Short term, we'll continue to slowly add girls into the home until we reach our maximum of six. I expect that will happen in the next three months or so. We are still learning the lessons necessary to provide the best care for these girls."

"And long term?" Jason asked after they gave their orders to the waitress.

"Long term, we're going to need to expand our number of beds. Unfortunately, child sex trafficking is so common that six beds are not nearly enough to meet the need within Brookview, much less our region of the state."

"Are you thinking of enlarging the house?"

"No, that's one lesson we've learned. When we added the fourth girl a few weeks ago, the amount of drama in the home increased exponentially. While we were able to handle it with additional staff, we've realized that there are only so many girls you can put into one space. We're hoping we can handle six girls at a time, and if so, that will be our maximum."

"So what are you going to do?"

"Since we have room on our current property, we're exploring the possibility of building a second facility that will hold between four to six additional girls. Also, adjacent to Hope House is some undeveloped land that, Lord willing, we might be able to purchase someday to continue to increase the number of girls we can serve. But that's several years down the road."

"I'm sure I don't need to remind you that the Lord has a plan."

"No," Eric chuckled. "I'm not at all worried about that. As you've often told me these past six months, my role is to follow. His is to lead."

"I'm glad at least some of my advice has been helpful."

"It's all been quite helpful, which brings up something I wanted to mention. I know that Monday is usually your day off. Since we've reached some level of spiritual stability at

Hope House, I was thinking we could begin meeting less often so that you could enjoy more time with your family."

"I'm sure Heidi would welcome that. How does every other week sound?"

"Perfect."

*****

"Eric remembered not to use Allison's name when he mentioned that she had run away from the house," Riel said, turning to Solen in their usual location near the ceiling of the restaurant. "What are the developments regarding the search for Allison since Adren helped the Hope House staff find her online listing?"

"We've been attempting to assist the task force members in their search for her, but the absence of believers on the task force is hampering our efforts," Solen responded. "I just sent Corel to evaluate the situation and change our strategy if necessary so that we can make sure she is rescued by the end of the week."

"Will she be returning to Hope House?"

"Probably not. Eric is correct that the court will likely send her to a secure facility. We will use her time there to attempt to soften her heart to the point where she can receive the love and care Hope House has to offer her."

"Do you have a candidate to replace her?"

"Our efforts to spread the reputation of Hope House through the regional angelic nexus are beginning to bear fruit. The next girl to be admitted to Hope House will come from another city and will arrive later this week. Her name is Deborah."

"The need for expansion may come sooner than Eric thinks," Riel replied.

"Our Lord wisely doesn't share His complete plans with His sons and daughters since Eric would be overwhelmed if he knew the eventual plans for Hope House. The Lord intends for Hope House to grow until it is restoring over fifty girls at a time. By that point, it will serve as a model facility for other homes within the region, and around the country."

"The need for these homes is a reflection of the fallen condition of man, though many refuse to acknowledge it," Riel noted.

"As we both know well, man's fallen state changes only through faith in Jesus, so suffering and abuse will continue until He returns. Those who faithfully study the Scriptures understand this and are not surprised by the continual spread of evil."

"But our knowledge of that truth doesn't lessen the anguish of witnessing that suffering," Riel sighed.

"No, but it does make the work of Christians like Eric that much more glorious. Without the suffering, the Gospel would cease to be Good News, and few would see their need for the Lord."

"Thankfully, the Lord is calling people from all over the country to start homes like Hope House."

"Yes, and I just learned the Spirit's called a woman from Brookview to start a home similar to Hope House, but for adult women."

"I'm sure Valden and his ilk will be thrilled to learn that a second God-called restoration home is coming to their region."

Solen chuckled, "Benzal is still raging about his demotion over the incident with Travoz and his inability to shut down Hope House. Dravon is now his superior, and from everything I hear, Dravon is relishing his revenge on his old master."

"Speaking of Travoz, have you learned anything of his fate?"

"I heard through the angelic nexus that his watcher abilities are being put to full use somewhere in the Arctic region," Solen responded with a smile.

"Fitting." Riel smiled back. "In spite of thousands of years of rebellion, they still haven't learned the danger of pride."

"For the Lord and His glory!"

*****

Heather grabbed Angelica and Sheniah's breakfast dishes and rinsed them in the sink before putting them into the dishwasher.

"Sheniah, do you want to finish that Bible study before I head to court this morning?" Heather asked.

"Yeah, I guess."

"Don't sound too excited," Heather replied jokingly. "Why don't you get your Bible and I'll meet you in the living room. You're welcome to join us too Angelica if you want."

"Nah, I've got some other things to get done before school."

"If you change your mind, we'll be in the living room."

Heather snatched her Bible from her bedroom and returned to the living room, sitting down on the couch just as Sheniah came into the room and found her favorite chair.

"If I remember right, weren't you asking about hell?" Heather started.

"Yeah. I want to make sure Roberto's going to hell for what he did to me."

"I'm not so sure we're supposed to want someone to go to hell," Heather responded as Tavia walked into the room. "Isn't that right Tavia?"

"Isn't what right?"

"Is it right to want someone to go to hell?"

"Whoa. I don't think so. Jesus taught his disciples that they should forgive those who sinned against them."

"How can I forgive Roberto for all the terrible things he put me through?" Sheniah asked with visible anger.

"There's no question you girls have been deeply hurt in many ways," Tavia began. "But forgiveness is not about letting the other person off the hook. Jesus will judge each person for what they've done, good or bad."

"So, He'll be sending Roberto to hell, right?"

"Only if he doesn't repent and put his faith in Jesus."

"Good, he deserves to go to hell."

"Sheniah, you should remember we all deserve to go to hell," Tavia continued. "It's only by God's grace that He forgives what we've each done wrong. But as I started to say, when we forgive someone who has wronged us deeply, we do it for ourselves, not for them."

"That's right," Heather interjected. "I've been working through forgiving my mom the past couple of months. It's helping me be less angry and bitter."

"Exactly, Heather. When we don't forgive someone who has horribly wronged us, we only hurt ourselves by allowing anger and bitterness to take over."

"I don't understand," Sheniah responded. "What's wrong with being angry at what I've been through?"

"It's one thing to recognize you've been wronged and feel initial anger because of it. It's another to allow your heart to become filled with anger and bitterness. That's when you become an unhappy person. In six months, wouldn't you rather be happy than bitter and angry?"

"I guess so. I never thought of it that way."

"I've felt much better the past several weeks since I began forgiving my mother," Heather declared. "It just makes everything seem brighter."

"That's one way to put it," Tavia chuckled. "Sheniah, when you forgive someone like Roberto, you lessen the control he has over you."

"What do you mean?"

"When you are full of anger and bitterness about what Roberto did to you, those emotions are controlling you. So, in a way, Roberto is still controlling you. Forgiveness frees you from that control by helping you get rid of those emotions. Does that make sense?"

"Kinda. If I don't think about Roberto, I won't get mad. Is that it?"

"Close. The important thing to understand is that forgiving Roberto doesn't mean that what he did wasn't wrong. Forgiveness is only necessary when someone has wronged us. Instead, forgiveness means releasing your desire for Roberto to suffer as a result of that wrong and turning him over to Jesus."

"But that's hard to do."

"It is hard, and some would say even impossible without Jesus."

"But it's worth it," Heather said. "I'm much happier than I was a couple of months ago. When I was bitter and angry with my mom, the only person I was hurting was me."

"Heather, are you ready to go to court?" Melinda asked as she walked into the room.

"Yeah, just finishing some things with Sheniah. Let me put my Bible back in my room, and I'll be ready," Heather answered as she got up and walked out of the room.

After she had left, Melinda turned to Tavia and Sheniah. "Heather's come a long way in the past three months. I'm sure she can give you some good advice, Sheniah."

"Yeah, but she can be a little pushy."

"We all can when we get excited about something," Melinda said as she turned to walk out to the car.

"So, what were you talking with Sheniah about?" Melinda asked as Heather joined her in the car.

"Forgiveness."

"A good topic. I'm so proud of your progress this past couple of months. You're becoming a different person."

"Yeah, I guess I was a little angry when I first got here."

"Rightfully so; but you've moved past that anger with forgiveness," Melinda noted as they pulled out of the driveway. "Not everyone does that. Some keep and use that anger to fuel more bad behavior."

"Thanks. I really hope my mom comes today. I haven't seen her since the initial court hearing months ago."

"I should tell you I heard yesterday that the authorities arrested Ted for possession of child pornography."

"Really? So they put him in jail?"

"That's my understanding."

"Maybe now my mom will believe me."

"Heather, I'd be careful getting your hopes up. I think it would be wonderful if your mother suddenly stopped supporting Ted and believed your story. However, I should warn you that it's also possible that she'll remain loyal to Ted."

Heather was silent for several minutes.

"Am I that difficult to love?" Heather finally replied sadly.

"Absolutely not. Heather, the problem is with your mother, not you. For whatever reason, your mother has a strong need for Ted that causes her to choose him over you. You have to remember that. You are a wonderful person, dearly loved by God. Your mother is blind to that because of her need for Ted."

Heather sat quietly, looking straight ahead as her eyes began to tear up.

*****

"How do you think Heather will handle this latest development?" Corel asked, joining Taron above the car as it traveled toward the court.

"Heather has made tremendous progress in the past three months. She'll be disappointed and hurt, but I don't believe it will derail her faith. Her love for the Lord is strong enough now to help temper the upcoming storms."

"The enemy removes an earthly father to create a void and advance his plan, but that tactic also allows the Lord to fill that same void as only He can."

"And Heather has greatly enjoyed that loving fellowship these past several months. Were you successful in leading the task force to Allison?" Taron asked.

"Since no one on the task force is Spirit indwelled, they all remained resistant to my thought suggestions. I ended up assuming human form in the guise of an IT consultant to direct one of the members to the latest online listing featuring Allison."

"Her demonization has sufficiently hardened her heart making her temporarily impervious to all attempts by the staff to love and care for her," Taron noted as they arrived at the courthouse.

"But her grandmother has been praying for Allison faithfully these past several months. Those prayers are enabling several direct mediations with Allison so that she can see her true condition and need for Jesus. Solen has asked me to undertake another intervention just a few days after she arrives at the lockdown facility."

"I pray your efforts will be successful and that she makes a decision to submit to the Lord Jesus, freeing her from her current bondage. I know that Heather spoke to her several times in the week leading up to her running episode. The Spirit used those interactions to begin softening Allison's heart," Taron acknowledged.

"Your prayers and mine will join those of the saints since Solen plans to activate the prayer chain. Solen was right that Heather would prove to be a powerful force helping free other girls."

"Which is why she will remain at Hope House far longer than she expected. Though she initially won't understand, as I help her work through the pain of abandonment, she'll eventually experience the joy that comes from helping others."

"She doesn't yet realize how each painful experience she endures further empowers her to speak into the hearts of others in a way no one else can."

"That's the essence of the Lord's plan. Take the suffering of the lost and help them find freedom so that they can help others find freedom."

"The freedom found only in the Gospel of Jesus Christ."

"For the Lord and His glory!"

*****

Heather sat down next to her attorney on the right side of the courtroom just as the CPS lady took the seat on Heather's left. The prosecuting attorney also came in, taking her usual place opposite Heather. Heather watched anxiously for her mother but didn't see her before Judge Parker arrived.

After the usual ceremony of standing as the judge entered the courtroom, Heather quickly surveyed the guest gallery again for her mother as she sat down.

No sign of her mother. The judge pounded his gavel.

"This is a continuance hearing in the case of 'State vs. Wallace.' Are all parties present and ready to proceed?"

"We are, Your Honor," both attorneys replied in unison.

Judge Parker put on his reading glasses and scanned over the papers in front of him.

"I see from this report provided by the therapist at Hope House that you seem to be doing very well young lady," the judge said as he looked up at Heather.

"I guess, Your Honor," Heather replied quietly.

"I understand that your grades are improving and that you are progressing very nicely through your therapy. I'm delighted to see this. Are you happy at the facility, Heather?"

"Yes, Your Honor. They are treating me very well, but I still would like to go home when possible."

"Of course. What is the status of the investigation of the stepfather?" the judge asked, looking at the woman sitting on Heather's left.

"Your Honor, I've submitted a report detailing the arrest and charges related to possession of child pornography to the court. They should be in her file."

Judge Parker shuffled through several papers before stopping and reading.

"Thank you. I've found it. Is the stepfather still in jail?"

"No, Your Honor. He was released on bail yesterday afternoon."

"And who provided the bail?"

"The defendant's mother, Nancy."

Heather looked at the back of the courtroom, confused and saddened once again at her mother's actions. Judge Parker watched her for a short time before looking into the visitor gallery.

"Is the mother present?" he asked loudly.

After a short period of silence, he sighed and began writing a note.

"I assume you informed her of this hearing?" the judge asked Heather's attorney.

"Yes, Your Honor, on multiple occasions."

"I decided not to issue a subpoena for this hearing to further assess the degree of involvement of this woman in her daughter's life. Her actions and lack of attendance here have solidified my opinion on the matter. The defendant's mother is hereby ordered to begin weekly meetings with a court-appointed family counselor to evaluate her future ability to serve as parent and guardian for the defendant."

Judge Parker looked directly at Heather.

"Young lady, I'm afraid your mother's actions and lack of attendance here have left me little choice. I cannot allow you to go back into that home, especially with your stepfather awaiting trial on charges of possession of child pornography. Do you understand?"

Heather nodded her head yes, on the verge of tears.

"I also want to tell you again that I'm very pleased with your progress at Hope House. I can tell you've been working hard and I want to make your time at the facility as pleasant as possible. Is there anything this court can do to help accomplish that?"

Heather hesitated a minute before answering. "Would it be possible for me to have visits with my best friend?"

The judge looked over at one of the court workers on his left.

"Michelle, please get the information on this friend, and if everything checks out, go ahead and arrange it."

"Yes, Your Honor," the woman replied.

Judge Parker returned his attention to Heather.

"I know that you want to be back with your mother, but it's this court's responsibility to make sure your mother is adequately protecting and caring for you. As you've just heard, we're attempting to make that determination as soon as we can, and if possible, return you home. Until then, I think it is best to keep you where you are doing well."

Turning to the other side of the courtroom, the judge asked, "Is this acceptable to the prosecution?"

"Yes, Your Honor."

"And the GAL?"

"I also agree, Your Honor."

"Very well; the defendant will remain at her current placement until Child Protective Services and this court make a final determination regarding the home situation. A follow up hearing will be scheduled in ninety days. This hearing is adjourned."

Heather sat quietly, thinking over the events of the morning as Melinda drove back to the house.

"Are you sure the Lord will never abandon us?" Heather asked.

"Remember that verse in Hebrews I showed you? God has promised that He will never leave us or forsake us."

"I guess it's just really hard to believe with my experience."

"God is different than our parents, Heather. He loves you more than you can imagine, and He has made you His daughter. That will never change, even throughout eternity."

"I sure hope that's true since I can't depend on my mom or my dad. I just don't know what I've done to cause them to abandon me," Heather said sadly through tears.

"Heather, as I've told you before, the problem is not you; it's them. Neither your mother nor your father is acting like a normal loving parent. They each have their problems which keep them from loving you the way they should."

"At least I have a few friends that have stuck by me. I can't wait to talk to Sue!" Heather exclaimed, shaking off her sadness. "How long will it take to arrange the visit?"

"Probably only a few days. The court caseworker said she'd get on it right away."

"The FaceTimes have been helpful, but it's not the same as talking in person."

"I agree, which reminds me I wanted to thank you for all that you said to Allison before she ran away."

"But it didn't keep her from running."

"No, but don't underestimate the impact you had on Allison. No one can understand what you girls have experienced unless they've been through it themselves. Allison ran because of her emotional bonding to her trafficker, not because you weren't helping her."

"Have they found her yet?"

"Yes. Unfortunately, I just heard from the task force that they found her at a local motel with her trafficker. She's back in juvenile detention, awaiting a hearing."

"Will she be sent back to Hope House?"

"Probably not. Allison has a long history of running away, so she'll probably be sent to a lockdown facility. But don't forget that both Angelica and Sheniah are watching you closely."

"Really? I had no idea. They don't say much to me."

"Sheniah is changing slowly and opening up, and I know that a large part of that is because of your new attitude and example. I've even seen small changes in Angelica the past couple of months that you've helped bring about."

"I have to admit; it does feel good to be able to help someone."

"I know it's selfish of me, but I'm thrilled you're going to stay with us at Hope House for the time being. I believe you can make a difference in the lives of other girls that come to us while you're here. You've found something that they need to find themselves."

"You mean finding the Lord?"

"Yes, and through the Lord, aren't you also finding something else?"

"I'm not sure what you mean."

"You're finding freedom, aren't you?"

"You mean from Derrick and Melanie?"

"That was only the first step. Now in the Lord, you're finding freedom from other things that control you, like sin."

"Yeah, I guess so."

"And the exciting thing is that as you continue to find your freedom, you can also help the other girls find their freedom."

"I never thought of it that way."

After a few minutes of silence, Heather continued. "I guess something good can come out of all this yuckiness. Maybe I should become a therapist like you!"

"That's always a possibility," Melinda chuckled. "You'll have a lot of time to think about it. But remember, you are in a unique situation to take the horrible things that have happened to you and turn them into something that can help others. That's got to make you feel good."

"Yeah, it kinda does. Just wait till I tell Sue all about it!"

For the Lord and His Glory!

For more information on human trafficking and how to report suspicious behavior, go to https://humantraffickinghotline.org.

CPSIA information can be obtained
at www.ICGtesting.com
Printed in the USA
LVHW111435151019
634126LV00002B/430/P